RIKA INFILTRATOR

RIKA'S MARAUDERS – BOOK 5

BY M. D. COOPER

Just in Time (JIT) & Beta Readers

Jim Dean
Lisa Richman
David Wilson
Alastar Wilson
Timothy Van Oosterwyk Bruyn
Scot Mantelli
Scott Reid
Marti Panikkar
Gene Bryan
Mikkel Ebjerg Andersen

Version 1.0.0

ISBN: 978-1-64365-010-4

Cover Art by Tek Tan
Editing by Jen McDonnell

TABLE OF CONTENTS

FOREWORD 5
PREVIOUSLY... 7
MAPS 12
BARNE AND SILVA 15
ATTACK FORMATION 24
ADMIRAL GIDEON 32
GROUND POUNDERS 35
MEMPHIS SPACE AND AIR 41
THE DROP 50
ON THE WALL 55
TAKE THE FIGHT 58
BERSERKER 76
BRING IT HOME 81
LAST STAND 94
CHASING RIKA 99
CAPTIVE 105
LOST 109
ORDERS 112
AMONG THE MISSING 117
PULLING UP STAKES 125
STOWAWAY 129
PURSUIT 139
THE JUMP 144
CHORES 149
FAMILY 153
VISITORS 171
BACON 176
ACCESS 180
EPSILON 186
A CHAT WITH SOFIA 193
THE PROBLEM 201
A GAME OF SNARK 208
DRAGON'S LAIR 212

UNEXPECTED PASSENGERS 221
A SURPRISING DIVERSION 226
JUST VISITING 239
PIPER 241
GETTING REAL 251
AN UNUSUAL EVAC 260
REUNION 270
AFTERMATH 275
MECH TYPES AND ARMAMENTS 283
3rd MARAUDER FLEET 4th DIVISION 293
7th MARAUDER FLEET 1st DIVISION 294
9th MARAUDER BATTALION 296
THE BOOKS OF AEON 14 303
ABOUT THE AUTHOR 307

FOREWORD

Something that's always a bit fun with the books that are being narrated is that I'm often listening to a book that is two or three releases behind the one I'm writing.

While writing this book, I listened to Alison's narration of Rika Redeemed (as well as a bit of Rika Triumphant), and was reminded of some fun and interesting interactions between the characters. While I don't really want to put Rika through more of what she went through in the Politica (she'd probably show up and kick my ass), I did want to give her a chance to really shine on her own once more.

That's really where she does her best, after all.

We're also going to get to see the fight for Genevia from the eyes of more Marauders than ever before. Chase will be getting some more time in the limelight, as will Smalls, Alison, Kelly, Leslie, Silva, and even Vargo Klen!

We're also going to get introduced to some new tech that Finaeus provided the mechs with, as well as some great old standbys that the Marauders are all too happy to use against their enemies.

And lastly, we'll get to see a bit more of Rika's journey down the path that Tanis set her on, with hints of where that may take us in the future.

We're getting close to the end of the Rika septology, with Rika Unleashed and Rika Conqueror still to come—but fear not, these seven books will not be the end of our time with Rika. There's a whole new series on the drawing board, ready to come hot on this one's heels.

Michael Cooper
Danvers, 2018

PREVIOUSLY...

It's hard to believe that Rika's journey started only a scant fifteen months ago, on Dekar Station—on that fateful day she was sold at auction to an unknown buyer. While it was arguably the lowest point in her life, it was also the event that turned everything around for her.

When she woke, she was on Pyra, a planet that would play a pivotal role in the next year of her life. There, she met Team Basilisk, a Marauder spec-ops group that had been tasked with assassinating the Theban president.

While Rika spearheaded that operation, she never completed the mission, unable to kill President Ariana. It was then that we learned what Rika was really made of.

When the Nietzscheans—Rika's hated enemy from the war that forged her—attacked Pyra, she and Team Basilisk were instrumental in driving them back. It was at that time that Rika both became a Marauder, and was reunited with Chase—a man who had always treated her like a person, even before she had a face and felt at all human.

Not long after, Rika saved a little girl named Amy, and then saved her former mentor, Silva. As though that weren't enough, she saved the Politica from the tyrant Stavros, and freed all the mechs he'd captured over the years.

With a new force of mechs at her disposal, Rika was tasked by General Mill (leader of the Marauders) with training them on the world of Iapetus, in the Hercules system.

There, she and her mechs thwarted a sinister plot hatched by the Nietzscheans, and carried out by Theban and Septhian traitors, to overthrow the system and claim it for the empire.

Following that, Rika and her Marauders boarded and captured a fleet of Nietzschean ships that were hiding beneath the clouds of a gas giant. The coup granted her a fleet of five vessels, and the massive dreadnought, *Fury Lance,* became her flagship.

The blood hadn't finished drying from that battle before Rika got word that Pyra and the Albany System were under attack once more.

The fact that Silva and Amy had taken up residence in the Albany System lent to her immediate departure from the Hercules System for Albany.

Upon arrival, Rika found that a new player had entered the battle: the Intrepid Space Force. Rika's AI companion, Niki, had told her of the *Intrepid*, so Rika joined up with the ISF, and led a secret mission to rescue the ISF's leader, a woman named Tanis Richards.

When Rika and her team found Tanis on Pyra's surface, they witnessed things they had never imagined: a human ascending into a fifth-dimensional being.

This was just the beginning of an eye-opening experience with Tanis, who—with her people's advanced tech—aided in upgrading the mechs into new '4th Gen' models. Tanis also hired the Marauders, supplying them with more ships, and tasking them with taking the fight to Nietzschea—a mission Rika was all too eager to accept.

Before Rika's full force was ready, Tanis received word of a system named Sepe where the Nietzscheans were regrouping. Seeking to deny the Nietzscheans any advantage—and as little direct intel of the battle in Albany as possible—she sent Rika and her original five ships to defeat the enemy at Sepe.

When last we left Rika and her merry band of Marauders, they had just defeated the Nietzschean forces in the Sepe System, and lifted the empire's boot from that system. During that encounter, Rika's mind was expanded, and she learned of new, latent abilities she possessed as a result of the enhancements the ISF made to her mind and body.

While she was recovering from that experience, Tanis contacted her through a quantum communication system she'd implanted in Rika, charging her with a new mission to take the fight deeper into the Nietzschean Empire.

A week later, Rika's fleet departed Sepe, on their way to the Blue Ridge System—once a Genevian System, now within the borders of the Nietzschean Empire.

And a ripe target for Rika's Marauders...

Prominent Members of the Marauders

Though there is a full list of all the mechs, pilots, and members of the Marauders at the end of the book, this is a listing of some of the more prominent characters and their current role in the battalion.

9th Marauder Battalion Leadership

Rika – Colonel, battalion commandeering officer
Alice – Lieutenant Colonel, executive officer
Silva – Lieutenant Colonel, training commandant
Barne – Sergeant Major, command sergeant
Leslie – Captain, intelligence officer
Niki – AI, Lieutenant, operations officer

M Company Leadership

Chase – Captain, company commanding officer
Karen – Lieutenant, company executive officer
Tex – First Sergeant
Aaron – Gunnery Sergeant
Potter – AI, Chief of Tactics and Strategy

The Seventh Fleet, First Division

Heather (Smalls) – Captain of the *Fury Lance*
Ona – CWO, bridge crew aboard the *Fury Lance*
Garth – CWO, bridge crew aboard the *Fury Lance*
Travis – Captain of the *Republic*
Ferris – Lieutenant, commander of the *Undaunted*
Vargo Klen – Lieutenant, commander of the *Asora*

Buggsie – Lieutenant, commander of the *Capital*

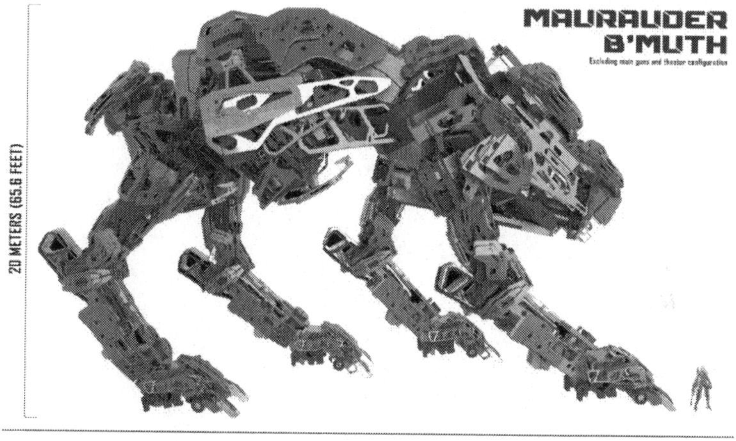

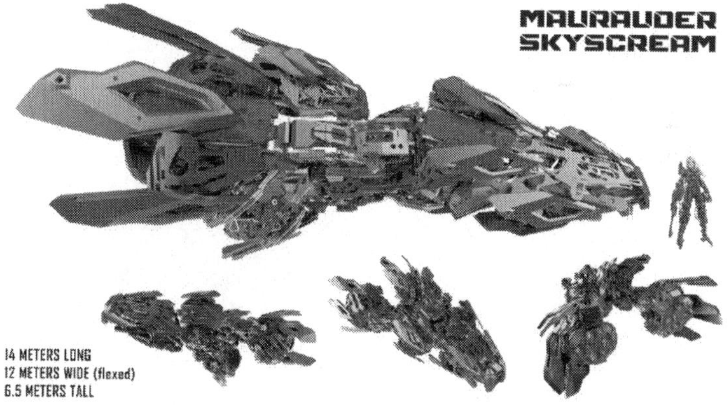

MAPS

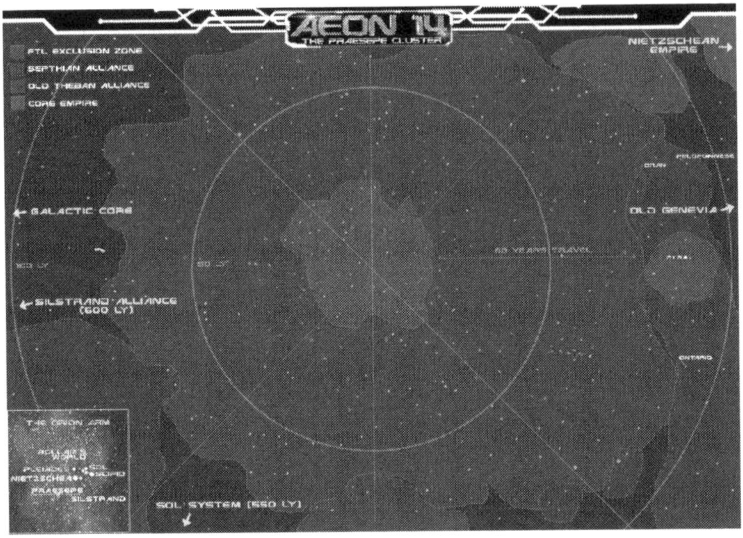
AEON 14
THE PRAESEPE CLUSTER
FTL EXCLUSION ZONE
SEPTHIAN ALLIANCE
OLD THEBAN ALLIANCE
CORE EMPIRE
NIETZSCHEAN EMPIRE
GALACTIC CORE
OLD GENEVIA
SILSTRAND ALLIANCE (600 LY)
ONTARIO
SOL SYSTEM (550 LY)

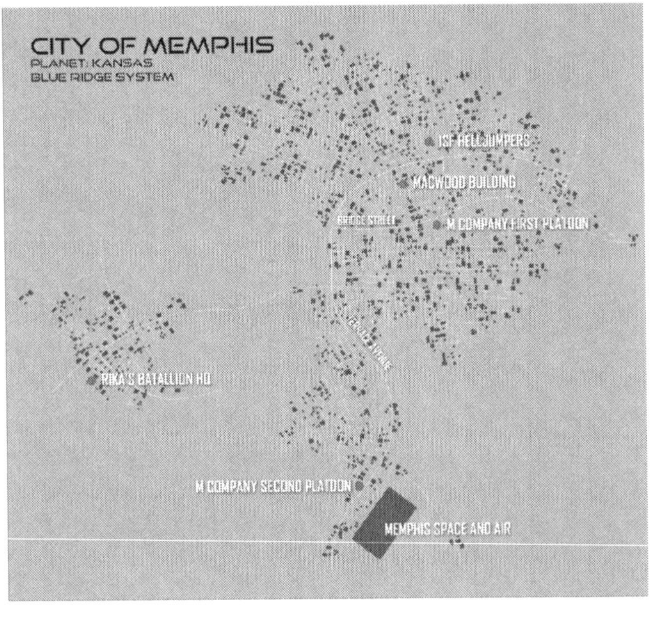
CITY OF MEMPHIS
PLANET: KANSAS
BLUE RIDGE SYSTEM
ISF HELLJUMPERS
MACWOOD BUILDING
BRIDGE STREET
M COMPANY FIRST PLATOON
RIKA'S BATALLION HQ
M COMPANY SECOND PLATOON
MEMPHIS SPACE AND AIR

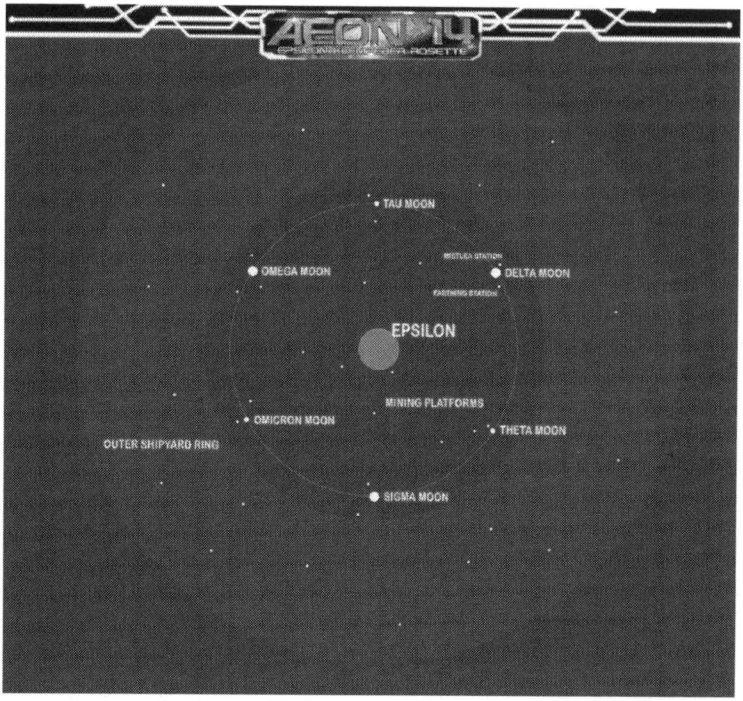
AEON 14
TAU MOON
OMEGA MOON
DELTA MOON
EPSILON
MINING PLATFORMS
OMICRON MOON
THETA MOON
OUTER SHIPYARD RING
SIGMA MOON

BARNE AND SILVA

STELLAR DATE: 10.12.8949 (Adjusted Years)
LOCATION: A1 Dock, ISS *I2* in orbit of Pyra
REGION: Albany System, Theban Alliance

Silva leant her back against the bulkhead next to Lift Bank 771 in the *I2*'s massive A1 Dock, and closed her eyes, breathing out a long, ragged breath.

Amy was gone—sent to New Canaan, where she'd be taken care of by Joe and Tanis's daughters. The knowledge should have given her peace, and she was honored that Admiral Tanis's own family would be watching over her daughter.

But the goodbye had felt so final.

In minutes, my daughter will be thousands and thousands of light years away.

After spending so much of her life away from Amy—and only recently being reunited—the thought of being separated across such a vast gulf was almost too much to bear. Without the ISF's jump gates, it would take decades to reach New Canaan, a perilous journey that would be all but impossible.

Stop thinking like that, Silva admonished herself. *We're going to win this war, the ISF will still be around, and I'll bring my boys to New Canaan to join their sister...not necessarily in that order.*

The lift chimed, and Silva opened her eyes, surprised to see someone standing next to her.

"General Keller!" Silva snapped off a salute. "I'm sorry, I didn't realize you were there."

The purple-skinned woman gave a kind smile, gesturing for Silva to proceed her onto the lift car. "Don't worry about it. I heard you sent your daughter to New Canaan; it's not an easy thing, to send your children away...or leave them behind."

Silva nodded while giving the general a sidelong look. "You sound like you have experience in that area. Do you have kids, General?"

"Please, call me Jessica. I spend so much time away from the *Intrep*—I mean the *I2*—that being called 'General' is hard to get used to. Especially here. This ship is more like a home than a workplace for me."

"Fair enough," Silva replied. "I'm not used to people saluting me...not even a little bit. So I get where you're coming from."

Jessica laughed. "Tanis drafted me into her merry little military almost a century ago, and I'm *still* not used to it. Probably because she keeps sending me off on side-projects. But to answer your first question, yeah, I have sixteen kids."

"*Sixteen*!" Silva gasped, looking the general up and down. "I guess I shouldn't be surprised you look so good, you have the tech to repair any damage that would cause."

Jessica glanced down at herself. "Well, this is a relatively new epidermis—I'm on my fifth or sixth now, depending on how you count—but my children are all AIs. Though I did bear half of them within a sort of expanse, and it felt entirely natural. Iris, who was the AI that I was paired with at the time, bore the other half."

"Iris 'bore' them?" Silva asked, trying to clarify and understand what Jessica was telling her.

"We were at a place called Star City—which doesn't describe the magnitude of the place at all," the purple-skinned woman explained. "Anyway they had these powerful AIs known as 'Bastions' that were protecting it from the Orion Guard, but there was only one left. The city needed more, but they weren't in a position to make the AIs themselves, so Iris, Trevor, and I had a little mental threesome, and bore our brood."

Silva shook her head, laughing softly. "I won't even pretend to know how that works."

"It's kinda weird, but kinda not weird, as well. Suffice it to say, I miss them a lot. Now that we have the—uh, well, I can't talk about that...but I'll be going to see them again before long, pretty freakin' excited about that.

"I bet," Silva replied, unable to miss the glow that Jessica's skin had taken on as she spoke. The general was almost blinding to look at.

"Shoot, sorry about that," Jessica said, apparently noticing Silva's squint. "So yeah, long story short, being separated from your kids is awful. I mean, I got to be with them as they grew up, but when I left...well, I was worried I'd never see them again. It's been over ten years now."

"Wait," Silva held up a hand, counting out the years. "How is it that you got to raise them? Does that happen really fast with AIs? I'm not really familiar with AIs that are partially born from human minds."

"Well, Star City has some pretty wild tech—"

"Damn, that really says a lot, coming from someone in the ISF."

Jessica snorted. "I suppose it does. Just goes to show, there's always someone out there that's above and beyond you. Either way, they had this thing called 'The Dream'—sort of an accelerated life simulator that they were using to go through lifetimes of mental growth in days. Essentially a great big reincarnation machine. We were in for three days, and I got to watch my kids grow for over twenty years. Tanis is the oldest, she—"

Silva couldn't help but laugh. "You named your oldest 'Tanis'?"

The general cocked her head and shrugged, an embarrassed smile on her lips. "I didn't know if we'd ever make it back, and I wanted to honor my best friend."

"Was she?" Silva asked. "Honored?"

"I think so?" Jessica chuckled. "Tanis plays it close to the chest a lot—plus she has a lot on her mind. I can't wait to introduce them someday. My Tanis is *a lot* like her namesake."

The lift chimed, and Silva realized it was at her deck.

"Thanks for the chat, General—er, Jessica. It was really nice meeting you."

"You too, Silva. Good luck on what lies ahead. You Marauders have your work cut out for you."

It was Silva's turn to laugh. "Stars, do we ever, but it'll be good work. There are a lot of Nietzschean asses that need kicking, and Rika's Marauders are just the mechs for the job."

The general's skin glowed brightly, and she waved as the doors closed, leaving Silva with her thoughts once more, this time focused on completing the work of training the latest batch of mechs that had arrived from the Politica, and then joining the fight, at Rika's side.

* * * * *

Silva's thoughts were interrupted by Barne's booming voice, echoing across the platform. Despite having taken a lift and talking with General Keller for a time, she was still in the *I2*'s A1 Dock, seven full kilometers from where she'd boarded the lift.

Sitting atop the platform was the *Terminus*, a Nietzschean heavy destroyer captured in the recent battle around Pyra that was now a part of Rika's fleet.

Technically, it was the Marauder's 7th Fleet, 2nd

Division, but everyone called it Rika's fleet—even the Marauders who had shipped in from the Ontario System in Septhia to lend a hand with the training of the mechs who were joining in.

Not that the mechs needed training from squishies when it came to fighting. Their biggest obstacle was learning how to work together in larger units. A few weeks prior, Barne had assigned a platoon of the new mechs to help clear out a group of Nietzscheans that were still holed up on Pyra. When the enemy saw thirty mechs, including four K1Rs, forming up outside the small town they were holding hostage, they surrendered before the first shots were fired.

From there on out, Silva and Barne had worked with the ISF and the local Theban forces, using some of the hairier jobs as training missions for the new mech units.

The team helping load the *Terminus*, however, was not one of those units. It was a squad consisting of FR-2's and 3's who had not yet gone into the mech-tubes to get their 4th generation upgrades.

They'd also not yet gone on any team building missions, and were barely able to function as a group. Silva imagined he had brought them along because they were otherwise unengaged, but as she listened to him bellow at the FRs, she wondered if he just wanted to blow off some steam.

"I once saw a squishie with an arm blown off and the other holding in half his intestines walk faster than you lazy oafs!" the Sergeant Major bellowed. "I shoulda had the Colonel's daughter move this gear before she shipped out! It would be done by now. Once saw that little girl shoot down a pinnace, kill seven Niets, and then save a wounded teammate while eating a sandwich. And that was on her first day!"

"Sergeant Major," one of the FR-3s, a rather cocky

woman named Pence, said as she set down a crate on an a-grav float. "How did Amy have a 'first day'? She's not in the Marauders."

"Not in the Marauders?" Barne stalked across the platform to where Pence stood next to the crate, a finger raised in the air as he closed with the woman. "You're in Rika's Marauders when Rika says you're in. Not a moment before, not a moment later. The old lady says she's in, she's in. What about you? Has Rika personally called *you* a Marauder?"

"Uh…well…no. I've never met her."

"Well then shut yer gob, Pence, and get a move on! Colonel Sil—well, shit, look, there she is, and you're all just dicking around still. Get a move on and load this fucking ship!"

Spittle flew from Barne's mouth, spraying across Pence's face. To her credit, the woman did look terrified of the sergeant, and ran to grab the next crate.

Barne turned toward Silva, his face nearly split in half with an ear-to-ear grin.

<*Stars, I love this job,*> he said with a laugh. <*I mean…I'm getting paid to kill Niets and yell at people. This must be what heaven is. Think we died in some recent engagement, and I'm in heaven?*>

Silva couldn't help but smile in response to the Sergeant Major. <*Maybe we are. Gotta say, the looks on the faces of that last group of Niets in that cruiser we hit was pretty priceless. They just about shit themselves when you came barreling around the corner.*>

<*I have it on good authority that there was no 'just about' about it.*>

<*Gah…then maybe you should tone it down a notch.*>

<*Why?*> Barne asked. <*I have FNMs like this lot to square away, I need to keep my shit-scaring game on point.*>

Silva shook her head, looking over the platform. <*How much longer 'til we're ready to roll?*>

<*Shouldn't be more than five minutes. The rest of this stuff is for a Theban cruiser that's waiting outside the* I2.>

<*I tell you,*> Silva said, looking out beyond the edge of the platform and across the A1 Dock, where hundreds of other ships rested on platforms, cargo drones flitting between them. <*These ISF people really know how to run an op. On its best day, the GAF wasn't half this well-oiled.*>

<*Half?*> Barne asked. <*Try a tenth. Granted, they didn't have AIs with brains the size of a destroyer keeping things running. Have you heard about the AIs on ships like this one?*> The Sergeant Major looked around as though a lightning bolt might strike him at any moment.

<*Are you referring to Bob?*> Silva asked. <*Because I talked with one of his avatars yesterday, and even* **that** *felt like my mind was being prised open with an electron blade.*>

<*Weird shit, that's for sure,*> Barne replied with a nod. <*AIs with human sock puppets, an ascended half-AI leader...sure glad these folks are on our side.*>

<*Not to mention willing to just give us as many ships as we can crew.*>

Barne snorted. <*Well, I mean...they're Nietzschean ships. If I had other options, I'd pawn these shit-boxes off on someone else, too.*>

<*Pretty sure you'd better not call the* Fury Lance *a shitbox. That thing is Rika's pride and joy.*>

Barne's grin took on a cunning slant. <*No, pretty sure Chase's new mech-body is Rika's pride and joy.*>

Silva groaned and shook her head. <*Can always count on you to make things that much more crass, Barne.*>

<*Another perk of the job, my dear Colonel, another perk of the job.*>

* * * * *

Twenty minutes later, the *Terminus* was boosting away from the *I2*, on its way to join with the rest of the 7th Fleet's 2nd Division.

Silva watched the ships that made up the R2D, as the mechs had begun to call it, with pride. Though the 1st Division would always have a place of pride in the hearts of Rika's Mechs—which was well earned, since they'd seized the ships while they were beneath the cloud tops of a gas giant—it was only five ships.

The 2nd Division boasted fifty-nine ships, all but two being Nietzschean vessels. Three of those were dreadnaughts the size of the *Fury Lance*. In all honesty, it was a tiny smattering of ships when compared to the vast fleets that the ISF—and the Nietzscheans, for that matter—were able to produce, but the ships belonged to Rika's Marauders, and of that they were all immensely proud.

While many of the mechs hadn't met Rika in person, they all knew she was the reason none of them were slaves to Stavros's Politica anymore. Each and every one of them knew the story of what Rika had done to save them—Silva made sure of that—and they were ready to follow their chosen commander into battle.

The ships of the 2nd Division were arrayed in a diamond formation, the dreadnaughts on the central axis, one at the forward end, one aft, practicing various close-formation maneuvers. Silva was no fleet tactician, but she understood that the dance the ships were involved in was more to practice coordination and precise maneuvering than something they would do in combat.

That many ships that close in actual battle would simply be an invitation for heavy beamfire and relativistic missiles.

"Looks good, doesn't it," Barne commented as he

approached the forward holodisplay on the bridge. "Rika's gonna split her knickers when she sees this."

"Split her knickers? What does that even mean?"

"Uh…I guess it makes more sense for men."

"Barne! You're on the bridge, you should set an example."

The sergeant snorted. "Trust me, I set the right kind of example. I've been at this a long time. Besides, I may be near the top of the heap, but I'm not an officer like you. I don't have to be all spit and polish all the time."

"I suppose," Silva allowed. "You're right, though. Rika is going to be more than a little happy to see all these ships." She paused and glanced over her shoulder before continuing privately. *<How do you feel about the ship captains that Marauder HQ sent us?>*

<Don't worry,> Barne replied. *<Billy here's good people. So are the rest. Chair warmers like that Alice may be plants, but General Julia and Marauder HQ want us to win out there. She sent us space jockeys that know their shit.>*

Silva watched the ships in the 2nd Division shift vectors and spread out into a flying X formation, the arms becoming convex, and ships moving along them until the X was four separate lines, reforming into the diamond afterward.

<They do look good,> she admitted. *<The ships.>*

Barne laughed. *<I knew what you meant. We're gonna bring the fight to the Niets, and they're gonna regret the day they ever said 'boo' to Genevia.>*

ATTACK FORMATION

STELLAR DATE: 10.12.8949 (Adjusted Years)
LOCATION: Battalion HQ, Memphis, Kansas
REGION: Blue Ridge System, Old Genevia, Nietzschean Empire

<*Chase!*> Rika called out from the command bunker—which was a fancy name for the basement of a deli on the west side of a city named Memphis on the planet Kansas.

When Chase replied, his tone was terse, and Rika could hear a simmering rage. <*What, Rika?*>

<*What are you doing at that position, is what! There's nothing over there.*>

Chase didn't reply for a moment, then the command net updated to show his company's first platoon—which he was accompanying—engaged with a Nietzschean armored column that also shouldn't have been there.

<*Shit, where did they come from?*> Rika asked.

<*Asshole factory, I imagine. This is where you sent us, though,*> Chase replied. <*Would be nice if you could send some backup. Crunch took a rocket to the leg, and he's bitching like mad.*>

<*I didn't…hold a mike.*> Rika checked the order log and saw that Lieutenant Colonel Alice had altered the orders Rika had given Chase, sending his platoon on a new route to their objective.

She turned to where Alice stood in the corner of the basement, hunched over another holotable. "Colonel Alice, why did you send Chase down 42nd Street?"

Alice glanced up, no concern evident on her face. "It was a faster route, and the intel showed no enemy activity."

Rika drew in a deep breath. "That's because we had a transmission hiccup. If you'd actually *looked* at the scan data, you'd've seen that it found *nothing* there. The only thing we have from 37th to 51st street is the city database's standard maps for that area."

Alice finally found the grace to look embarrassed for her mistake. "Shit…it wasn't flagged, Colonel Rika."

<*Stars!*> Rika said privately to Niki. <*I shouldn't have to fucking babysit my XO.*>

<*I'll watch her,*> Niki replied, also sounding rather upset. <*Let you know if she does anything stupid.*>

<*Stupid*er*, you mean,*> Rika replied to Niki before switching back to Chase. <*It's SNAFU here, Chase, sorry about that. What do you need?*>

Chase's reply took several seconds. <*Sorry, was putting holes in a Nietzschean transport. Honestly, I could use a B'muth or two right about now; this place is crawling with Niets. Oh, and I think I need Alice to go fuck herself.*>

Rika was having similar thoughts regarding Alice. It was becoming clear that the reason the woman had survived the Genevian war with Nietzschea was an overabundance of caution, and just enough intelligence to avoid any truly dangerous missions.

It wasn't quite enough to rate the woman as cowardly, but by Rika's estimation, she was right on the cusp.

Considering that my orders and most of my supplies are coming from Tanis and the Allies right now, I really wonder if I could just send Alice packing, and tell Marauder HQ to pound sand if they complain, Rika thought as she pulled up options, looking for the best way to reinforce Chase.

<*OK, Chase, Ferris is coming around the planet in the next thirty minutes. He has two B'muths. You send coordinates, and he'll drop them. They'll be unmanned, though, so you'll need to get crews in them yourself.*>

<*We'll set beacons,*> Chase replied, his tone still terse. <*Tell him not to miss the drop, or we're gonna get creamed.*>

<*He won't,*> Rika promised.

<I've got Ferris Linked up through the satcomm network,> Niki offered.

<Captain Ferris,> Rika said without pausing, though she thanked Niki with a mental smile. *<I need two B'muths dropped in Memphis. M company is going to set beacons on the standard freq as well.>*

<Ferris the ferryman at your service! You call, we make 'em fall,> Ferris sent back.

<Is that an affirmation, or just your standard jingle when anyone hits you up on comms?> Rika asked.

<Uh...can it be both, Cap—er, Colonel?>

Rika rolled her eyes, but couldn't stop a smile from forming on her lips. One thing she could always count on was Ferris messing up ranks.

<Why not, it's your lucky day,> she replied. *<Watch your approaches. We haven't taken out all of the Nietzschean anti-air, yet.>*

<Colonel Rika! You cut me to the quick. Besides, the Undaunted *has stasis shields. Niets can piss at me all day to no effect.>*

<I wasn't aware that you had any 'quick' left, after all the cuts you've suffered,> she shot back, unable to help herself.

<It's like you don't even know me, Rika. I'm ***built*** *out of 'quick'.>*

A laugh slipped past Rika's lips. *<Well, just remember that the B'muths don't have stasis shields—>*

<Swwwiiiiiing looow, sweet chaaaariot,> Ferris began to sing, and Rika sent him a long groan before closing the channel.

<OK, Chase, Ferris is on his way.>

<Glad to hear it,> Chase replied. *<I estimate there are several thousand Niets out here...two B'muths may not be enough. I know we're trying not to destroy this city, but can we maybe get some starfire?>*

Rika focused her holodisplay on the region that Chase was operating in. With the bad scan transmission, the only data they had was from the mechs on the ground and the drones they'd deployed.

Chase's company HQ element was deployed with his first platoon, putting a total of eighty-four mechs on the streets of central Memphis. They were spread out along seven avenues, advancing north toward the center of the city.

A kilometer ahead of them, the roads intersected an east-west thoroughfare named Bridge Street. It cut a broad swath through the city, even sporting a park filled with rocks and water features on its central boulevard.

North of Bridge Street lay a section of the city consisting of older, stone buildings. Which was, of course, where most of the Niets were set up.

Drone readings from the squads on first platoon's flanks showed that the Niets were moving east and west along Bridge Street, seeking to encircle the mechs.

<*Potter,*> Rika reached out to M Company's Tactics and Strategy AI, bringing her into the conversation with Chase. <*What do you make of the enemy's strength?*>

<*I estimate that we're looking at nearly two thousand Niets on the northern side of the thoroughfare, maybe a hundred or two on First Platoon's side. They've got some W7 cannons out there, and some goons in heavily armored mech frames. Those haven't advanced across to our side of Bridge Street, but the cannons turned the approaches into rubble with not a lot of cover.*>

Four red pins lit up on the display, noting the locations of the cannons. Then several dozen blue pins appeared, annotated by the estimated specs of the Nietzschean Goon-Mechs, or GMs—the Marauders' term for squishies in mech frames somewhat like a K1R.

The Niets hadn't used anything like the GM's back in the war—not that Rika had ever encountered, at least—but they seemed to have decided that the heavy mech-like armor was good for taking poundings and holding positions.

<*Ferris is going to be coming in too fast, and at a bad angle to hit*

those cannons,> Rika mused as she thought over her options. <*Smalls is up higher, and will pass over just after the B'muths drop. I have a suspicion that there's a lot more anti-air tucked away in the city than we've seen, as well. Enough firepower could take out the B'muths before they even hit dirt.*>

<*I share your suspicion about the AA. Smalls and the* Lance *are too high up for beams, though,*> Potter added. <*It'll have to be kinetics.*>

<*Smalls can make the shots,*> Chase said confidently. <*We're a klick back, anyway. Safe as houses back here—you know, if those houses were on fire and being shot at.*>

<*I'll sync up with Smalls,*> Niki informed the command team.

<*Break off several fireteams,*> Rika ordered Chase. <*Two per flank, and pull them back and around.*>

<*Flank the flankers,*> Chase said, and Rika could almost hear his grin over the Link.

Potter made a *tsk*ing sound, however. <*That's going to thin us up a lot. I see that you've instructed Ferris to drop the B'muths at the front of your flanks as well. Once we crew them, your line's going to be mighty thin.*>

<*You're right,*> Rika replied. <*I'll see about reinforcements. We haven't pulled the ISF Marines into the mix yet.*>

<*You gonna send me squishies for backup?*> Chase asked with a laugh.

Rika snorted. <*Don't forget, mister, you were a squishie 'til a couple months ago.*>

<*What an idiot I was. Mechs ru—shit, they're trying a sortie across Bridge Street. Gotta focus.*>

<*Going to drop Borden's ISF Helljumpers here.*> Rika noted a location behind the Nietzschean lines. <*They claim their drop pods can fool Nietzschean scan. Let's put that to the test.*>

<*Hell of a test,*> Potter replied.

<*Ha! I see what you did there. Getting all punny, Potter.*>

The AI let out a sigh. <*Obviously from all this exposure to you tin-heads.*>

Rika laughed and closed the connection, summoning Leslie and Alice to her side.

"Here's the situation with Chase and his first platoon," Rika said as they looked down at the holotank. "We're dropping B'muths and the ISF Marines; Niki is coordinating with Smalls to hit their cannons with kinetics. We need to take out the rest of their AA, too—once Fuller's 'toon takes the spaceport and gets us the Niets's artillery deployments."

"Shit," Leslie muttered, her tail twitching at the tip—a sure-fire sign that she was annoyed. "That's a tall order on the quick; especially with that many Niets out there. And here we thought Memphis would be an easy grab."

"Doesn't seem like there's any such thing," Alice replied, not a single note of apology in her voice for sending Chase into the lion's den.

The city of Memphis was just one theatre of operation for Rika's Marauders in the Blue Ridge System. Scarcliff and Crudge were up on Asmoian Station securing it with N Company. They were meeting with far less resistance up there than M company was seeing on the ground. Of course, N company had two platoons for a station with only ten million inhabitants, while M Company was taking on an entire planet with just four platoons.

The Marauders' saving grace was that the *Republic, Asora,* and *Capital* were easily holding back the small fleet of Nietzschean ships garrisoned in the Blue Ridge System. That left the *Undaunted* and *Fury Lance* free to help with the ground attacks—as their orbital paths permitted.

Dirtside, M Company's second platoon was on the southern end of Memphis taking on a battalion of Niets at the spaceport, while third and fourth platoons were even further afield, securing targets on the far side of the planet.

"We don't need a whole 'toon to take the spaceport," Alice said, highlighting first and second squad's positions. "We could move these two up to reinforce First Platoon's center."

Rika shook her head, wondering how Alice was missing the urgency to take the Nietzschean CIC at the spaceport. "No, speed is of the essence. If we don't get Smalls good targets yesterday, Ferris's B'muths will just be smoking craters in the ground, and First Platoon will be even worse off. Fuller's people need to keep their focus on the spaceport."

Leslie nodded slowly. "That's the right call. Half the Nietzschean supplies are there, as is their planetary operational command. Once Fuller gets that under control, we'll hamper the Nietzschean communications more than a little."

"So long as we can actually take the system-wide command center in that high-rise downtown," Alice groused. "They're going to have a lot more than just a few cannons."

<*Once Fuller gets us access to the network at the spaceport, we'll learn the location of their artillery and send targeting data up to the* Fury Lance,> Niki added to the conversation. <*As soon as they realize we have that, a smart Nietzschean commander would surrender. That high-rise will just be a big ol' wide open target.*>

Alice cocked an eyebrow. "So, kinetics from Smalls?"

"Or missiles," Rika replied with a shrug. "Whatever works best, depending on the targets."

Leslie turned the holo around, looking at it from different angles, then shook her head. "Even if we drop Borden and his folks behind the Niets—north of Terrace Avenue, to distract them—the center of Chase's line is still too weak…especially if the Niets bunch up in their center after the B'muths come into play."

<*I believe I made the same point earlier,*> Potter said, joining in the command net from First Platoon's location.

Rika nodded slowly. "Lieutenant, Chief, you're both all too

correct. I think it's time for us to pull up stakes and join the fun." She glanced at Alice, who wore standard Marauder armor that looked like it had never seen a moment of combat. "You got a helmet, Lieutenant Colonel?"

Alice pursed her lips. "Are you sure we should all go in? Who's going to run things?"

Rika rapped a knuckle on her head. "I can walk and chew gum at the same time, Alice. Don't worry, Niki and I can manage things just as well from the front as we can back here."

Alice didn't reply, and Rika wished she knew what was going on in the woman's head. The Lieutenant Colonel often made veiled comments about Rika and Niki's pairing, as well as Rika's neural upgrades. Nothing that approached insubordination, or even made Rika certain that the woman didn't trust what the ISF had done to Rika's brain, but they were slowly stacking up, building into a solid annoyance.

<*Corporal Yig,*> Rika called out to First Platoon's fireteam three/one, which had been attached to the Battalion HQ for security. <*Pull back to our position, and send someone out to scout a safe corridor to First Platoon's position. We're going to get in on the action.*>

<*Yes, ma'am. I'll send Goob out once he's done pissing on a Niet he killed.*> A chuckle came over the Link along with Yig's response. <*Give the guy his dick back, and he whips it out at every opportunity. Granted, Cole eggs him on a lot; it's like a game to her.*>

<*Stars, Corporal,*> Rika groaned. <*That* ***definitely*** *falls under the 'too much information' header. Tell him if he doesn't keep his armor bolted on, I'll make Bondo hack his junk off.*>

Yig's laughter intensified, and he replied, <*Colonel, I'll relay that order with far more glee than it warrants.*>

<*What happens in your fireteam stays in your fireteam.*>

A sense of confusion came back over the Link, then Yig exclaimed, <*Colonel!*>

Rika closed the connection, watching with approval as Leslie shut down the holodisplays and packed up the portable projector. In a minute, it would be like her HQ had never been here.

ADMIRAL GIDEON

STELLAR DATE: 10.12.8949 (Adjusted Years)
LOCATION: Nietzschean System Command, Memphis, Kansas
REGION: Blue Ridge System, Old Genevia, Nietzschean Empire

Fleet Admiral Gideon stared down from the four hundred and first floor of the MacWood Building. His gaze settled on the distant smoke rising near Bridge Street where the advancing enemy was skirmishing with the Nietzschean battalion holding that position.

"They're going to overrun our line there, sir," Colonel Sofia advised from his side. "Colonel Cole is organizing his reserve companies to flank the enemy, but I'm not convinced it will work."

Gideon glanced at the tall, yet somehow stocky-looking woman next to him. "What gives you that impression?"

"Well, sir, Cole's maneuver assumes the enemy wants to keep civilian casualties to a minimum. If that turns out not to be the case, they'll just pummel our flanking forces from orbit."

The admiral's lips pursed as he considered Colonel Sofia's words. The woman tended toward pessimism—which was one of the reasons he kept her around. He didn't need someone's lips around his asshole, he needed people who would tell it like they saw it. No punches pulled.

Sofia never pulled punches.

"Your thoughts, General Decoteau?" Admiral Gideon asked the man to his left.

"Well, our intelligence has flagged this motley crew as Marauders, a merc outfit comprised mostly of former Genevian soldiers—though I don't know how a bunch of mercs managed to steal a ship like the *Fury Lance*. However, because they're Genevians, our psycho-analysts think they're unlikely to cause mass destruction to one of their own former cities. So..." Decoteau paused to glance at Colonel Sofia. "Despite the colonel's worries, I don't think they'll perform orbital strikes on the city. Not without clear and significant targets."

"Like this building," Sofia added softly.

Gideon pretended he hadn't heard the colonel. It wasn't a new objection from her; the moment the Marauder ships had forced his garrison fleet away from the planet, she'd feared an orbital bombardment, and had advised evacuation to a bunker on the outskirts of the city.

Fleet Intel was still trying to sort out how the Marauder ships were able to withstand the attack from a numerically superior force with no damage. For all intents and purposes, it seemed as though the enemy's shields were impenetrable.

There had been a recent rash of rumors describing shielding such as what the Marauders possessed, but Gideon hadn't given the stories any serious consideration—until now.

Just the fact that a Marauder fleet was attacking a world within the Nietzschean Empire—and doing it with stolen Nietzschean ships, no less—was something that Fleet Intel was still struggling to come up with a good answer for.

Gideon knew the answer, but he didn't like it.

Somewhere, someone had screwed up. They'd overextended themselves, and suffered a loss so great, it had encouraged rogue elements like the Marauders to launch offensives.

But he knew of only one offensive large enough that its utter failure would bring about a response such as this.

The attack on Thebes.

That assault was the reason why Gideon only had a handful of ships available to police the Blue Ridge System. He'd been all but stripped bare.

Still, he was a Nietzschean, and far from defenseless. The Genevians had fallen before his people like so much ripe grain, harvested by their master scythes just a scant decade earlier. The mongrels would manage no better this time—especially not with a force comprised of a band of mercenaries.

"Pull a company from the spaceport," he ordered. "Hit those squibs from behind, and it will send them into disarray. We saw the dropships come down. Given the number of craft, there can't be more than a few platoons out there."

"There have been sightings of mechs," Colonel Sofia cautioned. "They'll be more dangerous than their regulars."

Gideon shrugged. "They can't have *that* many mechs. We killed most of those abominations at the end of the war, only let the women and more docile men live. I should know; I had to deal with a lot of that mess."

Sofia's jaw tensed, but she nodded. "Yes, sir. I'll pass the orders along."

"Make sure to tell Colonel Lucas at the spaceport to redistribute his troops so it doesn't appear as though he's sent a company to reinforce us here."

"Of course, sir," Sofia gave a sharp nod.

Gideon suspected she'd already been planning to tell Lucas that. Colonel Lucas often needed additional instruction. *Damn political appointees. Think they're officers just because their parents bought them their commissions.*

"What about the reserves north of the city?" General Decoteau asked. "I could bring them in to strengthen our position here."

Gideon half turned to the general. The man typically preferred to operate on the offense than defense, but Admiral Gideon remembered the look of worry in Decoteau's eyes when the Marauder ships had shed the fleet's beams as though they were pleasant rays of sunshine.

It was entirely possible Gideon's own face had displayed a

similar worry.

"Very well, General, call them in."

GROUND POUNDERS

STELLAR DATE: 10.12.8949 (Adjusted Years)
LOCATION: 1km South of Bridge Street, 48th Ave, Memphis, Kansas
REGION: Blue Ridge System, Old Genevia, Nietzschean Empire

"Crunch!" Chase hollered over his shoulder once he got off the line with Rika. "You can drive a B'muth, right?"

Crunch was sitting on a bench outside a restaurant bearing the name, 'The Green Pickle'. His features were hidden behind his helmet, but Chase imagined that the mech was probably a bit green, himself.

An enemy artillery round had come in almost right on top of Crunch. He'd been hunkered down with Kelly, going over positions for her fireteam, when it hit. He'd shielded Kelly and took the brunt of the explosion himself.

"You know," Crunch replied, his voice strained. "This is what we get for having more bio-parts. If I didn't have this stupid-assed half-leg, I'd be able to swap on a new one and get going. Now I have all this muscle and bone nonsense down there…which fucken hurts!"

"Can you lean to the left a bit, Sarge?" Private Harris asked from behind Crunch. "And steady your breathing. You're the perfect rifle mount."

Crunch half-turned, though with his helmet's three-sixty vision, he had no need to. "You fire that thing next to my head, Private, and I'll shove it so far up your ass you'll talk through its barrel."

Harris only laughed and repositioned next to a nearby groundcar, taking aim down the street.

"You never answered the question," Chase said, moving next to Crunch as Harris fired his PR-99 railgun at a group of Niets advancing down the street.

"I love this shit!" Harris cried out as he fired. It wasn't the first praise the private had lavished on the ISF-designed railgun. If the day progressed as it had been, it wouldn't be the last, either.

The weapon allowed the operator to dial in the desired speed of the projectile, with settings from five hundred meters per second, clear up to ten kilometers per second. It fired a variety of different pellet sizes; anything from a one-gram ball, up to a ten-gram slug. Several of the options fired the pellets as a single mass that broke apart in flight, spreading out into rail-driven grapeshot.

By the sound of the discharge, Chase could tell that Harris was letting fly with three-gram pellets moving at close to the max speed. That setting meant the private was firing at armor.

A pellet moving at that speed would punch right through a soft target—which included even moderately armored humans—with less damage than a conventional bullet. But fire it at a more heavily armored target, and it would punch through, super-heating the armor and causing significant destruction within whatever it hit.

Crunch had been watching Harris as well, and called out to the private, "Shit, Harris, you shoot like my mom! Put it where the thing's barrel meets the body."

"He was close," Chase chuckled. "And it is a kilometer downfield…behind a defensive barrier."

"No excuse," Crunch grunted. "And to answer your earlier question, yeah, I can drive a B'muth with just one leg. ISF upgraded 'em all to use neural hookups."

Chase nodded in satisfaction, doing his best not to flinch when an enemy round ricocheted off the concrete walkway nearby. "Good, one's going to drop on the next street. I'll help you hobble on over there."

"Corporal Ben!" Crunch called out as Chase helped him rise. "Make sure to keep an eye on Harris. I think he gets the ends of his PR-99 mixed up."

Ben only laughed in response, and Chase turned away from the fireteam to lead Crunch between the buildings.

"We're T-minus ten on the 'muths coming down," he told his injured teammate.

"Saw that," Crunch replied with a brief nod, wincing as he hopped along at Chase's side. "Glad they brought them down to such a convenient location."

"I could get you a little cart," Chase offered with a laugh.

"Is it insubordination if I tell my CO to fuck off?" Crunch grunted.

Chase could tell that Crunch was in a lot more pain than he was letting on, and he glanced down at the man's wound.

"Damn, a bit of the biofoam came off. Hold up, let me reapply."

Crunch nodded silently, and Chase applied the biofoam as gently as he could.

<*He's not using any of the pain suppressors the ISF gave you organics.*> Potter spoke privately into Chase's mind. <*Since the default suppressors from the GAF were removed, he's just taking it all head-on.*>

<*Shit! Are you serious, Potter?*>

<*I am,*> the AI affirmed.

"Sergeant," Chase said as the pair got underway once more, coming around the back of the Green Pickle restaurant. "You're using the pain suppressors, right?"

Crunch made a noncommittal grunt, and then gave a half-shrug. "They make me feel weird, like my senses are covered in a layer of foam."

"Is that somehow worse than agony?" Chase asked.

The sergeant didn't reply for a few moments. "Well, no…but Rika got her limbs cut off without any numbing."

"Yeah," Chase snorted. "And then she passed out. I need you functional, not slumped over unconscious, driving the

B'muth through a row of houses."

Crunch drew a breath like he was going to mount a defense against Chase's logic, but then he slumped his shoulders and nodded. "OK."

A moment later he seemed to straighten, and Chase resisted the urge to needle the mech about his obstinance.

The pair progressed the rest of the way down the alley, and came out onto the next block, which was named Burger Street—an oddity amongst the north-south numbered streets. Chase didn't see a single burger restaurant, so he assumed it was named for something other than food. Though that didn't stop him from feeling more than a little hungry at the thought of how good a double cheeseburger would taste right then.

They advanced toward the forward position held by Mitch's fireteam, and then Chase helped Crunch settle onto another bench.

"Need Bondo to get us some sort of field crutches, or something," Crunch muttered.

"Not a terrible idea," Chase said with a nod, and then jerked to the side as a round ricocheted off his armor.

He spun to see a group of Niets attacking from the storefronts across the street.

Return fire came from his left, and he grunted in satisfaction to see that Crunch had slid off the bench and was lying prone on the sidewalk, shooting at the enemies with unerring accuracy.

His moment of appreciation over, Chase dashed to the right, taking cover behind a car on the side of the road. Once in some modicum of cover, he slid his chaingun off his back and hooked it onto his right hip mount.

Crunch's armor was deflecting what incoming weapons fire managed to strike him, but Chase knew that wouldn't last. His chaingun spun up, and he eased around the car, spraying a hail of armor-piercing rounds at the storefront the Niets were set up in.

He could see figures dashing back into the store, as the enemy retreated from his barrage, but the attack didn't flag; a second wave of Niets appeared on the rooftops of three separate buildings.

Before Chase could raise his chaingun to respond to the new threat, sections of the balustrade running along the rooftops exploded. He turned to see Corporal Mitch advancing down the street with Private Lauren, both firing sabot DPU rounds at the tops of the buildings.

The pair of mechs were right at the edge of the minimum effective range—which was also the point where the uranium rods would hit with the most force.

Chase couldn't tell if they'd hit any of the Niets or just forced them back, but within seconds, there was no cover to be had at the roof's edge, and the enemy fire let up.

<*Hold a mike,*> Chase ordered, and fired a pair of his shoulder-mounted Birds of Prey—or 'Mini-Bops', as the mechs called them.

The miniature missiles streaked across the street and into the storefront. Each contained a plasma wave generator that sprayed molten star-stuff across a ten-meter radius. It was a brutal weapon, but they were facing a brutal enemy.

The two bursts were followed by screams, and the sounds of people flailing.

<*Clear the structure,*> Chase ordered.

<*On it,*> Mitch replied, signaling for Lauren to take the roofs while he stayed at street level.

The SMI-4 released a pair of drones to get a bird's-eye view before she leapt onto the closest building, her GNR firing an electron beam as she sailed through the air.

Chase walked back around the car, and offered Crunch a hand, pulling him back onto the bench. "Not sure why you can't just sit like a normal person."

"Just want you to wait on me hand and foot," Crunch replied, before gesturing over Chase's shoulder with his chin. "Looks like the ferryman is bringing us our presents."

MEMPHIS SPACE AND AIR

STELLAR DATE: 10.12.8949 (Adjusted Years)
LOCATION: Hornton Space and Airport, Memphis, Kansas
REGION: Blue Ridge System, Old Genevia, Nietzschean Empire

<*Jenisa!*> Sergeant Alison yelled at the SMI-4 in fireteam one/four. <*What are you doing up there? Scanning for hot guys? There's a whole platoon of Niets working their way up that row of shuttles. Lock that shit down!*>

<*Eh? What's that, Sarge?*> Jenisa sent back, a note of humor in her voice. <*I spotted a couple o' grease covered mechanics in a hangar halfway down the airfield. They're just standing there, watching the fireworks and lookin' good doing it. I totally think we should pay them a visit after we spank the Niets.*>

<*Stop thinking about spanking, and take out that platoon.*>

Jenisa groaned. <*Relax, Sarge. They're about to advance past a pinnace that has its refueling hatch exposed. Gonna hit it with a DPU and then throw an electron beam into a pressurized tank of hydrogen. Should be fun.*>

The SMI-4 highlighted her target on the combat net, and Alison gave a nod of approval. <*OK. Good, just make it snappy. Lieutenant Fuller is so anxious, he's practically crawling up inside my armor. We need to secure their CIC so we can get targeting data for Smalls.*>

<*Fuller's got a nice smile, he can crawl up inside my armor anytime,*> Jenisa giggled. <*OK, stop distracting me, Sarge, I have Niets to kill.*>

Alison rolled her eyes, and wished Jenisa could see it. She'd have to find the private after the engagement and give her an eyeroll in person for good measure.

An explosive round hit the side of the building that Alison was crouched beside, pulling her back into the present. She spun to see a group of four Niets approaching on her left.

<Haskell!> she growled. *<You're supposed to be on my flank. How come there are Niets shooting at me?>*

<We're a bit busy, Sarge,> Haskell replied after a moment. *<Whole fuckin' 'toon of the buggers came out of nowhere. They really don't want to let us get to the CIC.>*

<OK, just hold on. I'll get Fred's fireteam over there.>

Alison moved behind a stack of wheels while she sent the new orders to Corporal Fred. Once that distraction was out of the way, she checked her drone feeds to see that the four approaching Niets had split up to move around either side of her cover.

That's the problem with these idiots, she thought. *They never think about how high SMIs can jump.*

Alison extended her double-jointed knees and crouched down. She drew a deep breath, smelling a trace of the acrid fumes filling the air around the burning spaceport, and raced forward, planting one three-clawed foot on a wheel, then another on a tire.

She kicked on her booster jets, and sailed twenty meters into the air, high over the heads of her would-be ambushers.

Her GNR barked twice from her left arm, while the new PR-109 she clutched in her right hand fired a dozen high explosive rounds at the enemy with lethal precision.

The Nietzscheans were all dead by the time she hit the ground.

The moment her feet met the tarmac, the air was filled with the bellow of an explosion, and she knew that Jenisa's plan had worked in the mech's favor.

<I'm advancing,> she notified her squad. *<Fred, Haskell. When you get done wiping the Niets' asses, meet me at the southern side of the administrative building.>*

<Almost done, Sarge,> Fred replied. *<We just have to burp them and we'll—**shit!**>*

Alison didn't ask what had caused Fred's exclamation, and instead pulled his feeds to see a trio of enemy Terminator drones flying overhead, spraying HE rounds at the mechs.

<*Jenisa—*> she began, but the SMI-4 cut her off.

<*Got them in my sights,*> she announced, and a second later, one of the drones exploded; followed by the other two spliting up, each veering off in a different direction.

Alison tracked one of the drones on the squad's feeds and took aim where she expected it to appear around the hull of a heavy freighter, sitting on a cradle half a kilometer away.

The drone didn't emerge around the forward end of the freighter's hull when she expected, and Alison scanned the skies, looking for the thing. Then she caught sight of the Terminator as it pulled around a building on her right.

Whipping her GNR around, Alison fired a trio of projectile rounds at the drone, and one clipped it in the wing just as the Nietzschean robot fired a pair of ASM missiles at her.

Alison sprayed rounds from her PR-109 at the missiles, taking one out only seconds after it launched.

Her rounds missed the second one, and she felt a moment of terror as she struggled to track the wildly veering ASM before it reached her.

She was about to fire, when the incoming weapon exploded, and Alison looked up to see a Skyscream shriek past.

<*Stars, thanks, Bean,*> she called up to the SMI piloting the attack craft.

<*Just keeping you in one piece,*> Sergeant Bean called back. <*Wouldn't want to have to go down there and pick up all your bits.*>

<*You and me both,*> Alison replied, turning back toward the administrative building.

It lay across a hundred meters of runway that was used by surface-to-surface aircraft and any shuttles that came down on glide paths.

It was also completely devoid of cover.

Alison put her stealth systems through a pre-use cooling cycle, bleeding off as much heat as possible in an effort to bring the system back to maximum efficiency. The process flushed a chill through her, and she gave a shiver while reloading her PR-109, and then checked the auto-feeder on her GNR.

OK, ISF tech, don't fail me now.

With a slow, loping run, Alison took off across the wide-open space, praying that the stealth tech—which read as only eighty percent effective at present—and the battle raging around the spaceport would be enough to keep her from being spotted.

A Nietzschean Terminator drone swept past just a few meters above her head, with two Skyscreams chasing after—though the mech craft paused in their assault so as not to hit Alison with a stray shot.

"Shit," she whispered aloud in the confines of her helmet, hoping that no enemy targeting NSAI would pick up on the pause in the Skyscreams' attack.

She kept moving, ready for attacks that may come from the squat, three-story administrative building ahead of her, but nothing seemed to be aimed her way, and she reached the relative safety of its walls without incident.

<Alison!> Lieutenant Fuller's urgent tones came into her mind. *<We're cut off on our side; they've got a whack of their squishie-piloted Goon-Mechs over here. It's up to your squad to get in there.>*

<My fireteams are all a bit behind me,> Alison replied. *<I'm probably three, maybe five minutes from being ready to breach.>*

<No joy,> Fuller shot back. *<The B'muths are coming down in five minutes, and if we don't get Smalls some targeting coordinates, the Nietzschean W7's are gonna pummel First Platoon's line.>*

Alison looked over her fireteams' placements on the

combat net. They were all engaged with Nietzscheans; there was no way any of them could make it in time to back her up.

For a moment, she marveled at the estimation of the Niets' numbers. The combat net had a tally of seven thousand five hundred and twenty-two, a number that was climbing steadily as more and more of the enemy arrived at the spaceport from elsewhere on the planet.

All to battle eighty mechs. Well, it's almost a fair fight, but not quite.

<OK, LT, I'm going in. I'll have that data for you in five mikes.>

<Give 'em hell, Sergeant.>

Alison snorted. *<Like there's any other option?>*

Lieutenant Fuller flashed an acknowledgement, and Alison considered her best options for the fastest breach.

The schematics of the building—which they'd lifted from an off-planet database a week before—showed the main control room for the spaceport as being in an elevated hub in the center of the building.

Well, I can fight my way through the corridors, or I can just go up and over…

Alison slid her PR-109 onto its mounting hook, gauged the distance to the top of the building, crouched, and leapt twenty meters into the air, landing on the balustrade.

It bent under her weight, and she nearly lost her balance before she leant forward and rolled onto the roof in a mostly graceful move.

The surface was coated in a black, tar-like substance that had become tacky in the day's heat, and Alison came up with a black strip running down her side, and another on her back.

She hoped no one was watching the roof, when a pair of turrets rose up a dozen meters away, and opened up with armor-piercing rounds.

*****

"I still don't have any updated targeting data," Chief Ona said, twisting in her seat to meet Captain Heather's gaze.

"Do the currently selected targets reflect your best estimations?" Heather asked as she rose from the command chair and stalked to the holotank, which currently showed a top-down view of Memphis.

"Yes, ma'am. Those twenty locations are where I think their hidden AA and surface-to-surface guns are…based on the scans we've run, which are limited due—"

"I understand why we can't get a good reading on the city," Heather said, cutting the chief off. "They've improved their counterscan tech a lot since the war. A *lot* a lot."

"I've got the *Lance*'s fire control set up to hit the suspected locations. If we get targets that are too far off, it'll take a minute to reorient," Ona replied.

"Ferris is coming in hot," Heather noted, gesturing at the secondary tank that showed the Marauder destroyer's position as it dropped toward the planet. "He won't get a second run at this in time to help, so if we don't have updated data from Fuller's 'toon by the time the 'muths hit, we fire at the targets you've extrapolated."

"Aye, ma'am," Ona replied with a nod.

Heather shook her head, the ghost of a smile tugging at her lips. Sometimes the reality she was now living was almost too much to swallow. She was standing on the bridge of what was once a Nietzschean dreadnought, giving orders to squishie naval personnel who were perfectly cordial and deferential to her.

Feels good, she thought while pacing to the other holotank, and then back to the one at the center of the bridge. <*Lieutenant Fuller,*> she called down to the planet's surface. <*Am I gonna have updated data? We're T-minus five here.*>

<*There's a fucking brigade down here,*> Fuller said, his mental

tone laden with stress. *<We'll smash through them, sure. But five minutes? I've only got one mech outside their command center.>*

<Who is it?> Heather asked, wondering if one mech would be enough.

<Sergeant Alison.>

<Ali?> Heather laughed, a grim smile forming on her lips. *<Shoulda told me it was an SMI. We'll be standing by for her feed in a mike.>*

* * * * *

Alison fired a trio of rounds at one turret with her GNR, while lobbing a thermite burn-stick at the other. Her aim was true, and she raced across the rooftop, watching with her three-sixty vision as the thermite burned away half of one turret. The other continued to track her, spraying rounds in her wake and finally caught up to her, rounds slamming into her armor and the rooftop around her. One caught the back of her right knee, and the joint jammed.

Motherfucker! Alison thought, twisting midrun to fire her GNR's electron beam at the defense system.

It was a hair too close for such a shot, but Alison wasn't ready to see how much more of a pounding her armor could take.

The bolt of lightning lanced out and burned away the top of the turret; it must have hit a magazine, because the automated weapon exploded, flinging shrapnel all around her. She stumbled as a chunk of metal hit her, then she resumed her limping run toward the bulge that covered the CIC's main room.

As luck would have it, there were angled windows along the perimeter of the bulge.

Probably providing light and visual corroboration of incoming flight paths.

"Handy for me," Alison whispered as she swapped her GNR back to depleted uranium rounds, and fired one rod and then another at either side of a window's frame.

The reinforced glass held, but she prayed her rounds had bent the frame enough.

Five seconds later, she crashed into the window, and the entire assembly tore free and fell into the spaceport's central command room.

Screams sounded around her, and Alison took rapid stock of her situation as she rolled to her feet: there were seven people in the room, two were armored soldiers, and the other five were only wearing light combat gear. One bore a colonel's insignia, two were captains, and the couple were chiefs.

Alison wasted no time, firing half a clip of projectile rounds at one of the soldiers, the shots tearing a gaping hole in his right hip and up into his abdomen, while she lobbed a pair of burn-sticks at the other, turning the woman into a shrieking effigy.

Localized fire suppression systems kicked on and put out the burning soldier, filling the room with a white haze. Alison used the distraction to draw her PR-109, and fired three rounds, one into the head of each of the officers.

Eleven seconds after she'd smashed her way into the room, Alison limped over to the pair of chiefs, a gun leveled at each.

"I want the location of every battery in Memphis in twenty seconds, or I start tearing your limbs off."

* * * * *

"I've got joy!" Chief Ona cried out, half leaping out of her seat as she thrust a fist in the air.

"Count?" Heather demanded as the chief began updating the targeting data.

"Four more than I'd estimated; I had a third of their

placements off. Give me thirty seconds to get all the rail launchers realigned."

"You got it." Heather nodded in relief, and watched Ferris's destroyer begin its braking burn on the other holotank. *<Captain Chase, I have good targets from Fuller's platoon. We're firing in T-minus twenty seconds.>*

<Good!> Chase replied, relief obvious in his voice. *<Fucken Niets are lobbing everything they have at us, trying to wipe us out before Ferris gets here.>*

<Don't worry, Captain. It's not like we're the GAF space force up here, slackin' off with dicks in our hands. Mechs have your back.>

<Damn straight, Captain. I've got your targets on my HUD. Fire when ready.>

THE DROP

STELLAR DATE: 10.12.8949 (Adjusted Years)
LOCATION: Burger Street, Memphis, Kansas
REGION: Blue Ridge System, Old Genevia, Nietzschean Empire

Chase closed the connection with Smalls, and watched the skies, a smile gracing his lips as he saw the streaking light from the white-hot tungsten rounds appear in the sky.

No sooner had he spotted them than the rail-fired rods slammed into the ground, fire and fountains of debris rising into the air all around the city, smoke and ash following after.

<*You're in the clear, Ferris,*> he sent to the ship's captain.

<*Never doubted it,*> he replied. <*I get the call, I deliver the package.*>

Chase watched the remaining bright light streaking through the sky, the glow around the *Undaunted*'s shields now outshining the local star—called 'Blue Sky' by the locals—as the destroyer dipped down into the planet's ionosphere.

The Marauders had never dropped a ship with stasis shields into atmosphere before, but the ISF had told them this would happen if they did. The stasis shields were annihilating most of the atoms they came into contact with—not to mention the fire striking the ship from the Nietzschean AA emplacements.

The ship only carried two B'muths, and it was on Ferris to make sure they dropped intact; that meant he'd come in low and brake hard at the last minute. Chase gauged the *Undaunted*'s angle of descent and was surprised to see that the ship would come to within only a few hundred meters of the ground.

Whole city is gonna need to scrub down from **this** *fallout.*

Not only that, but, though the sound from the ship's

passage was still far behind the light heralding its arrival, Chase knew when it reached them, it would probably blow out half the windows in Memphis.

<*Ferris!*> he called up. <*You're too low. There's still a million civilians in the city. You're gonna deafen them!*>

<*Don't worry, Captain, check this out!*> Ferris replied in his customary, nonchalant drawl.

As Chase watched, the *Undaunted* shifted to the south and rotated. The destroyer fired its engines at what had to be a fifty-*g* burn, splashing flames and plasma across what Chase knew to be an uninhabited stretch of the planet's surface.

<*Well, now you're going to start a massive wildfire,*> Chase informed the ship's captain, trying to keep the exasperation from his voice.

<*Ye of little faith,*> Ferris scolded.

Chase saw the cruiser's engines cut out, and then a strange visual distortion swept across the area the craft's engine wash had burned. Then the *Undaunted* flashed overhead, and two objects dropped from its rear bay.

At that exact moment, the sound of the starship's descent into the atmosphere finally reached their position, and Chase felt the ground shudder as wave after wave of thunder crashed over them.

Boosters on the undersides of the B'muths fired, slewing the squat, four-legged walkers erratically as enemy smallbore anti-air fire streaked through the sky all around them. Then the twelve-meter-tall walker destined for Chase's side of First Platoon's formation slammed into the surface three hundred meters further up Burger Street.

"Clever bugger," Crunch muttered. "See that? He used the grav ramscoop to make a pressure wave that put out the fires from his engines."

"Ferris is one of a kind," Chase agreed with a nod as he looked across the street to see Mitch emerge from the closest storefront.

<*All clear in there, Captain,*> he announced.

<*Up here, too,*> Lauren added as she appeared at the edge of the rooftops. <*I think two managed to get away, but the rest of their squad has gone to meet their maker.*>

<*We riding in the 'Muth?*> Mitch asked.

Crunch snorted. <*Fat chance. You're going to get me to it, and then cover our flanks while I drive that sucker right into the Niets' faces.*>

Lauren chuckled. <*Sound strategy, Sarge.*>

<*Damn skippy it is,*> Crunch shot back, and Chase imagined the sergeant glowering under his helmet. <*Now help me get to the B'muth—the captain has better things to do than be my personal crutch. And get Wolf and Matthew to secure the damn thing, Mitch.*>

<*Already on it, Sarge,*> Mitch said as he crossed the street, gesturing for Lauren to stay on the rooftops, and provide overwatch.

Chase was only half listening as he checked in with the other squads, ensuring that the second B'muth had dropped safely.

<*Niets tried to rush the package,*> Sergeant CJ replied to Chase's inquiry. <*Unfortunately for them, they ran into an immovable object.*>

<*You get a grav barrier up?*> Chase asked.

<*No,*> CJ snorted. <*Ferris dropped the 'Muth right next to The Van, and he mowed those Niets down like he was smashing piñatas at a birthday party.*>

<*The Van?*> Chase chuckled at CJ. <*You borrowing Corin's K1R again?*>

<*Borrowing? My squad doesn't need The Van; I've got Rouse and Knight in their K1R-MBM setup. You know what they say: two mechs in one body is better than one. The Van was just taking his fireteam across to flank the flankers on Rika's orders. Just a lucky*

coincidence for him.>

<*Works for me. Who you putting in the 'Muth?*>

<*Captain!*> CJ exclaimed. <*Do you really think I'm going to let my meatheads drive the B'muth? That sucker's all mine.*>

<*I've coordinated our approaches,*> Potter interrupted their conversation. <*Crunch is going to be a few minutes before he is ready to roll.*>

<*How're things up front, Lieutenant Chris?*> Chase asked First Platoon's leader.

<*Oh, you know, Niets still can't shoot for shit, but you get enough of them spraying and praying, and things turn a bit hairy. We're holding, but Kristian here is gonna wet himself soon, so you'd best get the show on the road.*>

<*You're a real fucknut, you know that, LT?*> Staff Sergeant Kristian muttered.

Chris barked a laugh. <*Damn straight I know that.*>

<*We're just waiting on Smalls to drop the second round of joy,*> Chase advised. <*Hole up until we see their cannons go up.*>

*****

"Positive confirmation on all primary targets from Potter," Chief Ona announced. "Firing on secondary targets in fifteen seconds."

"Good work, Ona," Heather said, a near-giddy smile splitting her lips. "Gotta say, raining starfire down on Niets is the highlight of my week."

"It never gets old, ma'am," Ona agreed as her hands danced over her holodisplay, acknowledging the three NSAIs' calculations, and approving the firing solution.

"I have the new low-orbit surveillance satellites in position," Chief Garth announced. "Getting…what the heck!"

Heather saw it as well. There was a mass of heat signatures moving north from the spaceport to First Platoon's position.

Garth zoomed in and overlaid optics. "Gotta be almost a thousand Niets," he said, twisting in his seat to face Heather.

"Looks like they peeled a battalion off from the spaceport," she said.

"Firing on secondary targets," Ona announced, and a series of vibrations ran through the ship as the rails let fire once more.

"Ona, get the targeting NSAIs to work up solutions for that battalion. Most of the Niets are taking Terrace Avenue. Let's slow them down."

"With pleasure, ma'am."

<Chase,> Heather called down to M Company's commander.

<What's up, Heather? Nice shooting, by the way, those W7s are just twisted steel. We're starting our maneuver to cut off the Niets trying to flank us.>

<You may want to adjust your tactics,> Heather advised. *<You've got a thousand Niets about to crawl up your ass from the spaceport. We're gonna give them a pounding, but some will get through. We'll feed Potter the scans.>*

Chase chuckled before responding. *<Nice one, 'pounding in the ass'. I see what you did there.>*

<You're all class.>

<I've been around you mechs for too long.>

<You know, you ***are*** *a mech now.>*

Another laugh came across the Link from Chase. *<I guess we know why it's getting worse, then. You do your pounding. I'll get a squad to cover our six, and hopefully it'll be enough. I don't like the idea of being surrounded.>*

<You know Rika's orders. If things get desperate, we change our tactics.>

Smalls didn't like the idea of a full-scale bombardment of the city, but they couldn't take down Nietzschea using kid gloves. *Innocent blood is going to get spilled no matter what. Then again, we were all innocent once.*

ON THE WALL

STELLAR DATE: 10.12.8949 (Adjusted Years)
LOCATION: Nietzschean System Command, Memphis, Kansas
REGION: Blue Ridge System, Old Genevia, Nietzschean Empire

Gideon was on the far side of the room from the windows, reviewing intel from the analysts two floors down, when General Decoteau's loud string of curses grabbed his attention.

He was about to chastise the man, when a glowing light on the horizon caught his attention.

"What is it!?" he hollered while rushing to the window.

It was Sofia who answered first. "The enemy…they took the CIC at the spaceport, sir."

"What does that have to do with whatever's incoming?"

"They know where our anti-air is," Decoteau replied. "We're already tracking incoming rounds."

The general tapped the window, and an image came up between them. Gideon recognized the *Fury Lance*.

A Nietzschean Harmon-Class Dreadnought. It still rankled that these mercenaries had such a vessel.

Those thoughts were short-lived, as the dreadnought realigned itself in its geostationary orbit, and began to fire kinetic salvos from its railguns. Ground-based tracking triangulated the incoming rounds, and placed energy estimates on the screen: one-ton slugs moving at over thirty kilometers per second. Each shot would hit with the energy of a one-hundred-ton nuclear bomb.

"Analysis shows them to be shield crackers," Colonel Sofia commented quietly. "They'll punch right through the grav shields around our AA emplacements."

"We're sure that's what they're firing at?" Gideon asked.

Sofia nodded. "Hard to be completely certain until they're

within a hundred klicks—but what else could it be? If they wanted to hit us *here*, they didn't need to take the CIC at the spaceport. The locals would have told them our location without hesitation."

"Why bother?" Gideon mused. "They have those shields, our starships and orbital defenses couldn't touch them."

Sofia gestured to the light that was growing increasingly bright on the horizon. "They're dropping something. Probably heavy armor to reinforce their flanks."

Gideon clenched his fists, struggling to keep his rage at bay. To be outclassed and outgunned by Genevian mercenaries was unacceptable. *It will be a cold day in the core of Blue Ridge's star before I am defeated by a rag-tag group such as this.*

"Decoteau," he turned to face the general. "You have armor, do you not?"

He grimaced. "I have two platoons with mobile heavy-gun platforms in the city; the rest of my heavy armor was pulled up for the attack on the Theban Alliance. There's a company on the far side of Kansas with the new hover gun-skiffs, but it'll take time to get them here."

Gideon looked at the holodisplay to his left, which portrayed the possible armor the Marauders could be dropping with their inbound ship. At the top of the list was a pair of the Genevian Behemoth walkers.

"Yes, get them here as fast as possible. We're going to need it."

The admiral turned from the window, and paced across the room atop the MacWood Building. Two dozen aides were present, from master sergeants and chiefs to a bevy of captains and majors. They all stood still, watching the display of the incoming kinetic rounds, and the approaching destroyer that would be dropping off more ground pounders of some sort or another.

"Well!" he hollered at the assembled men and women. "Do you have any fucking clue what we should do? Or should I just send you out to the front lines? If I have to come up with everything myself, what do I need you for?"

Colonel Sofia turned from the windows, her expression settling into a deep scowl. "It's time for scorched earth, Admiral. These are Genevians, attempting to liberate a Genevian city. We shell a part of Memphis, and warn them to stop their advance or we continue. There are billions of people on Kansas, and we hold them in our hands."

Gideon's jaw clenched, and he glared at Sofia with undisguised disgust. Scorched earth meant they'd lost, and he wasn't prepared to concede that yet.

Behind her, streaks of light fell from the heavens, and slammed into the Nietzschean anti-air emplacements spread throughout the city. The building shook, and plumes of fire, ash, and smoke rose into the air.

Every eye in the room was on Gideon, and he felt a small pang of fear.

"OK. Do it. Take out a residential district with the guns on the north end of the city. Then send a broadcast to the entire city as well as the enemy: the Marauders halt, or we start wiping out the civilian population across the globe."

TAKE THE FIGHT

STELLAR DATE: 10.12.8949 (Adjusted Years)
LOCATION: 300m of Bridge Street, 46th Ave, Memphis, Kansas
REGION: Blue Ridge System, Old Genevia, Nietzschean Empire

Rika and her team were approaching the front when the second salvo of kinetic rounds from the *Fury Lance* rained down on the city. They struck targets all around Memphis, but most notably, they hit the four cannons on the far side of Bridge Street.

As she reached the company's forward command post—occupied by Lieutenant Karen and First Sergeant Tex—another full salvo fell, striking targets further south in the city.

<*Is that the strike on the Battalion of Niets coming up from the spaceport?*> she asked Potter.

<*It is. I don't have enemy casualty estimates yet—too much atmospheric interference to see through.*>

<*Keep me updated on their numbers,*> Rika replied, then walked into the salad restaurant where Lieutenant Karen, M Company's XO, stood near a blown-out window, surveying the terrain ahead.

"Having fun yet, Lieutenant?" Rika asked.

"Gobs, Colonel," Karen replied, glancing at Leslie and Alice. "Brought the whole gang, eh?"

"Yup. Yig's outside, giving Aaron and his folks a hand. How are things looking on the ground?"

"Just peachy," Karen replied as she took aim with her GNR, firing a sabot round at a distant target. "Chase is staying on the right flank with the B'muth, and Lieutenant Chris and Staff Sergeant Kristian are on the left flank, which has been taking a pounding. The Niets really want to take down the walkers."

"They massing in the center at all?" Rika asked as she tapped the platoon's forward feeds and surveyed the Nietzschean formations on the far side of Bridge Street.

"Hard to say," Karen replied. "They're hitting the flanks harder, but not as hard as they could be, based on what we've seen. Granted, it could be that Smalls' shots killed more of them than expected."

"Like things ever go that way," Lieutenant Colonel Alice interjected snidely. "They'll be building up, waiting for us to pull troops to reinforce the flanks. Then they'll hit us in the center and split our force."

Rika nodded.

It made sense. The Niets had far greater numbers, and they were treating the mechs like a conventional enemy, expecting that they could simply overwhelm them.

The problem with the enemy's logic was that, numbers-wise, the mechs were *already* overwhelmed, but still holding steady. Just under one hundred Marauders were facing off against at least five thousand Niets that were holed up in the city center, maybe more.

Being at a numerical disadvantage was where her people shone.

"Sounds like the perfect time to punch through *their* lines," Rika said. "Care to scout ahead, Leslie?"

Leslie chuckled, her shoulders rising and falling twice before her body disappeared, rendered invisible by her stealth flow armor. *<Like you even had to ask.>*

"We'll follow in five," Rika said as she looked over at the mechs and Alice. "Everyone green on stealth capability? I want to get behind their lines before we hit them."

"I got tagged a few times," Karen reported. "Left side is repairing—gotta love ISF tech—but I'm only seventy percent effective."

"OK," Rika glanced out the windows at the hundred-meter

stretch of road between them and Bridge Street. "You stay here and keep up pretenses. We'll keep to the left side of the road, so take your pot shots on the right side."

"And Leslie?" Karen asked. "Will she be on the left side, too?"

Alice cocked an eyebrow. "She's already off-comms. Going to have get out there to tell her to stay left, Colonel."

A burst of air slipped past Rika's lips. "Don't worry about Leslie, she'll already be on the rooftops. That woman never travels on the ground if she can help it."

Five minutes later, Rika and Alice left Karen's command post, joined by Tex, Kelly, Shoshin, and Keli. Gunnery Sergeant Aaron elected to stay behind with Karen.

Rika signaled Corporal Yig, instructing him to take Goob, Cole, and Fiona over the rooftops on the right side of the street, but to stay away from the edges.

When they reached the southern side of Bridge Street, Rika flashed a single pulse to her team, ordering them to halt, and considered her options.

Bridge street was a wide thoroughfare, easily seventy meters across, with a park occupying the central boulevard. Rock formations, water features, and abstract art filled the park area, and just a cursory look identified several Niets tucked into the landscape. A sweep with her IR overlay showed a total of thirty-seven, but she imagined there were more of them out there.

She sent another ping to the team, this one telling them to switch to random scramble channel A8.

<Spread wide on the crossing. Yig, once we're on the north side, set your team up atop that clothing store on the right. Kelly, you and yours get on that restaurant on the left. Alice, Tex, and I will head down the center and set up behind that furniture store they've reinforced. Ears open for any intel from Leslie. In twenty, we hit them.>

Yig and Kelly sent acknowledgements, and then Rika eased out from cover and began to carefully cross the street.

It had been late the previous night when the Marauders dropped on Memphis, and few civilians had been out and about when Rika's platoons hit the dirt—courtesy of a surprise drop that was aided by the fact that the Niets still didn't know Rika's stolen ships were no longer crewed by Nietzscheans.

She imagined that this would be the last time they could use that particular bit of subterfuge. The chaos caused in the Nietzschean fleets by the Battle of Albany could only last so long.

The result, however, was that most of the civilians had been at home when the fighting started—something Rika had planned on, what with Kansas having once been a Genevian world—and the streets were clear of any vehicles.

With only a short time on the ground, Rika had not been in contact with any local Genevian leaders—or resistance, if there was any. She hoped that when the dust settled, the Genevians would be in a position to take control of their world and, in short order, their star system.

Although, if they weren't, the Marauders would still have to move on. If the people couldn't rise up and take what was theirs, she couldn't stay and coddle them. The attack on Kansas was primarily for intel; intel that would be in the local Nietzschean command's databases—and possibly their commanders' heads.

<*Note to self, when we hit Nietzschean worlds, we do it during the day. Some cover on streets like this would be nice,*> Rika commented to Niki.

<*Really? That seems a bit savage.*>

Rika breathed a sigh inside her helmet. <*OK, not really—unless it's a necessity for other reasons. But the core Nietzschean worlds must be filled with nasty people, right? Can we be less cautious with* ***their*** *civilians?*>

<*I'll leave you to make that call when we get there.*> Niki's tone was a strange mix of concern and disdain. <*AIs have no love for Nietzschea, but I imagine that the bulk of their population is just like people anywhere else—just trying to get by.*>

<*Fair enough,*> Rika allowed. <*But a lot of the soldiers we fight come from their rank and file, and most of them have bought the party line. 'Master morality' and all that bullshit.*>

She checked over her new ISF-issued AC9CR rifle to make sure it was ready to do her dirty work, then and began to cross the road. Thanks to the ISF stealth tech, she had made it across the eastbound side of Bridge Street and stepped onto the curb, creeping along the sidewalk until she reached a paved pathway that ran across the grassy expanse.

She had to step more carefully on the hard surface, but it was her best option, since her feet would sink deep into the loamy soil and crush the grass—a dead giveaway to any observant Nietzschean.

She'd made it five meters along the path when a pair of Nietzscheans rose from behind a statue nearby and walked toward her.

Her first instinct was to shoot them where they stood, but she stayed her hand, knowing it would give the entire group's advance away.

<*There's no way they've spotted you,*> Niki confirmed. <*They're just going on a patrol.*>

Rika shifted to stand at the very edge of the path, the two Niets passing within centimeters of her as they strode past. As they moved toward the street, Rika saw more Niets slip out of cover, and move across the park to the street.

<*You've got company coming,*> she warned Karen, risking the EM signature.

<*How many, Colonel?*> Karen replied.

Rika chuckled. <*An entire company, Lieutenant, like I said. We'll be in position shortly and hit them from behind; should scare the shit out of 'em.>*

Karen replied with an affirmative ping, and Rika sent a double pulse to her team, informing them that the time to reach their assigned positions just cut in half.

Which meant she had three minutes to make it to her spot.

Tex and Alice's acknowledgements put them ahead of her, on another path that ran across the center boulevard. Rika walked as quickly as she dared down her own path, avoiding another dozen Niets as she went, before crossing the northern side of Bridge Street and moving down the adjacent street to the furniture store.

That would be where the enemy was coordinating the assault from. Her group would disrupt things there, while Yig and Kelly's fireteams would knock the Nietzschean company on its ass.

Three minutes later, Rika was at the entrance to the furniture store. Alice and Tex pinged their locations, and she marked them on her HUD.

Tex was front and center, ready to blast his way past the barricades the Niets had set up on the street. Rika considered reminding him that it wasn't the best use of his stealth gear, but decided that it would provide one hell of a distraction, and she could use it to her advantage.

Alice was situated atop the building across the street from the furniture store. The out-of-the-way position didn't surprise Rika overmuch—she was still shocked that Alice hadn't put up a fight about coming along in the first place.

For her part, Rika had decided to slip into the furniture store itself, easing past the door when a Nietzschean soldier walked out. Within, she saw several low-ranking officers milling around the front. She carefully moved through their midst and into a section of the store displaying artful seating arrangements—some of which had Nietzscheans sitting in them.

<Lazy bastards. They have a company about to engage, and they're lounging around,> Rika said to Niki while clenching her teeth. *<I won't feel bad at all about mowing these assholes down.>*

<Their network security is good,> Niki commented, ignoring Rika's statement. *<Not sure if I can slip in before you need to attack.>*

<Don't worry, I wasn't expecting you to. We're just going to crush these dickheads the old-fashioned way.>

<Well, try not to destroy their NSAI node in the corner, I want to interrogate it.>

Rika saw the black obelisk in a far corner of the room and nodded. *<Noted.>*

Near the NSAI was an ornate wooden table with two majors and a colonel standing next to it. A holodisplay above the table showed their view of the battlefield, and Rika was glad to see that it largely reflected the strengths and positions she had believed the Niets to hold. It also vastly overestimated the number of Marauders out on the southern side of Bridge Street.

From what she could see, the Niets didn't believe that the force they were fighting consisted exclusively of mechs. Even more amusing was that they'd tagged several mech fireteams as entire platoons—and in one case, a whole company—of soldiers.

<I'm not sure if that benefits us or not,> Rika commented to Niki.

<See those tags along the side of the holo? Those are expected advance points for reinforcements. They've called in an entire brigade to hold Bridge Street.>

<Dammit,> Rika said. *<That could cause issues…and probably shred this whole part of the city. We need to—>*

Her statement was interrupted by a Nietzschean suddenly rising from a nearby couch and walking right into her, spilling a cup of coffee across her stealthed form.

"What the…" he said, stumbling backward. "Intruder!"

She knew she had only seconds before the Niets all spotted her. Relying on Niki to send out the call to the Marauders to begin the assault, Rika backhanded the soldier who had ruined her cover, while simultaneously firing three quick shots at the officers standing next to the wooden table.

The first two rounds punched holes in the heads of the colonel and one of the majors, but the third major—a brutish-looking woman—moved with surprising speed, and ducked behind the table.

Rika had no time to go after the Niet, as rounds struck her armor from a dozen shooters. She pulled her AC9CR rifle off her shoulder, and fired on the closest group of Nietzscheans.

Her opening salvo of rail-shot was punctuated by the front of the store exploding in a hail of brick, steel, and glass.

<*You always did know how to make an entrance, Tex,*> Rika commented as she sprinted to a new position and took cover behind a cluster of armoires.

<*Just earning my keep,*> he grunted, the words punctuated by blasts from his railgun and the whine of his chaingun.

Rika tapped Alice's feeds to see that the lieutenant colonel was still atop the building across the street. After Tex's explosive entrance, there weren't many Niets standing out there, but she was keeping the remaining few suppressed.

Trying not to be actively disgusted with Alice, Rika pulled up the feeds from Kelly's and Yig's teams, noting with satisfaction that they'd hit the enemy in the rear right as the Nietzscheans had finished crossing Bridge Street, but before they had formed up to advance down the adjacent avenues.

Even though it was only nine mechs against nearly two hundred enemies, Rika considered the odds to be just about even.

<*Can you get over to the NSAI so I can drop some breach nano on it?*> Niki asked Rika.

<Sure, just checking on the kids.>

The AI laughed. *<You're one of the youngest mechs in your battalion.>*

<Not true,> Rika replied, as she peered out from her cover and fired a series of rounds at a group of Niets who were retreating in the face of Tex's onslaught. *<Plenty of the mechs are younger than I am.>*

<Thirty-two.>

<Thirty-two is plenty.>

<Clear up here,> Tex announced.

<Hostiles down outside,> Alice added.

Rika's HUD showed no more motion in the room, though EM still pinged from the armor of several of the soldiers. And of course there was the major who was hidden under the table, apparently thinking Rika still couldn't see her.

Rika kept an eye peeled for any hidden enemies while moving toward the NSAI tower. Once there, she placed a breach kit on one of the data access ports, and let Niki get to work. She followed along with what the AI was doing, enjoying her newfound ability to understand the quantum intelligence's actions.

While picking up some new tricks from the AI, Rika turned to the planning table and the Nietzschean officer below it.

"I can see you," she growled. "You're the last woman standing; no one's coming to help."

The Niet didn't reply, and Rika reached under the table and fired a light pulse blast from the emitter in her left hand.

A muffled cry came in response, and then a wavering voice followed. "OK, OK. I'm coming out. No need to pummel me."

Rika snorted and took a step back, glancing toward Tex, who was approaching through the furniture store. "Don't give me ideas."

The stocky woman emerged and scrambled to her feet, pressing her butt against the table as she sought to put as much distance as possible between herself and Rika's towering form.

<They don't make Nietzschean officers like they used to,> Tex commented as he pulled a pair of restraints from a pouch on his thigh.

<You can say that again,> Rika replied. *<Lock her down. We'll see what the NSAI knows before we try to get anything out of this one.>*

Tex grunted, and gestured for the Niet to come around the table. "Get over here, squishie. It's your lucky day."

"Lucky?" the woman asked as she edged around the table.

"Yeah! Colonel Rika, here, told me I'm not allowed to rip out your spine, so you get to keep wasting air."

The Niet swallowed loudly as Rika turned her attention to the table's holodisplay.

Rika's HUD showed Potter's overview of M Company's status: Yig and Kelly had pinned the Niets across Bridge Street, where Karen and Aaron and elements of second squad had caught them in a vise. Several groups of the enemy had already surrendered, though a few squads were holding out against the pummeling that the mechs were delivering.

<Rika.> Leslie's voice came into her mind. *<You've got company coming.>*

The holo before Rika lit up as Leslie spoke, showing a brigade moving in from the city center. She cursed silently while reviewing Leslie's feed.

When the new enemy forces reached Bridge Street, the mechs would be forced to either retreat, or engage in a level of combat that would be detrimental to the city and the civilians hiding in their homes and businesses.

<Chase, you see this?> Rika asked.

<Damn…I do now. Things are about to get intense!>

A laugh slipped past Rika's lips. *<That's one way of putting it. I'm going to take Kelly's team and push through with Leslie.*

Borden and his ISF Helljumpers have hit dirt a kilometer behind this new battalion. We'll meet up with them and cut the head off this snake.>

<*How hard should we push against this wave of Niets?*> Chase asked, not bothering to make an attempt at dissuading Rika from her plan of attack.

<*Make them earn every inch, but don't waste lives on it. Don't cluster around the B'muths, either; once you knock out the flankers, keep those things further back, or they'll draw too much fire from the enemy.*>

<*And if the Niets mass on Bridge Street, can I call for starfire?*>

Rika looked at the view before her on the map, noting that most of the businesses on the north side of Bridge Street would be empty. <*Targeted kinetics only. On Bridge Street, or sixty meters north of it. No further.*>

<*Understood,*> Chase replied. <*I'll coordinate with Smalls.*>

<*Good.*>

<*Rika…?*> His voice carried a note of hesitation.

<*Yes, Chase?*>

<*Just…you be careful, OK? Don't do anything stupid.*>

She chuckled, shaking her head. <*When have you known me to do anything stupid? Besides, isn't it insubordination to say that to your CO?*>

Chase sent a long groaning sound. <*To your first question, almost all the time, and to your second, no.*>

<*No?*>

<*No. Now go kick Nietzschean ass, and don't get anything shot off.*>

<*I'm a mech. We're specifically made to get stuff shot off and keep on fighting.*>

Chase groaned. <*Your head, Rika…don't get your head shot off.*>

<*Well, yeah…and you keep the company safe. We kill the Niets for their transgressions, not us.*>

<*Rika's Marauders! Roo-ah!*> Chase replied, a laugh coming through the Link. <*Don't worry, I know how it's done.*>

Rika closed the connection and smiled as she gazed around the furniture store, squaring her shoulders and preparing herself for what was coming next. Then she reached out to Alice and Tex. <*I'm going to take Kelly's team and meet up with Leslie. We're going to slip around the Niets and take out their HQ with the ISF Marines.*>

<*Understood, ma'am,*> Tex replied.

<*You sure?*> Alice said at the same time. <*That seems…nuts.*>

<*Better than destroying Memphis or retreating. That HQ is our target, anyway. The whole reason we're here.*>

<*OK,*> Alice said grudgingly. <*We'll hook up with Corporal Yig's team, and then return to Karen's position once they finish taking out that company.*>

<*Good,*> Rika replied before turning to the NSAI column. <*How's it look, Niki?*>

<*I've got their force deployments. Now that we know about the battalion coming up our asses, our intel lines up with the data here. They're trying to pull in forces from elsewhere on the planet, but nothing will be here in time. They've committed what they have to stopping us at Bridge Street, so right now, there's just a single company guarding the tower their HQ is set up in. If you can slip past the bulk of their forces, I don't see this as being a huge problem for you.*>

<*Excellent.*> Rika gave a curt nod, and glanced at the NSAI tower. <*Need me to trash that thing?*>

<*Nope, I seeded a virus in it. If the battalion command comes through here and hooks up with it, they'll be in for a rude surprise.*>

"What should I do with *her*?" Gunnery Sergeant Tex asked, gesturing to the Nietzschean major.

Rika sighed. "Knock the coward out and leave her, we can't be bothered to haul around garbage. Better to have a worm like her back with her people than in our way."

"Fucken Niets," Tex muttered as he walked toward the enemy officer and gave the woman a light kick in the back of the head.

"Shit, Tex," Rika said, leaning over the table. "You didn't break her neck, did you?"

"Colonel," Tex placed a hand over his heart. "I would never do such a thing to a poor, defenseless Niet. She may have a bit of a concussion, but her bones are all intact."

Rika shook her head and turned just as Leslie materialized in front of her. "*Shit!*" she exclaimed. "You trying to give me a heart attack?"

"If that's what it takes to get your ass in gear," Leslie replied. "Our window to slip past the Niet battalion is closing."

"Right, let's go."

A minute later, both Rika and Leslie were on the rooftops, invisible and deadly as they leapt from building to building, moving deeper into Memphis's city center.

The brick and stone flat-topped buildings gave way to older structures with steepled roofs, and Rika's and Leslie's progress slowed, as both women had to be more deliberate in their leaps from roof to roof.

<*This world has such a fascinating history,*> Niki noted as Rika leapt across a fifty-meter gap, landing as lightly as she could on the apex of a stone building's roof.

<*Oh yeah?*>

<*Did you know it was a lost world at one point? The people lost spaceflight, and went nine hundred years without any communication with the rest of humanity. They regressed all the way back to a pre-industrialization-level civilization.*>

Rika gave a soft whistle within the confines of her helmet as she followed Leslie to the next rooftop.

<*They're on major trade routes, though. How did they go so long without any visitors?*>

<There are indicators that a few may have come by over the years, but no one is sure. Problem is that all the nearby systems were decimated during the second wave of the FTL wars, so no one knew this place had survived—though it was barely survival, if what I see in their history books is true.>

<How'd they get uplifted, again?> Rika asked, catching a halt signal from Leslie, and moving into the lee of a spire on the rooftop.

<Believe it or not, the old Asmovian Empire used to stretch out this far. They sent scouts through the area and found this place just as it was getting back into space,> Niki explained.

<Asmovia…those were the people who genetically changed their skin to be blue, and had a thing for horns, right?>

Niki laughed. *<No, those are the Asmarians. They're still around, too, though they mostly stay in their home system. Some sort of weird religious thing about it being the star where their god Baal lives. Anyway, the Asmovians were on the far side of Genevia from here; they were conquered by the Kunta Triumvirate six hundred and twenty-seven years ago.>*

<Wait…Kunta was the precursor to Genevia,> Rika said, wishing she'd paid more attention to the nations and empires that had hewn their way through space before the Age of Reconstruction.

<It was, yes. Eventually, their parliamentary government managed to pull enough power away from the ruling triumvirate to reorder the Kunta into a democracy of sorts. They renamed it 'Genevia', and it meandered along until it became the republic you grew up in.>

<And got crushed by the Niets,> Rika added.

A sigh came from her AI, causing Rika to frown.

<Sometimes I can't tell if your single-minded hatred of the Nietzscheans is a strength or a weakness.>

<Easy. It's a strength.>

<You sure about that? You know Major Carol, the woman you

didn't kill back in the furniture store?>

Rika shrugged as she eased over the crest of the roof to watch a column of Nietzscheans double-time it past on the street below. <*The coward? Yeah.*>

<*Ever wonder what their story is? Soldiers like her?*>

<*What are you getting at?*> Rika asked.

<*Well, by her features, I'd peg her as Turan. They were a small, three-system alliance that the Nietzscheans subdued before they moved on to Genevia. They had a treaty with Genevia for mutual support against aggressors, but Genevia never came to their aid. In fact, there are a few stories like that. Genevians often complain that no one came to their aid when Nietzschea attacked, but half of their allies were already gone.*>

Rika's jaw tightened as she considered those implications. <*Why are you telling me this?*>

<*I just think you need to remember that some people you're fighting against may not have had a lot of options in life. Some of them, like Major Carol, may view Genevians as being just as bad as the Nietzscheans—something I imagine you can appreciate, given what your own government did to you.*>

<*Your point is diminished by the fact that so many of the people I've fought over the years may not have been born Nietzschean, but they* ***became*** *Nietzschean. They embraced the Niets' twisted morality.*>

<*Do you think they all had a choice?*> Niki pressed.

Rika gave a derisive snort. <*Yes, I believe they did.* ***I*** *would never have joined the Nietzschean military. I'd've sooner died.*>

<*Not everyone has the same strength of conviction that you do.*>

<*I've noticed.*> Rika was growing agitated with Niki's line of reasoning. <*Seriously, though, why are we having this conversation now?*>

<*Because maybe you should start seeing these people you're fighting as* ***people*** *and not just 'the enemy'.*>

<*Do you like it in my head?*> Rika asked Niki.

<Are you going to have us separated because you don't like my opinion?> Niki's tone was cool in the extreme.

<No, but my head might get shot off if I start thinking like that. It's my job to make life and death decisions all the time. If I start seeing the enemy as individuals who are just trying to survive, that gets exponentially harder.>

<Shouldn't it be hard?>

<It already is.> Rika clenched her teeth and slowed her breathing. *<Look I get it, this is a 'the war will consume you' conversation. And maybe it will, but I wasn't looking forward to much of a life before I got back into the shit anyway.>* Despite her best efforts, Rika's tone contained a large dose of vehemence.

Niki didn't reply, and Rika sighed, the fight gone out of her.

<Look, you make valid points. Can we just have this conversation another time? What we have ahead of us is enough to consume my mind for now.>

<OK, Rika, I understand,> Niki replied.

The AI's tone was rather sullen, but Rika decided it would have to do for now.

The Nietzscheans on the street had passed by. Leslie signaled for Rika to begin moving once more, and after several minutes, they had progressed through the older stone buildings and reached a newer section of Memphis, featuring tall towers sheathed in a glowing polymer that resembled marble, but with shifting patterns of light and dark working their way across the structures.

<A bit of a change,> Rika observed, noting the high-rise that the Nietzscheans had claimed for their system headquarters. *<They always seem to hole up in the tallest structure they can find. It sort of defies logic.>*

<It fits their 'lording over' modus operandi,> Niki replied.

Leslie pinged her location as Rika landed on the last steepled roof in the older section of the city, and Rika moved close to the scout so they could communicate on a tightbeam.

<*We're going to have to approach the Niets' tower at ground level,*> Leslie said. <*We could do a-grav, but they'll probably be watching for stealthed attackers, and a-grav would light us up.*>

Rika looked over the route they'd need to take. Seven blocks north, then three west. Each and every one of them patrolled by the enemy.

<*No one ever said this gig would be easy, did they,*> Rika commented. <*I almost want to call in for a pair of Skyscreams, and just blast our way in.*>

Leslie sent a 'negative' flag over the Link. <*You'd need to call in a few dozen; they'd shoot us down before we got halfway.*>

<*There's the sewers,*> Niki suggested.

<*They'll have the sewers monitored, and if we get trapped down there, we're done,*> Rika replied.

<*Plus it'll ruin the stealth we'll need to get into the tower,*> Leslie added. <*There's nothing for it but to work our way through the streets.*>

Rika nodded and eased toward the edge of the rooftop. <*Streets it is.*>

She was about to jump down, when the distant *thuds* of artillery came from the east.

<*Niki, we don't have anyone deployed to the east, do we?*> Rika asked while checking the deployments again.

<*No…no one—oh, shit. Listen to this.*> She passed a feed to Rika and Leslie that was flagged as originating from the Nietzschean HQ.

"All Marauder forces, this is Admiral Gideon of the Nietzschean Military Service. We have just fired an artillery barrage on a residential area in East Memphis. You will stand down and cease all aggression, or we will continue shelling civilian targets. You have five minutes to comply."

<*Short and to the point,*> Leslie commented when the transmission had ended. <*I assume we're not complying?*>

<No. We didn't come this far only to fall back when Nietzscheans behave like Nietzscheans,> Rika said before calling up to Heather. *<Smalls, do—>*

<We're already on it,> Captain Heather interrupted, rage evident in her voice. *<They've deployed counter surveillance that is messing with our satellites, but we're working around it. We'll find that new artillery and wipe it out.>*

<Good,> Rika replied. *<While you're at it, relay this message planetwide: 'To all Nietzschean motherfuckers occupying the Genevian world of Kansas. Know this: you're facing a force consisting entirely of Genevian mechs. We will rip the spines out of anyone found to have been shelling civilian targets. If that's you, go ahead and suicide now—or just stay with your artillery and wait for us to rain starfire on your heads. Either way, you will die.>*

Heather snorted. *<One hell of a missive. Consider it sent. Now, go gut their commanders.>*

<With pleasure.>

BERSERKER

STELLAR DATE: 10.12.8949 (Adjusted Years)
LOCATION: 2km South of Bridge Street, 44th Ave, Memphis, Kansas
REGION: Blue Ridge System, Old Genevia, Nietzschean Empire

<*Form up!*> Chase ordered. <*Delta 9 pattern, I want those approaches covered.*>

Corporal Ben signaled his acknowledgment, and Chase saw Whispers, Kim, and Harris move to their assigned positions.

With the Nietzscheans closing on all sides, his options had become more and more limited, which was why he was two kilometers from the front line with four other mechs, getting ready to take on the remainder of the enemy battalion that had left the spaceport half an hour earlier.

<*Smalls, can you task a satellite to get me a better picture? How many are out there—just the company's worth I can see, or more?*>

<*We'll try to get one closer, but it's tough. The Niets have a few positions in the hills, and they're using them to fire beams at the satellites. Not enough to take them out, but they're causing ionization, and making it hard to get a clear picture.*>

<*Noted,*> Chase replied. <*Whatever you can get me would be great.*>

He surveyed the city to the south of his position, noting that most of the area consisted of warehouses and commercial buildings. It would make covering the area easier than if it were residential terrain, but from what meager intel he had, it was apparent that the enemy was advancing in a line over two kilometers across.

Stars, there's just no way we can secure that much ground.

<*Captain?*> Whispers ventured. <*May I offer a suggestion?*>

<*I'm all ears,*> Chase replied, hoping the private would have

a brilliant idea that would save the day.

<*You're a great company commander, Captain—a thousand times better than the ones we had in the war. But you're still thinking like a squishie.*>

<*I am?*> he asked, wondering if the mechs didn't see him as a full member of the battalion because he used to be fully organic.

<*I don't mean any offense by it,*> Whispers said, his mental tone hushed. <*But you're establishing lines, working out how to hold the enemy back from a position; those are squishie tactics.*>

<*I'll admit, it's what I was taught,*> Chase allowed. <*What am I missing?*>

<*Fear. Not only do the Niets fear mechs, but we have stealth tech. Have us spread out more, two hundred meters apart. Then, when the Niets are all around us, give the signal, and we go berserk on them.*>

Berserk, Chase tasted the word. <*You mean we just wade in and shoot anything that moves?*>

<*Well, we do a lot of jumping. While we do that, call in the second platoon's Skyscreams to strafe the northern edges of the enemy force. It'll ruin them. Trust me.*>

Chase looked south at the approaching enemy, still four hundred strong.

<*I do.*> He switched to address the entire fireteam. <*Whispers has suggested we go berserk on these Niets, and after careful consideration, I think he's on to something. I've assigned new positions. When they reach the markers I've set, we go hog wild on their asses.*>

<*Now you're talkin', Captain!*> Harris cried out.

Ben gave a more formal acknowledgement. <*On it, sir.*>

Chase moved out of the cover he'd selected and into the middle of a wide intersection.

The Niets were moving cautiously along the perimeters of buildings, but from what the overhead drones relayed, a platoon would have to cross this street. Chances are they'd split their forces on either side, giving him his perfect berserker moment.

He didn't have long to wait before the enemy began to appear around a corner a block to the south. Two fireteams moved up the sides of the street, crossed the intersection, and then continued north. The rest of the platoon came behind—four squads, between thirteen and fifteen Niets in each. A man with lieutenant's bars on his armor was in the middle of the formation, and Chase tagged him for one of the first shots.

A minute later, half the Niets were at the intersection, the first squads moving across the open space.

Chase sent out a five-count to his team, and when the counter on his HUD hit zero, he opened fire.

Chaingun in his right hand, and PR-109 in his left, Chase sprayed rounds at both squads while unloading half his remaining Mini-Bop missiles at the Niets further back, one homing in on the lieutenant.

The barrage spent the last of the ammunition for his chaingun, and he discarded the weapon. In the few seconds since he'd launched his assault, several of the Niets had tracked his shots and begun firing at where he stood.

Their counterattack was not to be simple, though. His position in their midst meant that the Niets were far more likely to shoot their comrades than their target, and Chase compounded that by moving backward, keeping enemies on both sides while continuing to fire with his PR-109.

The Nietzscheans he was shadowing reached the northern side of the intersection, taking cover behind benches and several of the trees that lined the street.

Chase lobbed two grenades at each side, and then leapt into the air, triggering a stealth system flush, and landing invisibly on the southern side of the intersection. Once there, he fired another barrage of Mini-Bops, taking out an entire squad in seconds.

Twenty-five seconds had passed since Chase had first opened fire, and nearly half the Nietzscheans were injured or dead.

An entire squad on the south side of the intersection broke and ran, leaving just a smattering of enemies remaining on that side of the road. They bravely fired on Chase, but with his stealth systems and speed, they only tagged him twice before he was upon them, firing into their midst at point-blank range.

When that group was down, he turned back to the remaining Niets on the north side of the road, only to see them fleeing east and west.

<*How you guys faring?*> Chase asked the other mechs.

<*Just dandy!*> Kim announced, while Harris chimed in with, <*Peachy keen.*>

<*You two need to update your vernacular,*> Whispers intoned.

Chase was about to reply, when movement to the south caught his attention, and he turned to see two Goon-Mechs lumbering into view.

A laugh that was half elation and half raw fury escaped his throat as he charged toward the new enemy, knowing that he was being driven by adrenaline and the taste of victory rather than logic.

Finally, a challenge!

* * * * *

"Got them! Finally!" Chief Ona cried out from her station. "Last one of those counterscan disruptors is toast."

Heather watched the satellite view clear up, and zoomed in on Chase's position, knowing that if he got smashed, Rika would be very displeased.

Instead of seeing his group retreating from the approaching battalion, Heather let out a gasp of surprise to see the five mechs—each a few hundred meters from one another—

chasing the fleeing remnants of the Nietzschean battalion south, back toward the spaceport.

"Well I'll be," Heather muttered. "Chase finally figured out how to be a mech."

"Ma'am?" Ona asked.

"Nevermind. Hit those final artillery emplacements that are targeting civilians. I'll get Second Platoon's Skyscreams to mop up the remains of that battalion. "

While she did that, Heather put the overhead view of Chase's fight with the pair of Goon-Mechs on the central holo, a grin forming on her lips as she watched him leap atop one and drive his lightwand through the central housing, exposing the Nietzschean pilot within.

The enemy attempted to knock him down with its kinetic slugthrower, firing the thing wildly as it flailed against the mech on its back, but Chase was well anchored, and grabbed the barrel, aiming it at the other 'mech' and tearing one of its limbs free with friendly fire.

Garth was cheering, and Ona was grinning, even while she keyed in the final commands to strike the last of the Nietzschean surface artillery.

"Good day to be a Marauder, isn't it?" Heather asked her bridge crew.

"The best, ma'am," Ona replied as she let loose another barrage from the *Fury Lance*'s railguns.

BRING IT HOME

STELLAR DATE: 10.12.8949 (Adjusted Years)
LOCATION: The MacWood Building, Memphis, Kansas
REGION: Blue Ridge System, Old Genevia, Nietzschean Empire

It had taken Rika and Leslie over twenty minutes to make it to the high-rise that Nietzschean Command was holed up in. The edifice stood over two kilometers high, housing over five hundred levels, any of which could hold their quarry.

The exterior appeared to be windowless; just the smooth, shifting, marble-like sheath. The only apparent entrance was the main doors at the front, but Rika and Leslie both knew that there would be a back entrance, as well as the underground maglev tunnel that ran to the tower.

The pair had discussed using the maglev at one point, but had decided that those tunnels were only a step up from the sewers. Neither wanted to be trapped underground with hundreds of Niets overhead.

Colonel Borden and his ISF Helljumpers were a kilometer further north, stalling another battalion of reinforcements, and the two women decided to use the distraction and approach the building at ground level.

Following Leslie's location pings, Rika slipped around the side of the MacWood Building, carefully avoiding a squad of Niets who were setting up a crew-served railgun and grav shields on the street. Once at the back of the structure, the two Marauders found a set of large bay doors for the building's loading dock. Though they were open, they were guarded by a platoon of the enemy who were well entrenched.

However, their preparedness didn't involve high-energy active scan, and the two stealthed women carefully edged past the guards at the loading bay entrance, and into a broad space filled with cargo trucks, four empty heavy Goon-Mech frames, and two heavy rail batteries, both aimed at the opened doors.

<*Drop breach kits on those mech-frames. I'll breach their controls, and we'll use them for a diversion later,*> Niki instructed Rika and Leslie.

<*What makes you think we'll need a diversion?*> Leslie laughed over the tightbeam that Niki had established once they were inside.

The question was rhetorical, and no one responded.

Rika selected her two mechs, then crept through the bay until she reached them, and deployed the breach nano. <*Using the ISF's tech feels like cheating sometimes,*> she said to Niki.

<*Weren't you just telling me how keeping heads on shoulders was the goal?*>

The AI's mental tone carried a note of humor, and Rika laughed in response. <*I didn't say I'm above cheating.*>

Once the GM's internal NSAIs were breached, the two infiltrators moved to a service elevator in the back of the bay.

<*Think we should just go to the top?*> Leslie asked as they pressed the call button and waited for the car to descend.

Rika shrugged. <*If* ***my*** *city was being attacked and I had two companies of mechs on my doorstep, I'd be in a bunker somewhere far away. But these Niets probably think they can hide behind the shields they've set up around this building and the fact that we don't have a history of willfully killing civilians.*>

As she spoke, the lift arrived and the doors opened. Rika and Leslie were partially obscured by the mech frames and haulers in the bay; with any luck, no one would look too carefully at the service elevator, and wonder why it had come down and opened its doors.

<*So, what you mean is that we should start with the top floor,*> Leslie inferred as she keyed in the command.

<*You got it.*>

The elevator car's doors began to close, then a voice called out. "Hey! Hold that lift!"

Rika froze and pressed herself against the wall, knowing Leslie would do the same. She was tempted to reach over and mash the 'door close' button, but a figure burst into the elevator before she could.

"Huh…" the uniformed man said as he glanced about the empty car. "Stupid Genevian tech. Always fritzing."

He turned to the control panel, and entered his desired floor as the doors closed. Once his floor, '239', lit up on the display, the man—a corporal, by his insignia—turned to face the door. He'd just let out a long breath and widened his stance, when he turned his head back to the display.

"Floor five-oh-one, too?" he muttered, approaching the panel. "Shouldn't be able to go right up—oh, good. It's going to stop at four-ninety for inspection."

<*Well, shit,*> Leslie muttered. <*I did think it was a bit odd that we could just ride on up. I was taking it as a sign that fate was on our side.*>

Rika sent an affirmation. <*As soon as this guy gets off, we need to select a stop a few floors down from four-ninety. I don't favor a bunch of Nietzschean goons announcing our visit.*>

<*You know who you're talking to, right? I* ***live*** *for stealth.*>

A snort almost escaped Rika's lips. <*Yeah, but you're into Barne, so…*>

<*Took you long enough to bring that up again,*> Leslie said as the elevator car slowed and stopped at floor two-thirty-nine.

<*None of my business who gets horizontal with who.*>

<*Who says we get horizontal?*> Leslie shot back with mirth in her tone. <*Way more fun to do it against the wall.*>

<*Les!*> Rika groaned. <*I just meant that since Jerry…*>

<*Yeah, I knew where you were going with that…I was trying to crassly head it off. I still miss Jerry. A lot. But he's not coming back, and Barne…well…he's changed lately.*>

The Nietzschean corporal walked off the lift, and once the

doors closed, Leslie quickly keyed in a stop at floor four-eighty-five.

<*It's the tail,*> Rika said with an audible laugh. <*He's totally into the tail.*>

Leslie sent her an image of rolling eyes…just the eyes.

<*Leslie, yuck, why are those so bloodshot? What's gotten into you today?*>

<*You deserve that. Barne may be into the tail—I mean, it's pretty damn awesome—but in reality, it's you, Rika.*>

<*He's into me?*>

<*Shit, silly tin-head. No.* ***You've*** *changed him.*>

Rika estimated where Leslie was standing and gave her a light punch in the shoulder for 'tin-head'. <*I guess he is a lot less of an asshole than he used to be. But a lot of that change has come from the ISF; they've given us real hope for the first time. We're not just scratching out a living, dreaming of taking the fight back to the Niets. We're actually doing it.*>

<*OK, first,* ***ow!*** *And second, sure, that's a part of it. But it was really what you did at the Politica. You were willing to sacrifice everything to save those people. You could have killed Stavros a dozen times over, but you wouldn't sacrifice all those mechs and even his stupid-ass goons. A lot of commanders would have written them off as collateral damage. But not you.*>

Rika stood in silence for a moment as the lift began to rise. Finally, she said, <*'What you do to the least of these, you do to me'.*>

<*That sounds deep,*> Leslie said. <*What's it mean?*>

<*Something my father used to say,*> Rika replied with a shrug. She tried not to think of her parents, of how her life used to be. Though it didn't hurt as much as it used to, it still highlighted a hole inside herself that she knew would never close. <*It means that you're only as good a person as the way you treat the most vulnerable people…or creatures. People do what they can get away with; they're either policed by their own ethics, or by society.*

Watch how they treat a child that annoys them, or a homeless person, or a wounded animal—when they think no one is watching. That's the real person.>

Leslie didn't reply right off. <*That's some stiff judgement. I don't know how well I'd stack up. I've had some…bad moments in my past.*>

The lift slowed to a stop at floor four-eighty-five, and the doors slid open to reveal an empty hall. Rika stepped out first and unslung her AC9CR.

<*Good thing we've already paid for many of our sins.*>

<*Too bad we keep committing new ones,*> Leslie replied.

Rika wondered about that statement. Though Leslie often portrayed a carefree exterior, and rarely spoke of her past, there was a deepness to the woman. Something borne of a past that Rika suspected was troubled long before the Nietzschean war broke out.

Neither spoke further as they traversed the level, heading toward the stairwell on the far side. Since the other staircase was a secondary access route, it was less likely that it would be patrolled by humans, and the ISF tech would allow the two women to slip past any automated sensors the Niets would have deployed.

Several of the rooms they passed contained Nietzschean officers and chiefs of varying rank clustered around holotanks and planning tables. Few were in the halls, and those were easily avoided.

Every one of them looked worried.

Good.

When Rika and Leslie reached the secondary staircase, Niki bid them halt while she deployed nanoprobes, checking for additional security.

<*Nothing other than cameras and EM/IR sensors,*> the AI reported after a minute. <*You're clear to ascend.*>

Rika slipped in first. Though Leslie was the better scout, if they hit significant opposition, they were going to want a mech's heavier guns at the fore.

The stairs were steel, and Rika stepped lightly to avoid any sound. Though the ISF's stealth tech would dampen the noise, she didn't want to take risks when they were this close to their prey.

After two minutes, they reached the four hundred and ninetieth floor, and Rika saw a bored looking guard standing next to the door. There didn't appear to be any active scanning systems present, so Rika stepped right past him and moved onto the next flight.

The moment her right foot met the third step, she felt the slightest amount of give.

Behind her, the guard's head snapped up, and he muttered a curse before unslinging his rifle and moving toward Rika's position.

<*Shit…pressure sensor. It was in the wall mount, and I didn't spot it in time.*>

<*I got him,*> Leslie said, and a moment later, the man's head twisted at an unnatural angle, a sickening crunch filling the stairwell.

<*I've got nano on him. Give me a minute, and I'll call it in as a false alarm,*> Niki announced.

<*Keep moving,*> Leslie added. <*I'll stay here and make sure no one checks in. Or survives if they do.*> The scout had that bloodthirsty tone in her voice—the one that scared Rika a little.

<*OK. Follow after as soon as Niki gives the all-clear.*>

<*You bet, Colonel,*> Leslie replied.

Rika waited for Niki to give a green-light on the rest of the stairs, and then proceeded to climb them as quickly as possible. Chances were that even if Niki managed to hijack the dead guard's Link before someone came to check the stairwell out, a visual inspection would still have been ordered.

At least it'd better. If I were running security here, and no one checked an alarm while the city was under attack, heads would roll.

She'd just climbed past the four hundred and ninety fifth floor when Niki signaled that she'd sent the all-clear. The message came a moment before the sound of a rifle firing from below.

<*Annnd it's too late,*> Leslie commented as Rika heard pounding on the steps. <*Two Niets came to check things out. Didn't have helmets on, and now they're dead Niets. I'm moving up a flight and planting some mines on the stairs. I'll keep them busy.*>

<*Stay safe,*> Rika advised. <*Disappear and follow after me if things get too hairy down there.*>

<*Rika, they're just Niets. I'll be fine.*>

Rika wanted to admonish Leslie further for her blasé attitude, but knew that the scout was just trying to help Rika stay focused on the objective: take out the Nietzschean leadership, and force the rest of the enemy to surrender and cease the slaughter of civilians.

There was no guarantee it would work, but even if it was only partially effective in getting some of the Nietzschean field commanders to stand down, it would be worthwhile.

With her objectives firmly in mind, Rika kept moving as quickly and as silently up the stairs as she could. When she rounded the landing below the five hundredth floor, she could see a security arch at the top of the next flight.

<*You got this?*> she asked Niki.

<*Already spotted it with the probes. It has some high-grade encryption, better than the Niets usually use on systems like this; a good sign that the brass is still up here. Going to take a minute or two.*>

The sound of weapons fire came from below, and Rika shook her head. <*No dice. We don't have time.*>

Two guards were stationed on either side of the door that stood beyond the security arch. The stairwell ended at level five hundred—which meant access to the top floor was somewhere beyond the pair of Niets guarding the door.

<*You sure?*> Niki asked.

<*Yeah, gotta get this party into full swing sooner or later, anyway,*> Rika replied, then took aim with her GNR-41C and fired three rounds into the helmeted head of the guard on the left before repeating the action on the right-hand guard.

To her surprise, the projectiles didn't penetrate either guard's faceshield. She toggled the GNR to fire an electron beam, getting a shot off at the guard on the right—burning a hole clear through his head—before the other Nietzschean had recovered and opened fire on her.

<*Guess the e-beam draws a bit of a line to where I am,*> Rika said with a laugh to Niki as she leapt into the air, sailing over the security arch.

The machine began to wail as it detected her motion.

She came down next to the remaining enemy, and activated the lightwand built into her left wrist. The Nietzschean didn't have time to react, and his head fell from his shoulders half a second later.

<*Damn, Rika, you're scary fast,*> Leslie noted, and Rika saw the blood-spattered shape of the scout advancing up the stairs behind her. <*Is that from the SMI-4 upgrades, or the other stuff they did to you?*>

<*A bit of both, I think.*> Rika kicked open the door and strode into the hallway beyond, firing her GNR at a pair of lightly armored Nietzscheans rushing toward her.

The weapon was still on its electron beam setting, and the shots burned holes clear through the torsos of the two lightly armored soldiers.

Rika barely spared them a second glance as she dashed down the corridor, angling toward the center of the level, where she suspected the stairs to the top floor would be.

All around her were the trappings of luxury. Some of it

looked to have been there since before the Nietzscheans took up residence in the building, but other items—mostly the art and a few pieces of furniture—didn't fit the overall décor, and Rika suspected they were the spoils of war and later corruption.

Behind her, the report of Leslie's rifle sounded again, followed by the dull *thud* of her mines detonating.

<Well, we're not getting back down that way,> Leslie said. *<Though I suppose we could always jump a few flights…except the rubble looks like it's blocked things off at around the four-hundred-eightieth floor.>*

<We won't need to retreat from here,> Rika replied calmly as she gunned down a trio of Nietzschean officers who thought firing sidearms at a mech was a wise life choice.

Rounding a corner, she caught sight of a foyer with a broad staircase that swept up to the next floor, splitting at the halfway mark and curving to either side.

At the base of the stairs were two heavy mech frames, their four-meter-tall bulk almost more than could fit in the space. They were flanked by soldiers who were clustered around crew-served railguns, and protected by grav shields.

Rika's stealth effectiveness read at ninety-five percent, and she judged that as good enough to move into the open area at the staircase's base.

All of the Niets—twenty-seven, counting the pair inside the mech frames—were on alert, heads swiveling as they watched the room and the approaches—including the one Rika was easing through. She knew this to be the point where they were most likely to detect her, and was almost clear, when one of the soldiers cocked his head, and then fired a round directly at her.

<Spotted!>

The bullet ricocheted off her body, causing no harm. But in the following moment, all hell broke loose.

Rika leapt into the air as rail-fired slugs streaked through the space where her body had been seconds before. Her left hand fired rail shots from her AC9CR rifle while she sprayed ballistic rounds from her GNR at the nearest Niets.

The moment her feet touched the floor, she ceased firing and flung herself to the right, narrowly avoiding a spray of slugs from one of the Goon-Mech's chainguns.

As she sailed through the air, everything seemed to slow down, and a calm certainty came over her. *There is nothing these Nietzscheans can do to stop me. I am their death.*

It would be easy.

She lobbed a pair of smart grenades at the wall to the right of the stairs, angling them above the enemy's grav shields. The small balls of death bounced off the wall and headed straight for the crew-served weapon. She didn't watch to ensure they hit, trusting the 'nades to detonate once they attached to the gun.

Her focus was on the two heavies. The one on the left was advancing, conveniently blocking the left-side crew-served weapon, while the one on the right contented itself with spraying more rounds into the open space.

Rika took a moment to wonder if there were other Niets working elsewhere on this level. As best she could tell, the weaponry being fired at her would chew clear through the building—and anyone in their path—in short order.

Good thing we're near the top, she thought. *Otherwise these idiots would bring the whole building down.*

A moment later, the grenades went off, the grav shields containing the blast and flinging the nearby Niets about like rag dolls.

Rika used the moment of distraction to rush the right-hand heavy. Her DPU sabot rounds could penetrate the metal monsters, but there wasn't enough range in the foyer to fire them, and she wanted to save the charges on her electron beam for whatever may come next.

I'll do these bastards up close and personal.

The GM must have spotted her movement—likely from disturbances in the smoke that was starting to fill the room—because it jerked its chaingun toward her.

Rika would have thanked the mech's operator if she'd had the chance. The weapon mount made for the perfect landing place, and she clamped on with both feet, bending three of the barrels and fouling the weapon.

At the same time, she dropped her AC9CR back onto the hook on her back and ignited her lightwand, driving it into the main body of the thing, sinking the blade down to the hilt.

With the hole torn into the operator's pod, she disabled her lightwand and pulled her AC9CR free—briefly considering getting another set of arms—and fired on a pair of Nietzscheans rushing down the stairs, while her right foot pulled free of the gun mount and grabbed another grenade from the pouch at her waist, driving it into the hole that her lightwand had hewn.

She ran across the heavy as it scrabbled at itself, trying to knock the grenade free. She landed on the second GM, ducking behind its bulk as the grenade inside the first one detonated. Her GNR snapped three times, ballistic rounds firing into the greatly-widened opening on the first GM.

The second heavy spun around, attempting to fling her off, its movements making it impossible for the Niets operating the left-side crew-served weapon to fire on her, for fear of striking their comrade.

Rika grabbed another pair of smart grenades and set them to hit the Niets furthest from the shielded gun. The heavy swung an arm up at Rika, and she narrowly avoided getting a chaingun to the head.

The grenades detonated, and she kicked off the flailing beast to sail over the grav shield and land directly behind the crew-served railgun.

One slash with her lightwand, and the operator was dead. She locked one foot onto the gun's floor mount, and then slammed the other foot into the Niet managing the ammo. She clamped her three claws around his neck and twisted, breaking the woman's fragile bones before flinging her body at her comrades.

In the time it took to kill the two Nietzscheans, Niki had breached the simple biolock on the railgun, and Rika let out a primal scream as she fired it at the remaining heavy, tearing its limbs off before finally penetrating its armored body and killing the human inside.

A moment later, something struck her side, and she saw one of the Nietzscheans near the stairs firing a small-mass coilgun at her.

With a flick of her wrist, a smart grenade was sent sailing through the air to land on the soldier's chest. A guttural cry escaped the Niet before the top of his body exploded in a bloody spray.

Two of the soldiers on the far side of the stairs had disentangled themselves from their comrades, and were running past the now-flickering grav shield toward one of the exits. Rika didn't hesitate before gunning them down, not willing to risk the enemies regrouping with more of their scumbag friends and attacking anew.

On her right, two of the Nietzscheans who had witnessed her callous action opened fire—one with a heavy caliber slug thrower, and the other with a beam rifle.

Rika twisted to the side, spinning the crew-served railgun on its mount to point at the pair, firing the last of the rounds in its current string of ammo at the Niets, and tearing their bodies apart.

When the railgun's whine died down, a stillness fell on the foyer. Rika stepped out, around the grav shield, watching for any signs of life in the twisted wreckage of human and machine before her, nodding in satisfaction.

Easy.

Her stealth effectiveness was down to fifty percent, her armor dented and scored from the rounds that had struck her. She deactivated it; from here out, she wanted the enemy to see her coming.

<*You in one piece?*> Leslie asked. <*I nearly got hit by a salvo tearing through the walls.*>

<*I'm good. It's a bit of a Nietsoup in here, though.*>

<*Ugh…that's the worst kind. Don't tip the waiter.*>

Rika laughed at the scout's joke. <*Keep your level secure, I'm moving up to the top.*>

<*Already on it. I left a few surprises at the ruined staircase, and I'm heading to the main lift to head off any new guests.*>

<*Good. I'll holler if I need you.*>

<*Me too,*> Leslie replied.

Rika chuckled to herself, checking her AC9CR's charge and swapping its nearly spent rail-pellet magazine. Satisfied that the rifle was ready to rock, she checked her GNR for damage, ensuring that the firing modes were all functional.

Niki had already sent a passel of nanoprobes up the stairs, revealing a squad of Nietzscheans who had taken up positions in the hallway on the left-hand branch of the staircase. The top floor's halls curved, so she knew that both paths would lead her to her quarry. She took the right-hand staircase, not feeling the least bit of guilt over hitting the enemy in the rear.

Striding up the stairs and into the corridor like she hadn't a care in the world, she resisted whistling a tune.

Killing Nietzscheans was her business, and business was good.

LAST STAND

STELLAR DATE: 10.12.8949 (Adjusted Years)
LOCATION: Nietzschean System Command, Memphis, Kansas
REGION: Blue Ridge System, Old Genevia, Nietzschean Empire

Admiral Gideon tensed as the sound of weapons fire ceased. He glanced at the master sergeant next to the door.

"No one's in the corridor yet, sir," the man said, beads of sweat visible on his brow.

Gideon nodded silently, not blaming the sergeant for his nerves. They'd all watched the feeds from the base of the staircase.

The enemy they faced had impressive stealth gear, but as the fight progressed—all thirty-nine seconds of it—it became clear that the destruction was caused by a single attacker.

One of the Genevian human-hybrid mechs.

"What was that?" Decoteau asked a moment later. "It didn't look like a model I've seen before."

"An SMI of some sort," Sofia replied from her position behind a holotable, rifle held ready. "But different than any I've seen before. Faster, and that electron blade in her arm…"

"Just one…" a major on the far side of the room whispered. "What are we going to do?"

"Stow your shit," Sofia growled. "She's not invincible, and she took a lot of hits down there. Plus, we have our countermeasures ready. They should be sufficient."

Gideon wasn't convinced that Sofia's plan would work, and was wondering if it was too late to make a break for the express elevator at the far end of the corridor. The small voice in the back of his head was driving home the regret he felt for not taking Sofia's advice earlier. The bunker on the northern edge of the city was looking very inviting right then.

The staccato rhythm of kinetic rifles firing broke the silence outside the room, and was punctuated by a scream, then a shriek and some crying.

He doubted it was coming from the mech.

Seven long seconds later, a lightwand slashed through the door, cutting away the lock.

<*Hold until my signal,*> Sofia instructed. <*We need her to get inside the room.*>

Gideon swallowed. Being the bait had seemed like the right call five minutes ago when Sofia proposed this plan. He'd felt strong and in control, an inspiration to those around him—he'd also been convinced that the attacker wouldn't make it past the defenses on the stairs.

Now he worried he'd mess himself.

The electron blade slid out of the door, and he drew in a breath, holding it for three long seconds before the door exploded inward, followed by the mech striding into the room.

Her sleek, grey armor was darkened by carbon scoring and streaks of blood—from the looks of it, none of it was hers.

"Who's in charge here?" The woman's clear, strong voice rang through the room like a bell.

Gideon squared his shoulders, hoping he appeared more certain of himself than he felt. "Fleet Admiral Gideon. What are your intentions?"

The sleek mech took another step into the room. Her head didn't pivot to take the space in; he knew it didn't have to—her helmet would be feeding a surround view of the space into her mind.

The thing had eyes in the back of its head.

"My intentions are for you to surrender, Admiral Gideon. Order all your forces in the Blue Ridge System to stand down and cease all hostilities."

If Gideon hadn't seen this killing machine tear its way

through his troops just minutes before, he would have laughed in her face.

"And if I refuse?" he asked.

The mech took a step forward, swinging its right arm toward him, the meter-long barrel on its end aimed at his head.

"Then I blow your head off, and your second-in-command gets the honors."

It took every ounce of Gideon's willpower not to take a step back. He needed the mech to think him defiant and move further into the room.

Then she did. A quick step, followed by a second.

Colonel Sofia screamed "Now!" though it was not necessary. The EMP burst had already gone off, a targeted wave of modulated energy, washing over the mech.

Electricity arced across her body, and the mech stiffened, her three long fingers twitching as the EM wave continued to surge over her.

Then the EM burst cut out, and the woman let out a keening wail, her right arm jerking as though she were trying to fire the gun embedded in it.

To Gideon's great relief, nothing happened.

The mech fell still, and the tension fell out of the room, soldiers and officers rising from behind their cover. Then the mech took a shuddering step forward, a deep growl emanating from deep within the armored shell.

With a calm expression, Colonel Sofia rose and fired a CF-Net that wrapped around the mech. Upon impact, the net latched on and tightened, carbon-nano fibers drawing taut, pulling the mech's arms to its body. The Genevian horror wobbled for a moment, and then fell backward, slamming into the ground.

Gideon breathed a sigh of relief. He glanced at the windows to get an update on the status of the battle, only then realizing that, even though the EMP burst had been targeted, the wave of energy had still shorted out every display in the room.

And from the looks of it, had also killed three of the officers closest to the mech.

He glanced at Sofia, but she only shrugged. "Collateral damage."

"I can't believe she made it so far on her own," Decoteau said as he stepped toward the mech and gave it a kick.

"I wouldn't—" Sofia's words cut off as the mech twitched, a muffled voice coming from behind her helmet.

"I'll kill every last one of you fuckers!"

"Some mouth on that thing," Gideon commented, as a sergeant ran into the room, skidding to a halt when he saw the monstrosity on the floor.

A second later, he regained his composure.

"Admiral, sir!"

"What is it?" Gideon growled, annoyed at the interruption.

"The enemy, we have updated our assessment of their numbers and composition."

"And?"

"There are no more than two platoons out there," the sergeant reported.

"What?" Decoteau interjected. "How are they—?"

He cut off when Gideon waved a dismissive hand in his direction.

The sergeant took the gesture as his cue to continue. "They're all mechs. Every last one of them."

"*What*?" Sofia gasped, then gestured at the thing on the floor. "Like *this*?"

"Yes, that's their scout model. Most of them are the heavier mechs, but there are a few configurations we've not seen before. Their walkers also have shields far stronger than we've encountered in the past; not like their ships, but still strong."

"Sir." Sofia turned to Admiral Gideon. "We need to go. *Now.*"

Gideon didn't hesitate to nod. "I agree. But we need more intel on this threat; if I abandon Kansas with nothing more than wild stories…" He appeared to make a decision. "We're taking this mech."

The thing on the floor twitched at his words, but Sofia nodded. "Understood, sir."

CHASING RIKA

STELLAR DATE: 10.12.8949 (Adjusted Years)
LOCATION: Floor 500, MacWood Building, Memphis, Kansas
REGION: Blue Ridge System, Old Genevia, Nietzschean Empire

<Leslie! EM—> Rika's voice hollered over the Link, then cut out.

The scout let out a string of curses, then flung her last grenade at the wall, triggering it to bounce twice, then roll amidst the Niets that had been advancing up the primary stairwell from the floors below.

<Rika! Niki! I'm coming!>

She was running back toward the central room and its staircase to the top level before the grenade she'd thrown even went off.

When she reached the foyer at the base of the stairs and saw the carnage, Leslie felt a sense of awe sweep over her, though the feeling was short-lived, as weapons fire rained down on her from the level above.

"Fuck!" she swore as she ducked back into the corridor, reviewing the new enemies that her optics had detected.

There were at least a dozen of them up there, and by the sounds of the footsteps, another dozen were forming up at the head of the staircase's other branch.

A shot zipped over her shoulder, pinging off the wall, and Leslie realized that her grenade hadn't slowed down the first group of Niets as much as she'd hoped.

<Rika! Can you hear me? Niki?>

There was no response, and Leslie felt a sense of helplessness wash over her as she turned down a side corridor and retreated under intensifying enemy fire.

<Chase? Potter?> Leslie called out, but her comm relays

weren't responding. *The EM pulse Rika was trying to warn me about must have shorted them out. Why does she always have to run off without backup?*

Leslie continued cursing Rika's bravado and the Nietzscheans' cunning as she continued to fall back.

Through the nanoprobes she'd left behind, she watched a group of officers descend the stairs, and saw that several sergeants behind them carried Rika's bound form.

Leslie noted that Rika was struggling feebly, and breathed a sigh of relief.

She's alive.

Her need to survive warred with Leslie's desire to get Rika free. Her stealth armor reported only sixty percent effectiveness, and she knew that precluded sneaking up on the Niets and freeing her commander. Still, it would be enough to lose the squad of Niets that was trying to flush her out.

As she ran down the corridors circling the floor, Leslie tried to get close to the group of officers, only to have the feeds from her nanoprobes show them reaching the elevator bank well ahead of her, filing into a waiting car.

Stars, let them put Rika in the next car, Leslie all but prayed as she rushed back to the half-destroyed secondary staircase.

She came to the stairwell, and looked down to see a pair of Nietzscheans standing on the rubble that was piled up twenty floors below. Without a second thought, she leapt out into the empty space, firing her PR-99 at them as she fell. As luck would have it, the Niets fell across each other as they died, and she landed on their stacked bodies, then rolled off and dashed out into the corridor beyond. Without missing a beat, she raced across the four hundred and eightieth floor, firing indiscriminately at any enemy that got in her way, not even bothering to ensure they weren't gathering behind her.

Twenty seconds later, Leslie turned a corner and saw the lift doors ahead. There were two guards on either side, and she fired a series of rail-accelerated pellets, first at one, and then the other, before turning her weapon on the doors.

Shredded aluminum gave way, and she slammed into the doors and leapt across the lift to the lift-climb rail on the back wall. Below her, an elevator car was descending, and she glanced up to see another slide into place at the five hundredth level above her.

Leslie wished Niki was online to tell her where the lifts were headed. It was her hope that the group was going to the loading dock at the base of the tower. If that was the Niets' destination, they would have a surprise waiting for them—just as soon as she was able to Link up with the four mech frames she and Rika had hacked on the way into the building.

As the elevator car above began to descend, Leslie swung an arm out and caught one of the floor beams as it passed by.

Hanging from the bottom of the car, she looked down into the thousands of meters below, scanning the doors leading to each floor for any signs of activity. The last thing she needed were Niets shooting at her while hanging from the bottom of the car. No enemies showed their faces, though, and Leslie gave a silent thanks to the ISF that—even at partial effectiveness—their stealth technology was enough to fool the Nietzscheans.

Either that, or they don't have any sensors in the elevator shaft. That would be foolish in the extreme, but not terribly surprising. They're cocky bastards, after all.

As the cars descended, she watched the first one—presumably containing the enemy's commanding officers—pass below ground level, and let out a curse.

They must be going for the maglev line beneath the building.

Amid her descent, she was finally able to connect to the four mech frames they'd passed in the loading bay, and triggered their activation sequences. Once again wishing that Niki was around to help, she directed the crude NSAIs in the frames to get to the elevator shaft, and follow down once she'd passed their level.

Below, she could see the first car stopping, and assumed that it must have reached the maglev station below the building.

Sure enough, it slid to the side at the lowest level, making room for the car Leslie was hanging from. The view confirmed that this was the bottom of the shaft, and she quickly scrambled up the side of the car, hoping that she hadn't made any noticeable noise. She settled on the roof, waiting for the car to stop and its passengers to disembark.

Above her, she saw the four mech frames tear the lift doors off at the loading dock's level, and three of them clamber down the sides of the shaft.

She instructed the fourth one to wait, attempting to relay a signal through it while still at ground level. *<Potter, Chase? Are you there?>*

For a moment, there was no response, and Leslie worried she'd be entirely on her own.

Then Potter's voice came into her mind. *<Leslie! Are you OK? You sound worried.>*

<I'm OK, but the Niets captured Rika! They have her down at the maglev platform beneath the building. I'm in pursuit.>

<***What***!?>

Leslie was about to respond, when beamfire flashed above, and the mech that had been standing at the doors exploded, the lower half of its body toppling into the elevator shaft as the top half became shrapnel, spraying into the other three mech frames.

"Shit!" Leslie swore aloud, tearing off the access door on the car's roof and dropping down into the small space.

Rika was no longer in the elevator car, but two Nietzschean naval chiefs were, both frozen in surprise at the partially visible figure that had just dropped between them.

Leslie didn't even bother firing at the pair, instead racing out of the elevator as the bottom half of the mech frame slammed into it, smashing through the roof of the car, and crushing the two Niets.

She found herself in a long corridor that connected to the maglev platform. Ahead, she could see Rika's form being carried on the shoulders of the Nietzschean sergeants. She fired at them, hitting one in the legs, but then the enemy made it around a corner, forty meters away.

Passing an instruction for the remaining three mech frames to follow as best they could, Leslie took off down the corridor, cursing the need to slow as she approached the corner.

While still a dozen meters away, she flung two microdrones ahead of herself, their optics revealing four Niets crouched behind a barricade, their weapons aimed at the corner, ready to shoot anything that came around it.

Beyond them, she could see that the Nietzschean officers were already boarding the maglev, the soldiers who were carrying Rika double-timing it to reach the train.

Leslie snatched the empty grenade satchel from her waist and disabled its stealth before flinging it out beyond the corner. She didn't wait to see if the enemies fell for her weak ruse before easing around the edge.

As she'd hoped, the four guards were distracted by the flying satchel. Combined with her stealth, the weak diversion helped her make it past their barricade. Once clear, she picked up her pace, racing toward the maglev, though the doors began to close while she was still some distance away.

No! she screamed in the confines of her mind, driving her body to its limit in an attempt to reach the train.

Behind her, a voice cried out, and projectile fire streaked past her head.

She was nearly at the train when a pulse blast hit her in the back and sent her flying across the platform and over the edge.

She landed on the maglev rail as it activated, the magnetic field crushing her body against the lower half of the rail.

Pinned, tears of rage and frustration streaming down her face, Leslie stared at the departing maglev train.

The train that held Rika.

"Don't move, or I'll blow your head off!"

She looked up to see a Nietzschean standing at the edge of the platform, an ugly, snub-nosed coilgun pointed down at her.

"Think so?" she asked, wishing the Niet could see the sneer on her lips.

He looked like he was about to reply, when an electron beam tore through his chest, fired by one of the mech frames that had finally made it past the elevator car's wreckage.

The current on the maglev rail shut off, and Leslie clambered up onto the platform, watching as the Goon-Mech frames finished off the Nietzscheans.

Fuck...what do I do? She wondered.

Then an idea came to her, and she signaled the closest mech frame to open up its operator's pod. A minute later, she was inside the Nietzschean machine, racing down the maglev track.

"I'm coming, Rika," she whispered.

CAPTIVE

STELLAR DATE: 10.12.8949 (Adjusted Years)
LOCATION: Unknown
REGION: Blue Ridge System, Old Genevia, Nietzschean Empire

Rika felt consciousness slip in and out as she was jostled about for what felt like forever. Rough hands grasped her, wrenching her to and fro, the feeling barely perceptible over the pounding in her head.

Try as she might, she couldn't get a response from Niki. Her internal connection to the AI only flashed a routing error, and her external wireless connections—and her QuanComm connection—were also unresponsive.

She was barely able to move a muscle, and her mechanical limbs could have been fried for all she knew. Centrally located in her skull, directly below her reptile brain, were the heavily shielded repair mods; though she could access them, the systems only reported 'Assessing Damage' when she asked for status.

Fuuuuck! she silently raged, furious that she had allowed herself to fall into such a crude trap; her anger warring with the fear that was clawing at the edges of her mind.

She was utterly helpless, and in the hands of the Nietzscheans.

Time seemed to pass with excruciating slowness, though when she checked it, the chronometer still functioning within her mind told her that it had been eleven hours since her capture.

What!

Rika felt a fresh wave of panic. She wondered how her body had not managed to repair critical systems in that amount of time. She reviewed her internal system logs only to find signs that the Niets had tried to crack her armor several times, but that her anti-intrusion defenses had responded with nano attacks.

The ISF's nano had staved off any breaches, but the intrusion attempts had slowed her recovery significantly.

<*Rika?*>

Niki's voice came into her mind, sounding different than normal—a bit more like it used to before they were properly paired.

<*Niki!*> Rika shouted with joy. <*Are you OK? Do you know what's happened to us? Why do you sound different?*>

<*Easy, Rika. I'm OK. Well, mostly. A part of my direct I/O with you was destroyed by the EMP, so I had to re-route through your general Link—which I had to fix first. Then they tried to breach us… Stars, what a mess.*>

<*Where are we?*> Rika asked. <*Do you have any feeds?*>

<*I do, and you're not going to like it.*>

<*Niki…*>

<*We're on a ship, Rika.*>

The AI's words crashed into her like a K1R on a bender.

<*A* ***ship****? How in the stars…*>

<*I don't know any better than you. I imagine Nietzschean Command must have had some sort of evac vessel nearby. How it got past the blockade is beyond me.*>

Rika considered how that could have played out. The Niets had an effective bargaining chip with her in captivity; it could be that they'd simply told the Marauders that Rika would die if they attacked.

She hoped her mechs wouldn't fall for something like that. Her life was just as likely to be forfeit if the enemy got her outsystem.

<*It's on us to escape,*> Rika decided, pulling up her repair mods' assessments. <*Stars, we're still a mess.*>

<*Yeah, you're lucky there's enough power to keep the lights on,*>

Niki replied. *<We're in a cell of some sort. It's EM shielded, but I've sent a passel of nanocloud probes into the deck and bulkheads, looking for any power we can tap into. If we can do that, we can rebuild our nano supply, and send a batch to start eating this damn web they've wrapped you in.>*

<Then we'll show them that only idiots take mechs alive—of course they have no idea we have something like nanocloud even exists, let alone that we have it.>

Niki sent a feeling of emphatic agreement. *<Lucky for us the ISF developed a variant they were comfortable with sharing—and that we stayed in Sepe long enough for that courier to arrive. Oh, by the way, they got your AC9CR, and also managed to pull the barrel off your GNR.>*

Rika stifled a curse; getting angry wouldn't help her now, and she shouldn't have been surprised anyway. Disarming her as much as possible was a logical move on the part of the Niets. *Smart. For once.* She continued her assessment. *<Guards?>*

<There are four of them outside the cell. They check on you every twenty seconds in a rotation.>

Rika gave a soft laugh. *<Paranoid bastards. Not that I blame them.>*

Over the next half hour, she assisted Niki in finding a power source—a weak, but consistent magnetic field in the deck beneath them. They tasked the final nanoprobes to build a coil to tap the magnetic field using copper from her charging cable and threading it through a small hole they'd bored in the deck underneath her back.

<It's going to take some time to juice us up,> Rika commented as the trickle began to flow into her SC batts.

<More hours than I care to consider at this rate,> Niki agreed. *<But once we get more energy, we can build a connection that will support more amperage.>*

<Then we get free,> Rika whispered, hoping that the Niets

would leave her be for that long.

She harbored no illusions that they would.

LOST

STELLAR DATE: 10.12.8949 (Adjusted Years)
LOCATION: Intersection 48th and Bridge Street, Memphis, Kansas
REGION: Blue Ridge System, Old Genevia, Nietzschean Empire

"Shit!" Chase swore as Potter confirmed that a stealthed ship had broken atmosphere at an opportune time, and was already on the far side of the planet from the Marauder vessels.

<*Their stealth is poor, but with the atmospheric ionization from all the fighting, it was enough to get them by,*> Potter said quietly. <*I'm sorry.*>

<*Should I go after them with the* Lance?> Captain Heather asked over the command net.

Before Chase could shout 'Yes!', Lieutenant Colonel Alice joined the conversation.

<*No.*>

<*No?!*> Chase asked, pulling up Alice's location on the battlefield. She was still on the far side of Bridge Street, a kilometer away. *If I can get a line of sight on that piece of…*

He forced himself to take a deep breath.

<*Why 'no'?*> he demanded in a measured, perfectly not-murderous tone.

<*It could be a trap or a ruse,*> Alice cautioned. <*An attempt to draw us away from our target here.*>

<*Our target is the Nietzschean command officers,*> Potter reminded her. <*I don't see a high-probability scenario where they wouldn't have boarded their own their evac craft; even if Rika* ***isn't*** *onboard, we should be pursuing that objective.*>

<*What about Leslie,*> Chase asked. <*Have you managed to connect with her?*>

<*Not since that single burst,*> Alice replied. <*I imagine she's in*

pursuit.>

<*I'm sending Kelly and her team after her,*> Chase decided. <*We know from Leslie that the Niets took the maglev line from under the MacWood Building.*>

<*There's more than one line under that building, and the area is crawling with Niets,*> Alice warned.

<*You don't say?*> Chase thundered.

<*I was just going to suggest that we send in Yig's team as well,*> Alice replied, a steely edge to her voice.

Chase clenched his jaw. He wasn't certain he believed Alice, but this wasn't the time to take her to task—especially with her being in nominal command of the battalion. <*Oh, sorry.*>

<*The Niets are falling back, and we need to regroup. Kelly and Yig can check over their former HQ, while the rest of us establish our HQ at the spaceport. We can better coordinate the hunt for Rika and Leslie from there.*>

Alice's words made sense on the surface, but he wondered if it really *was* better to move to the spaceport. It was clear across Memphis, and it would take some time to get the B'muths over there.

Still, he couldn't countermand her, and he figured it would be wise to be in the same room as the woman when she was making her decisions—if for no other reason than the probable need to knock her unconscious and take command of the battalion.

<*Lieutenant Karen,*> Chase addressed M Company's XO. <*I'm going to take Potter and Aaron to the spaceport. You stay with First Platoon, and hold Bridge Street. See if you can establish a cordon to the MacWood Building to support Kelly and Yig if they need it.*>

<*You got it, Captain,*> Karen replied. <*Do you think the Niets will counterattack?*>

A trickle of sweat ran down Chase's temple, and he wished

he could remove his helmet to brush it aside.

<No, probably not. Especially since things are under control at the spaceport, and the Skyscreams control the air over Memphis. With their leaders gone, the Niets are broken. Now we just have to keep this city from devolving into chaos.>

<Fun times,> Karen replied. *<By the by, doesn't this run counter to the lieutenant colonel's orders?>*

<You're just securing the area for an orderly retreat,> Chase reasoned. *<Alice won't reach out to you directly; if she does, just tell her you're following my orders.>*

<You got it, Captain…and, Chase?> Karen's voice had grown softer, and he knew what she was going to say.

<Yes, Karen?>

<We'll find her.>

Chase gave a vehement nod in the shade beside a kitchen appliance store. *<Damn straight we will.>*

<Then we'll make the Niets pay.>

ORDERS

STELLAR DATE: 10.12.8949 (Adjusted Years)
LOCATION: Hornton Space and Airport, Memphis, Kansas
REGION: Blue Ridge System, Old Genevia, Nietzschean Empire

Alison snapped to attention as Lieutenant Colonel Alice entered the Nietzscheans' former CIC at the spaceport.

The woman was one of the few non-mechs in the Marauders, and the only one in the command other than Leslie. The other non-mechs were mostly engineers, pilots, and ship crew. So far as Alison was concerned, each and every one of them were fully-fledged members of Rika's Marauders—they bled oil just like the mechs.

But not Alice.

Everyone knew that she was a plant sent from Marauder HQ to keep an eye on them and make sure that Rika remembered she worked for the Marauders, and not Tanis and the ISF.

Bullshit, Alison thought. *Rika works for Rika. But everyone knows she's taking direction from Tanis.*

That was the scuttlebutt, at least. It was ISF intel that had enabled the Marauders to launch an attack on the Sepe System. Following that, Tanis had reached out to Rika with the information that the Blue Ridge System was all but undefended; a ripe target within Nietzschea's borders.

Of course, any goals here were secondary, now, what with Rika's capture by the Niets. Alison was beside herself with worry—along with the rest of the Marauders.

She'd heard Lieutenant Fuller and Staff Sergeant Chauncy talking about how they should just abandon Kansas—and the Blue Ridge System entirely, if needs be—to go after Rika.

The sentiment was one she shared wholeheartedly.

Still, Chase hadn't made the call to leave, so she would bide her time. But if the captain said the word, she'd pack up in a heartbeat.

No matter what the lieutenant colonel says.

"Sergeant," Alice said loudly in the otherwise empty room while glaring at the holotable showing the layout of the spaceport.

"Yes, Colonel Alice?" Alison replied, turning toward the woman.

"I need you to find the fastest, interstellar-capable ship in the spaceport. Something maneuverable that we can use as a pursuit craft."

"Ma'am?" Alison cocked an eyebrow. "Is there something wrong with our fleet?"

Alice looked up from the holo and met Alison's gaze. "Yes. It's a Nietzschean fleet, and they'll be looking for it. We need something they won't suspect, that is able to effect a pursuit and breach. You find the right craft and pick two fireteams to come along."

Alison's estimation of Alice shifted slightly. *This woman is going to lead the rescue of Rika?* That was something she could get behind.

"Yes, ma'am!"

"And, Alison," Alice said, taking a step closer, her eyes darting around the otherwise empty CIC. "Keep this to yourself. We think the Niets have breached our comms somehow—it was how they got the drop on Rika. The company commanders know we're doing this; Chase is onboard."

"So verbal orders only?" Alison clarified.

"Exactly, Sergeant."

Something about Alice's voice didn't seem right, but a gut feeling didn't warrant insubordination, so Alison nodded. "I've been inventorying the ships here, while we wait for things to settle down. I was curious if there are any Niet-owned ones that we could seize, and I found one that may fit the bill. It's a corvette-sized vessel. Interstellar-capable. It may be a bit small for yourself and nine mechs, but it has weapons, decent shields, and it can pull a hundred *g*s in a pinch."

Alice nodded as she looked over the ship that Alison had pulled up on the holo. "You're right about it being tight for ten. What if we cut that number? Can you assault a Nietzschean ship with just one fireteam?"

Alison barked a laugh. "Don't you recall Sepe? I only took two fireteams for a *dreadnought*; one will be plenty for a tin can full of Nietzschean brass running with their tails between their legs. All we have to do is free Rika, and she'll tear them limb from limb."

Alice grinned. "Excellent. Get your best fireteam to the ship, and make sure it's ready to go. I'll inform Lieutenant Fuller that I'm borrowing some of his mechs."

Alison saluted and left the CIC, feeling a bit uneasy about leaving without reporting in to Lieutenant Fuller herself. She was tempted to do just that, but he was clear across the spaceport, working with third squad to take out a final batch of Nietzschean holdouts. She didn't have time to hoof it over there and give him the information in person, so she would have to rely on Alice to pass on the news.

* * * * *

<*Captain Chase?*> Lieutenant Fuller's voice carried a note of concern as it reached Chase's mind.

<*What is it, Lieutenant?*> Chase asked as he strode into the spaceport's administrative building, ready to tear a strip off the lieutenant colonel for not responding to any of his inquiries over the last ten minutes.

<*A ship just took off from the spaceport…a fast interceptor*

corvette, from the looks of it. Did you authorize that?>

"Fuck!" Chase swore. <*Lieutenant, have your platoon sound off. I think our battalion XO has just gone off-mission.*>

Less than ten seconds later, Fuller was back. <*It's Alison and her fourth fireteam. They're missing.*>

Alison wouldn't go off on her own. This is definitely Alice's doing. Chase let a few choice curses for the woman flow through his mind. He didn't know what she was playing at, but she'd picked the perfect time to make her move; there was no way Chase was going to send a team after her when Rika was missing.

<*What should I do?*> Fuller asked.

<*Nothing. I'll handle it. I don't think Alison would go AWOL; Alice must have tricked her.*>

<*Stars…I wish we'd never brought that snake along.*>

<*You and me both,*> Chase replied. He reached the spaceport's CIC, and set Potter's hardened case down on the edge of a holotable. "You should really get a mobile frame sometime, Potter. Can you Link in from there?"

<*Yes and yes. It is a bit…awkward being carried around, but I also make for a smaller target. OK, I have access to the visual feeds. I can confirm that Alison and her fourth team joined Alice on that ship…the* Grey Goose.>

"Can you reach them?"

<*Their transponders are off, and they're not responding on comms.*>

Chase spun and paced across the room, feeling torn about leaving Alison in Alice's hands while Rika was also missing.

"What's wrong?" a deep-timbred voice asked from the entrance to the CIC, and Chase turned to see the ISF colonel, Borden.

"It's that damn Alice," Chase muttered. "She's taken five of my mechs, and snuck off. Anyone I send after her could be someone I need to get Rika back."

"Never liked her," Borden ground the words out slowly. "But Alison is good people. I'll go fetch them…and bring Alice back in shackles. You focus on getting Rika back from the Niets."

Chase pulled his helmet off and strode to the ISF Marine, extending his hand. Borden pulled his helmet off as well, the two men's eyes meeting.

"You're sure?" Chase asked.

Borden's usually stern expression cracked into a smile. "I beat Jenisa and Alison in a game of Snark; they owe me too many credits to let them off this easy."

Chase snorted. "Well, we can't let that ride. Lightspeed to you, Colonel."

"And to you, Captain. You need to get your fleet after Rika; this world can take care of itself. It was going to have to, anyway."

The ISF colonel turned and walked out of the CIC, leaving Chase to consider his words. The man was right; they wouldn't have stayed around for long—but they also would not have left the people high and dry, at the mercy of any remaining Niets and whatever thugs would be crawling out of their hidey holes.

<Lieutenant Klen,> he called up to the captain of the *Asora.*

<What's up, Chase? We going after those fuckers who took the Colonel, yet?>

<We are, but I have a special mission for you.>

A snort came over the Link. *<No can do, Captain. If the Colonel is in trouble, the* Asora *is leading the charge to get her out of it.>*

<What if the alternate mission came with a promotion?> Chase asked.

<A promotion?> Klen's tone was guarded. *<To what?>*

<How does 'Governor of Kansas' strike you?>

AMONG THE MISSING

STELLAR DATE: 10.12.8949 (Adjusted Years)
LOCATION: The MacWood Building, Memphis, Kansas
REGION: Blue Ridge System, Old Genevia, Nietzschean Empire

"Dammit!" Kelly swore as rail fire tore out of the MacWood Building's loading bay, spraying across the street and tearing into the adjacent tower. "Fucking Niets just don't want to come out and play."

Yig shook his head as the rail fire died off again. "We could hit them full force, but we're not going to get into the building if we bring it down on their heads. We need some sort of distraction."

"The Skyscreams are too far away, dealing with a bunch of Niets who still think shelling civvies is a good call," Kelly said, leaning back against a low marble wall.

"What do we need them for?" Yig asked. "You want them to get all the glory?"

Kelly gave the fireteam leader a saucy wink—which he couldn't see, with her helmet in the way, but she liked to do it just the same. "Well, we could get them to carry us up top and drop us on the roof."

"So we have to fight our way down the whole building?" Yig shook his head. "Sounds stupid."

"Well, we just drop down the lift shaft."

"Or we go two blocks west and get into the maglev tunnels over there." Yig gestured to a low building that was adorned with signs indicating the various maglev tracks and their destinations.

"There's a dozen tracks down there; we need to start from the source," Kelly shot back.

<*Have you two made it inside the building yet?*> Sergeant CJ's

voice interrupted their argument.

<Almost,> Yig said, at the same time that Kelly responded, *<Not even close.>*

<Dammit, what are you doing out there? Jerking each other off?> CJ bellowed—an uncharacteristic reaction from the sergeant.

<They've got serious rails in there with heavy shields. We'd have to take the building down to get past them,> Kelly explained. *<We're trying to figure out the best distraction.>*

<Well, you're in luck, because Crunch is halfway there. Is a B'muth a big enough distraction?>

Yig chuckled. *<Crunch in a 'Muth? That'll do.>*

"Great," Kelly muttered. "Just what I need."

"What? A 'Muth not good enough for you?" CJ asked.

A coarse laugh escaped Kelly's lips. "Oh sure, a B'muth is great, but Crunch already thinks he's saved my life twice. He keeps talking about the third time being 'the charm'."

"The charm?" Yig sounded confused. "The charm for what?"

"Marriage," Cole said with a snicker as she took up a position near the pair, firing on a Niet who had peered around a building's corner a block away. "Crunch has the hots for Kelly, wants to bed her with his new man parts."

Kelly could only groan as Yig burst into laughter.

"Stars, I can't *wait* to see this go down," he said when he'd finally regained control of himself.

Cole snorted. "Was that an intentional euphemism? If so, well done."

*****

Five minutes later, Crunch's B'muth lumbered around a corner, and came into view of the MacWood Building. The moment it was in sight, a pair of guided missiles fired from halfway up the building, streaking down toward the massive walker.

The missiles had barely left the building when point defense chainguns spun up on the back of the B'muth, destroying both in seconds.

Four more missiles streaked out from the tower, and the walker's guns made short work of them too, shrapnel raining down on the street to the cheers of Kelly's and Yig's teams.

The four-legged machine pivoted, and its main gun lifted off its back, firing a trio of ten-kilogram slugs at the locations where the missile fire had originated.

The rail-fired rounds tore clear through the building—and the high-rise on the far side, as well—before arching up over the city.

<*Shit, Crunch, we're trying not to bring the thing down!*> Kelly admonished.

<*I can do math and drive a walker, Corporal,*> the sergeant replied. <*The building's in no risk of crumbling. Now go tell those Niets to surrender before we shoot the building down on top of them.*>

<*That's what we're trying* **not** *to do—what you just said you're not doing,*> Kelly retorted.

<*Yeah, but we've just convinced them otherwise. Go, tell them they have one minute. It'll work.*>

Kelly shrugged and signaled Keli and Shoshin to cover her as she crept down the street. Her stealth was shot with all the blood and grime that covered her, and she hoped no Niets would try to take a pot shot from up high—something she supposed Crunch's railshots had discouraged.

<*Don't be timid, girl,*> Crunch admonished. <*I've got the building covered. They're not going to try anything.*>

<*Girl?*> Kelly shot back. <*I'll show you 'girl'.*>

<*That's what I'm hoping for,*> Crunch said, the grin that must have been on his face almost palpable in his voice. <*Third time, remember?*>

Kelly didn't dignify Crunch's statement with a response, and instead called out to the Niets inside the loading bay at the base of the MacWood Building.

"Hey, dickheads! The sarge in the B'muth really wants to blow some more holes through your building. I kinda want to get down to the maglev line below, but he outranks me, so if you don't all get your asses out here on the street—unarmed, mind you—then he's going to get his way and take the whole thing down. Not much I can do about that, so now it's up to you asshats. Think this thing is a big enough tombstone?"

She waited eleven seconds for the response, becoming more certain that the Niets must have a death wish as each moment ticked by.

Then a hand waved around the corner, and a moment later, over fifty Nietzscheans came out of the loading bay, and laid down on the street, hands behind their heads.

"Wow, you're all so well behaved," Kelly said as she stared at the enemy soldiers. "I should get you all some extra tasty dogfood later, a reward for being so good."

<*Really hamming it up out there,*> Crunch said.

<*Who said I'm hamming it up? We passed a big pet supply store a block back.*>

"Hey, where you going?" Yig said as he jogged to Kelly's side. "I'll take my team in. You secure these Niets, they clearly respect you."

"Yeah," Cole said as she approached the prone Nietzscheans. "They didn't listen to Yig at all when he tried to get them to come out. But you went all momma bear on them, and they just rolled over."

Kelly glanced at the enemy soldiers, nodding with appreciation at Shoshin as he moved amongst them, checking for weapons.

"Tell you what, Yig, we'll play Rock-Paper-Scissors to see who goes after Leslie."

"Best of three?" the corporal asked, and Kelly shook her head. "No. Sudden death. Winner takes all."

He shrugged, and they slammed their fists against their chests three times before showing their choices. Yig had his hand clenched in a fist, while Kelly swirled her fingers in a circle over his rock.

"What? No way!" Yig exclaimed. "Black hole has a thirty-day cooldown, and you…aww, shit."

"That's right, guard duty boy, I last used it thirty-one days ago." Kelly reached out and tapped him in the chest with a long, pointed finger. "Boom."

"Dammit," he muttered as he turned to the Niets. "OK, you assholes, I want the first row to go stand against that building and get out of your armor, then go and lay next to that fountain over there."

As Yig gave the Niets their orders, Kelly signaled Keli and Shoshin to follow her into the loading bay. "Let's go find ourselves a lost kitty."

Yig glanced at Kelly as she walked into the bay. "Hey, you mind taking Cole with you? She's likely to try and bench press a stack of Niets if she has to guard them for too long."

"Fuck, Corporal, I'm right here," Cole muttered.

"Am I wrong?" Yig asked her.

"Well…no…"

Kelly gestured for Cole to join her team, chuckling softly as they entered the bay.

"Cole's short for something, right?" Keli asked as she eased around one of the trucks, checking for ambushers—or just Niets who were too cowardly to exit the building.

"Yeah," Cole replied simply. "Is Keli short for something?"

"Sure…Kelly."

"Shut it," Kelly ordered as she leapt onto the platform at the back of the loading bay, and peered through the torn-open doors of the elevator.

<*Looks like something fun happened here,*> she said while sending a passel of drones down the shaft. <*Half a Niet Goon-Mech frame is down there…all shot to shit.*>

<*Any signs of motion?*> Shoshin asked.

Kelly stepped out into the elevator shaft, dropping the twenty meters to the bottom. <*Nope.*>

A minute later, the four mechs stood on the maglev platform, looking for clues as to which way the train had gone.

<*There,*> Keli said, pointing at scuff marks on either side of the maglev rail. <*Those match the feet on the GM in the lift shaft.*>

<*Weird,*> Shoshin grunted. <*Why are Niet bots chasing after a Niet train?*>

<*Maybe Leslie took control of them? Or they're chasing her, and she's after the train…*> Keli suggested.

<*Well, we have our track and our trail,*> Kelly said as she hopped down onto the track and broke into an easy lope. <*Let's see where it leads us.*>

It took Kelly and her team thirty minutes to get to the end of the track, thankful for the signs the Nietzschean mech frames had left on the tracks. When they reached the end of the line, they found themselves on a deserted platform, deep underground.

"One of the GMs went down here," Cole said from the far end of the platform, where she stood over the fallen form of one of the mech frames. "Shell's cracked. There was no one inside, but some Niets died doing the deed."

"Signs of a fight up this staircase," Keli said, her voice ringing out in the eerie silence of the platform.

<*Keli and Shoshin. You take that staircase, Cole and I will go up the one on the far end,*> Kelly said. <*And stop talking aloud.*>

<*OK, Boss,*> Keli replied. <*But this place is dead. No one's here.*>

<*Doesn't mean they didn't leave surprises,*> Cole shot back.

A giggle came from Keli over the Link. <*But I **like***

surprises.>

<*Shut up,*> Shoshin said as he gestured for Keli to follow him up the stairs.

Kelly met Cole at the far end of the platform, sparing a glance for the twisted—and still smoking—wreckage of the mech frame.

<*Takes a big boom to do that,*> she said while following Cole up the stairs.

<*Lotta boom. Seems to be the order of the day, though.*>

Kelly nodded. <*Got that right.*>

They climbed up seven levels, each one showing varying levels of combat, destruction, and carnage, until they got to the ground level, and came out into an utterly decimated courtyard.

<*Holy shit, Boss,*> Keli said from the far side, where she and Shoshin had emerged. <*Leslie let them have what-for.*>

<*Stop calling me 'boss',*> Kelly growled.

<*You got it, Mistress.*>

Kelly only groaned while keeping her GNR level, sweeping its barrel before her. Ahead was a landing pad—recently vacated, by the signs of refueling lines.

<*Got bodies here,*> Shoshin reported from behind a stack of supply crates. <*Nietzschean special forces. Ten of them.*>

<*Another mech frame here,*> Cole added from next to a coolant tank. <*Looks like this one was empty, as well.*>

<*There were four charging stations in the loading bay under the MacWood Building,*> Shoshin recalled as he walked toward a low structure on the far side of the landing pad. <*We need to find that last mech frame.*>

Kelly had deployed drones, and flipped through their feeds while her team examined the area. She set three of her drones to sweep over the low hills surrounding the bunker. A minute later, one of the eyes in the sky spotted a smoking crater a kilometer from the base.

<I'm going to check something out,> she informed her team. *<Keep sweeping the base.>*

A minute later, she was at the impact site. The remains of the fourth mech lay in the crater, the pilot's cocoon cracked open.

Empty.

Kelly saw something inside the cocoon, and prised the two halves apart.

<I've got blood on the fourth frame,> she reported, looking up at the clear blue sky overhead. *<I'm going to sweep the area, but I'm starting to think that Leslie hitched a ride.>*

<We'd better be damn sure,> Cole said. *<I'm not leaving 'til we know for a fact that the LT isn't here. 'Toon needs her tail for luck.>*

<You want all of her back, or just the tail?> Keli asked with a laugh.

<Keli! > Cole admonished. *<I can't believe you'd say that.>*

<Relax, Cole,> Kelly replied. *<That cat's over two centuries old and still has at least six of her lives. Gonna take more than some pissant Nietzschean brass to knock her down.>*

<They knocked Colonel Rika down,> Shoshin said quietly.

No one spoke for several minutes after that.

A half hour later, they were certain that Leslie was not at the bunker. The silver lining was that wherever the captain was, chances were that she was near Rika.

The two of them can take on anything, Kelly thought as she got ready to report in to Captain Chase. *They have to.*

PULLING UP STAKES

STELLAR DATE: 10.12.8949 (Adjusted Years)
LOCATION: MSS *Fury Lance* in orbit of Kansas
REGION: Blue Ridge System, Old Genevia, Nietzschean Empire

Dropping a battalion of mechs on a planet was a lot easier than getting them back into space again.

In the end, Chase had left the B'muths and a squad of mechs under Vargo Klen's command to finish the cleanup and keep Kansas from devolving into chaos. He had no idea how twenty mechs would manage to maintain order across an entire planet, but Chase told Squad Sergeant Abs that if things got too messy on the surface, they were to hightail it into space and leave the Blue Ridge System behind.

<*Stars, Smalls, is this the right move?*> he asked Captain Heather as he walked through the *Fury Lance* to the ship's bridge.

<*There's no right move here, Chase,*> Smalls replied. <*This is a shit-show, start to finish. Alice…well, she's just a bucket of puke to top it off.*>

<*Damn, Smalls…a bit too graphic, there.*>

The SMI-4 gave a throaty laugh. <*Sorry, cooped up too long up here. Next time we hit dirt, I'm going down to smash some Niets, and you can sit up here in the sky.*>

<*When we find those bastards that took Rika, we'll* ***all*** *go smash some Niets, and Potter can manage the ship,*> Chase sent the reply over the command network, and Potter replied with a laugh.

<*Stars I'm glad to be back up here,*> *the AI admitted.* <*I'd gotten used to a few meters of steel between me and the enemy. I think if I do go off-ship again, I'll take you up on a mech frame of some sort.*>

<*I'll get a hamster wheel for you.*> Captain Heather's chuckle spilled over the network. <*We'll get some chainguns on it, and*

you can just roll around and blast Niets.>

<*I don't think that would be very effective,*> Chase replied.

<*Just you wait and see. Carson's already working on one. It's going to be epic.*>

Chase resisted a groan. Chances were that Lieutenant Carson was doing no such thing, but he didn't have time to go check. Not only that, but the *Lance* was Heather's ship; he wasn't going to go checking up on her.

Even if I am the de-facto leader of Rika's Marauders right now.

The thought brought a weight with it, and Chase wished he could just lie down for an hour, try to catch his breath.

<*How long 'til we're underway?*> he asked Heather instead.

<*Not long, just have to get one last squad from Asmoian Station aboard.*>

<*OK, I'm going to send the* Capital *ahead. Buggsie already has her in a higher orbit, after chasing off the last of the Nietzschean cruisers.*>

<*You worried they'll come back?*> Heather asked.

He was, but he was more worried about Rika. <*Klen can fend them off. Worst-case scenario, he can just smash the Asora into their ships. He's good at crashing things.*>

<*You know I'm on the command net, right?*> Vargo Klen asked.

<*Know about it?*> Chase barked a laugh. <*I was counting on it. You good?*>

<*Yeah,*> Klen replied. <*Abs has already set up shop at Memphis's spaceport and is organizing a group of locals to help police the city and get things back in order. They've told her about a resistance that's off in the mountains, so they're going to try and link up. Seems like some of the old planetary senators might still be out there, too*>

Chase nodded in appreciation. <*Pass on my congratulations. Remember, no martyrs. We're just doing the bare minimum to keep the planet from devolving into chaos.*>

<Don't worry, Captain. We'll keep things in line. You get Rika back safe and sound.>

<That's a promise I can keep,> Chase replied.

*****

Twenty-seven minutes later, the *Fury Lance*'s mighty engines thundered to life, their thrum sending a vibration through the deck plates that no amount of a-grav dampener calibration seemed to be able to deal with.

Chase didn't mind, he liked the sensation. He could tell Captain Heather, did as well. *I wonder if Smalls tweaks the calibration just enough to keep the slight shudder in place.*

The *Fury Lance*'s captain approached him, standing across the holotank that displayed the Blue Ridge System.

"Those Nietzschean cowards gotta be heading to one of those three jump points," Heather said. "They're the ones that lead deeper into Nietzschea, *and* they're closer than any others."

Chase nodded. "They're the most logical. Agreed."

On the holotank, icons flashed showing the positions of the four Marauder ships.

Buggsie had the *Capital* boosting for the furthest point, while Travis was taking the *Republic* to the second furthest. Ferris had the *Undaunted* en route to a station which sat midway between the first and second points. It was still firmly under Nietzschean control, and a possible stopping point for Rika's abductors.

The *Fury Lance* was headed for the closest of the three points, a marker currently twenty-five AU from the ship. At their current thrust, it would take the *Lance* two days to make their destination.

"What's got you looking like that?" Heather asked. "Other than the obvious."

Chase glanced up at the ship's captain. "What makes you think there's something else? Isn't Rika being missing enough?"

Heather shrugged. "Just seems like you're having reservations."

He lifted a hand and ran it across his forehead, pulling it away greasy from sweat. "I hate the thought that Leslie could still be back there." He jerked his thumb back to where Kansas lay. "Not to mention the fact that fucking Alice took off with Alison and her team.... How did this all go so wrong so fast?"

"Alison can handle herself, and we know that Leslie isn't back on Kansas," Heather shook her head. "Kelly was thorough. You know that she of all people would not leave any stone unturned if it meant finding Rika. If she says there was nothing left at that bunker, then there was nothing left. Leslie got on the Nietzschean ship with Rika."

"As a prisoner?" Chase asked.

Heather only shrugged in response, and he sighed.

"I'm going to hit the san. Let me know if anything changes."

"You got it, Captain."

STOWAWAY

STELLAR DATE: 10.13.8949 (Adjusted Years)
LOCATION: NMSS *Spine of the Stars*
REGION: Blue Ridge System, Old Genevia, Nietzschean Empire

Even though Leslie's armor kept her warm, she couldn't help the shivers that continually wracked her body. She knew it was psychosomatic, the result of knowing that she was crammed into a small compartment with the ship's landing gear, enjoying the cold vacuum of space.

Or maybe it was that she was less than ten minutes from the end of her fresh oxygen supply. After that, she'd have to make do with only recycled air from her scrubbers.

Even though she'd been tucked away in the Nietzschean ship's folded landing gear for hours, Leslie still felt like her heart was pounding in her chest. The fight at the Nietzschean bunker had been one for the books, and she couldn't help but think it a shame that no one else had been there to witness it.

Using the three remaining Goon-Mechs, she'd taken out dozens of Niets, but hadn't managed to head off the enemy brass, or their precious cargo. In the end, the ship had lifted off from the pad, leaving Leslie on the ground to slog it out with a group of their special forces soldiers.

The GM had short-burst jump jets, and Leslie had used them to boost up to the departing ship, getting within ten meters, only to have it fire on her with its point-defense cannons.

The second shot had rent a hole in the pod, and Leslie had made a do-or-die decision.

She'd jumped the final distance.

At that point, they were over a kilometer in the air. She'd almost missed the ship, catching a single finger on a landing strut, before whipping her tail up and around the beam, barely clambering up its length before the strut had folded up into the ship.

I didn't bite it out there, and I'm not going to freeze to death in here, either! Leslie declared as she finally managed to breach the control systems for the maintenance hatch a meter above her head. *I may not be all brained up like Rika, but this isn't my first time hacking my way into a Nietzschean network—even if it's taken hours.*

Though the hatch was now unlocked, she still had to get up to it. Thanking the stars that she'd hadn't mech'd up along with Chase and Barne, Leslie wormed her way past the landing strut's armatures to the waiting hatch.

After keying in the access code she'd lifted from the ship's network, Leslie pushed the hatch open and squirmed into the tiny airlock. She cycled it, begging the stars to let the taps she'd placed in the ship's maintenance network keep the airlock activation from showing on anyone's board.

Last thing I need is to find the barrel of a gun in my face when the other side opens up.

She fought the urge to close her eyes as the airlock's inner hatch opened—not that it would have mattered. Though she hadn't gone full mech, she had taken her share of mods from the ISF, and one of them was the ability to parse three-sixty vision.

With her helmet pushing feeds into her mind, there was no way she could avoid watching the hatch open.

However, nothing but an empty service tube awaited her, and Leslie offered up a silent thanks to the stars and Jerry's soul.

She thought of him less these days, but Rika's comment earlier had brought him back to the fore.

I bet you'd love this, Jerry; kicking Nietzschean ass, just like we were always meant to. Only this time, we have ***them*** *on the run.*

Leslie carefully accessed the ship's schematics in the maintenance system she'd tapped, and downloaded the vessel's full layout.

She'd not seen the ship's name before, but the map denoted the vessel as the *Spine of the Stars.* It was a rather large name for a ship that was somewhere between a corvette and a destroyer.

It was small enough to boost out of a planet's gravity well without too much trouble, but large enough to carry the fuel to power its engines for a long burn while running the reactors hot enough to power the ship's three dozen beams.

A smile spread across Leslie's lips. Once, she would have considered three dozen beams on a ship this size to be almost overkill; that was before seeing the I-Class ships the ISF had built. Ten thousand ships like the tub she was on wouldn't even come close to an I-Class's firepower.

Leslie put the comparison out of her mind and focused on her next task: get her armor clean and repaired so her stealth would return to peak efficiency.

Once she could move about the ship with impunity, she'd assess the enemy's strength, and work out the best plan to free Rika.

Though Leslie would have liked nothing better than to blast her way through the ship and rescue the colonel as quickly as possible, chances were that her friend was in the most heavily guarded portion of the ship. There could be dozens of Niets and automated defenses waiting for her.

She'd have to wear down their numbers first.

* * * * *

"Who are you?" the man standing at the door to Rika's cell asked. "Where did you get those Nietzschean ships you attacked Kansas with?"

Rika was still wrapped in the CF net, laying on the floor of her cell, arms pressed against her sides. Her power reserves had been working their way up over the past few hours, and she activated her armor's external speakers to respond to the man.

"I'm Colonel Rika, 9th Battalion, 7th Marauder Fleet. As to where I got the ships, pretty sure it was from your mom. Right after I kicked her ass."

"A mech officer?" the man's voice dripped with disdain. "You Genevian mercs must be scraping the bottom of the barrel."

"That's where they kept us," Rika replied, her tone even. "Lucky for you. If we'd been allowed to operate at our full potential in the war, I'd have your emperor over my knee right now."

The man rolled his eyes and sighed. "I highly doubt that."

"So you have my name and rank, what are yours?"

The man straightened. "Fleet Admiral Gideon."

"Ah, the civilian killer himself." Rika gave a derisive snort. "Pretty damn small fleet. I take it the rest got sent to Thebes? I guess they left the dregs behind. How's it feel to be down at the bottom of the barrel?"

<*Easy,*> Niki cautioned.

<*Doing my best, here.*>

"I'm not going to share intel with you, squib."

"Squib?" Rika felt a laugh building. She did her best to stop it, every muscle still ached, but the chortle broke free nonetheless. "Well, this squib has killed more Nietzscheans than she can count. Gotta be closing in on a quarter million now. But that's nothing compared to what the Allies did to your people at Thebes."

She gained a modicum of satisfaction as the admiral's expression paled. "Allies?"

Rika gave a small nod—all that she could manage. "I guess

technically it's called The Scipio Alliance, but it's really run by Field Marshal Richards of the ISF. She brought a fleet in that obliterated the forces your moron of an emperor sent into Thebes. My fleet chased after the cowards that ran away to Sepe. We mopped the stars with them and left their surviving ships for the Sepians to use in case any of you dickheads decide to wander into their system again."

Halfway through Rika's recitation, Admiral Gideon began to shake his head.

"No, there is no way. Scipio is in a cold war with the Hegemony; there's no way they could send a force large enough to Thebes…not that they'd have any reason to."

<This guy really doesn't want to accept what's right in front of him,> Niki said with a laugh.

"Your intel's ancient, Admiral Gideon," Rika scoffed, reveling in the act of turning this Niet's world on its head. "Scipio is in an *active* war with the Hegemony, now. But you missed the key point—the ISF is the driving force behind the Allies. Well, them and the Transcend. Either way, they crushed your fleet with a numerically smaller force, and only lost a hundred ships doing it. You have no idea how outclassed you are."

The admiral's jaw tensed, and he shook his head. "Nice try, squib. But that tale's a thousand klicks too tall."

"Curious what the 'I' stands for?"

"In your fantasy fleet? Sure."

"Intrepid. Remember that ship that showed up twenty years ago in the Bollam's World System? Remember how it had impenetrable shields and defeated five fleets on its own?"

The admiral's eyes widened, and he shook his head. "They disappeared."

"Sure did." Rika wished the man could see her grin. "And then they got *busy*. Some folks found them and poked the hornet's nest. Now they're bound and determined to get payback while knocking down all the asshole empires. Think Nietzschea is an empire of assholes? I sure do."

The admiral didn't reply, and Rika saw him cock his head, his eyes losing focus.

<*Someone's interrupted your little bit of grandstanding,*> Niki commented.

<*Just when I was on a roll, too,*> Rika groused.

The admiral's face grew troubled, and he turned away, pausing to glance at Rika before the cell door closed. "We'll have to continue exploring your fantasies later."

"I look forward to it," Rika said as her parting rejoinder. <*Stars, that was weak. I should have come up with something way more quippy,*> she said to Niki.

<*Well, you're injured, I suppose it can be forgiven.*>

* * * * *

Leslie peered around the corner, checking to ensure that no enemies were in the corridor, biting back a curse when she saw a pair of men wrapped in one another's arms halfway down the passage.

She'd cleaned her armor off as best she could in a maintenance closet, bringing her stealth effectiveness up to seventy-two percent, but that overall number didn't represent even coverage. Patches of her armor had no stealth capability at all, making it all but useless at close range.

She paused to consider her options. *If I kill these two lovebirds, then I have to deal with bodies, and I start the clock ticking.*

Leslie decided to see if she could slip past the pair. Given how into one another they were, she might just manage. If not, she'd take them out and deal with the consequences as they came.

One of the men had untucked the other's shirt, and pushed

it up, his lips working their way across a well-muscled abdomen.

Leslie wondered at the state of discipline in the Nietzschean military, that couples would just bang out in the open.

Wouldn't surprise me if they just started fucking at some point.

She held back a laugh, half wishing they would. There'd be no way they'd notice her, then.

Moving quietly, and as slowly as she dared, Leslie was almost past the pair when a voice called out from behind her.

"Hey! What are you two assholes doing?"

Shit! Leslie thought, watching a burly sergeant stride into the passageway.

"Uh…hi, Sarge," the tummy-licking Niet said, rising to his feet right next to Leslie.

"I'll show you, 'hi, Sarge'. We got brass running for their scrawny li—what the fuck is *that*?"

Leslie could see that his eyes were fixed on her. More specifically, on a patch of armor on her shoulder that was completely visible.

"What?" one of the lovebirds asked, then his eyes fixed on Leslie. "Wait! There's—"

The man's words were his last, as Leslie extended her claws and tore out his throat with a single swipe. The other amorous Niet cried out in horror as a spray of blood splashed across him, though the utterance was cut short as he suffered the same fate as his former lover.

Leslie didn't give their deaths a second thought as she ran toward the sergeant, well aware that her form would be completely visible now, half covered in blood as she was.

The sergeant unslung a weapon, but he was too slow. Leslie was already at his side, clawed fingers stabbing through a weak point in his armor where his pauldron met his chest plate.

He cried out, but still had the presence of mind—and ample strength—to swing his rifle at Leslie's head.

She'd been ready for a counterattack, and blocked the blow with her right arm, while drawing her lightwand and slamming the blade into his neck.

It tore right through his light armor and jutted out the other side.

She took a step back and watched the large soldier crumple, before the sound of footfalls coming from around the corner sent her running further aft in the ship.

* * * * *

"We've got her cornered on the aft end of Deck 7, sir. She *might* have made it down to Deck 8, but we have it cordoned off as well," Sofia reported as Admiral Gideon strode onto the bridge.

"She?" Gideon asked, scowling at the display showing the bloody mess on the port side of Deck 9.

Sofia flicked a finger, and the holodisplay shifted to show a woman in black armor, half-covered in blood, sprinting through a passageway on the ship.

"Is that a tail?" Gideon asked.

"Yes. This is the woman who breached the MacWood Building with Colonel Rika. I can only assume that she was in one of the mechs that pursued us down the maglev line."

"Tenacious bitch," Gideon muttered. "I want her dead; we have enough trouble going on. Vent the entire aft half of the ship if you have to."

"She's in armor," General Decoteau joined in the conversation from where he sat at the back of the bridge. "Vacuum may do her no harm."

"Kill grav too, then," Gideon said with a sweep of his hand. "Whatever can disadvantage her."

"I advise against that," Sofia said, her voice deferential and cautious. "It's entirely possible that she's more adept in those conditions than our own soldiers."

"I don't care about our soldiers," Gideon shot back. "It *will* disadvantage her. One shot in the right place, and she sucks vacuum and dies. The same is true for our troops, but we have over fifty of them."

"Forty-eight," Decoteau said, both his tone and his posture shouting that he was entirely disinterested in the situation. "But who's counting."

Gideon was about to lay into the general, but saw that the pair of ensigns manning the bridge consoles were staring at the exchange with wide eyes.

"Attend to your duties," Gideon thundered before pointing at Decoteau. "You. In my office. *Now*!"

The general rose, his posture still one of insolence, and sauntered off the bridge and into the passageway.

Gideon's office was the first on the left, and Decoteau ambled in, the admiral storming after him, slamming the door once they were both inside.

"What the fuck is your deal, General?" Gideon demanded as Decoteau sat in one of the plas chairs next to the desk.

"My deal?" the general coughed out a laugh. "Well, I took a bullet today; that was fun. So I'm basically just waiting to die at this point."

Gideon frowned. "From the shot? You're already patched up. You'll be fine."

Decoteau's expression darkened, and he rose to face Gideon. "No, no I *won't* be fine. You saw what these Marauders can do; they dropped a company to take a planet. *A planet,* Admiral. And two of them—fucking skinny-assed women, at that—killed their way through our HQ, and almost took us out, too."

"Almost," Gideon shot back.

"Well yeah, we survived. But you seem hell-bent on giving them as many fucking chances as you can. You should have killed that mech colonel—or left her behind. That might have slowed them down. Now she's on our ship, and so is one of her friends. They killed hundreds of our soldiers already. Do you really think that the fuckheads on this ship—lazy assholes who've never seen combat in their lives—will stand up to one of them?"

"Watch it, Decoteau. Don't forget who you're talking to."

The general leant back in his chair and looked Gideon up and down. "From where I stand, it's a dead man walking. Only way we make it out of this is if we kill the mech, set the reactor to blow, and get on a shuttle. Any other scenario sees us dead within half a day."

Gideon couldn't believe what Decoteau was saying. The general wasn't the brightest, or most ambitious of men, but he had never seemed so…pathetic before.

"You're a fucking coward!" the admiral screamed. "I'll have you court-martialed!"

"You?" Decoteau snorted. "You'll be dead. You're not having anyone court-martialed."

Gideon ground his teeth together as his vision turned red. He took a step back, snatched his sidearm from its holster, and pointed it at the general's head. The man's eyes grew wide, then he slowly rose from his chair, the two men standing still for a moment, staring at one another in silence.

Suddenly Decoteau lunged for Gideon, and the admiral squeezed the trigger three times. After the general's body fell, he emptied the magazine into the former officer's head, turning it into a bloody pulp, smeared across the deck.

PURSUIT

STELLAR DATE: 10.13.8949 (Adjusted Years)
LOCATION: *Karl's Might* on outsystem vector
REGION: Blue Ridge System, Old Genevia, Nietzschean Empire

"You sure we're headed to the right jump point?" Jenisa asked while frowning at the navigation console. "The rest of the fleet is breaking up. Heading for these other three jump points."

"Smoke screen," Lieutenant Colonel Alice replied, her tone nonchalant. "We don't want to spook the Niets. If they think we're not hot on their tail, they'll let their guard down. Half the civilian ships in the system are headed for jump points right now. We're just blending in with the pack."

"Why not just come after them with the *Lance,* and crush them?" Fred asked. "I don't care what the Niets have, if they stay stealthed, the *Lance* can catch them, no problem."

Alice turned in the commander's seat to glare at Fred, who sat at the weapons console. "And what if they break stealth and do a hard burn for the jump point? Yes, the *Fury Lance* is fast, but we know there are plenty of corvettes and destroyers that are faster. You wanna lose Colonel Rika?"

Fred's cheeks reddened as he shook his head. "No, Colonel."

<Fred, take it easy,> Alison sent privately to the corporal. *<Something is off, I can feel it, too, but it could just be how secretive Alice is. We're used to more intel with our intel. If there's a chance we can save Rika, though, we take it. We're making good time, at least.>*

<Sorry, Sergeant,> Fred replied, only sounding a little contrite. *<I'll do my best not to poke the bear, but I don't like her. Not even a little bit.>*

Alison gave the lieutenant colonel a sidelong look. <*You're not alone. She gives cockroaches a bad name. Still, Rika has her in the chain of command, and we follow that chain of command.*>

<*What if she does something that puts Rika at risk?*> Fred asked.

<*Then I cold-cock her and take over,*> Alison replied equably.

Fred's laugh filled her mind. <*Can I be the one to do it?*>

<*Fuck no, Corporal. There's a chain of command.*>

* * * * *

Alison and her mechs crewed the bridge in two-person shifts, staying well-rested and alternating between card games and training sims, in which they practiced infil and takedown ops on ship-types similar to what Rika's captors were flying—or what Alison suspected they were flying.

All the while, Alice stayed on the bridge, excepting short san breaks. Alison had kept tabs on the lieutenant colonel, and so far as she could tell, the woman hadn't slept in the forty hours since they'd lifted off from Memphis's spaceport.

Under her direction, the *Karl's Might* continued to boost at the maximum velocity possible while maintaining the ship's stealth systems. The fact that the ship had stealth systems capable of functioning effectively under heavy boost was impressive in and of itself.

Though the *Karl's Might* was registered as a civilian craft belonging to Karl's Shipping and Trade, the mechs were certain that it was really a smuggler's ship, possibly even a pirate ship. Whenever they weren't on duty—or playing Snark—the mechs were scouring the ship, trying to find evidence of what the *Might* was really used for.

There was quite the pool for whoever found concrete proof of either option.

Fred and Kor were both of the opinion that it was just a

smuggler's ship, or perhaps a mostly legitimate courier vessel that sometimes hopped into systems that were less than friendly. Randy was on the fence, and had wanted to put fifty percent of his credit on either outcome, but Jenisa had scoffed at him, asking what the point of a bet like that was. In the end, he put in for smuggler.

Certain that the ship was a pirate craft, Jenisa had spent half her time tracing power conduits, trying to find where the hidden guns were located. Alison had recently discovered that the woman had pulled half the panels off the bulkheads in the lower decks, and made her put them all back on.

The last thing they all needed was Colonel Alice going on a rampage.

No matter what the outcome of the mechs' hunt for the ship's true purpose, Alison was certain of one thing: Karl was likely pissed that his ship had been taken by the Marauders.

The system's public feeds were running rampant with speculation over what was really going on. Some people thought that the Marauders were just pirates, while others were hailing them as saviors, come to lift the Nietzschean boot from their necks.

There was worry about trade, and the damage to Memphis, Asmoian Station, and the locations that Third and Fourth Platoons had hit.

The strangest news of all was that Vargo Klen was functioning as the system's governor pro-tem until the locals sorted themselves out.

Jenisa had laughed for a solid ten minutes when they got that news.

During that time, she'd managed to wheeze out seven words: "Captain Chase is off his fucking gourd."

Kor had commented that he had no idea what a gourd was, but he agreed that Chase was off something. Fred, however, had nodded sagely, saying that Klen had prior experience with system administration, but wouldn't elaborate, saying it was Klen's story to tell.

Despite the fact that the mechs were making the best of the situation they'd found themselves in, Alison worried about what they'd do if the ship they were pursuing jumped to a heavily populated Nietzschean system, deeper in the empire. The mechs were all too willing to breach an enemy ship, but they were less enthusiastic about assaulting an entire system—at least, with Alice at the helm.

"Any updates?" Alison asked as she entered the bridge and settled into the navigation station's low seat—too low for a mech to sit comfortably.

"Yeah, I picked up their shadow a few minutes ago," Alice said, gesturing to the bridge's secondary holodisplay, which showed a corvette class vessel very similar to the *Karl's Might*.

Alison plotted its route and shook her head. "They're going for this jump point, all right, but we're five hours behind. Even if we pour on full thrust, we won't catch them before they make the jump."

"I know," Alice said, scowling at the display. "We'll have to follow through. I sent a tightbeam to Chase; he's going to shift course as soon as the Niets leap out—we don't want them to know we're onto them."

Alison glanced over her shoulder at the lieutenant colonel. "Where could they be going, Colonel? There aren't a lot of systems in this direction…not for fifty light years. And then we'll be on the far edge of old Genevia…just a dozen light years from where the border with Nietzschea used to be."

Alice nodded. "Yeah, their trajectory is almost directly aligned with the Iberia System. Last time I was through there, it wasn't anything special, but maybe the Niets have a sector HQ out there or something. Either way, they're not going to get Rika."

Alison gave a resolute nod, but didn't feel nearly as certain as the gesture made her seem.

<*Kor,*> she reached out to the AM-4 on the team's encrypted combat net. It wasn't secured from Alice joining in, but they'd know if she did.

<*What's up, Sarge?*>

<*You were searching through the ship's supplies earlier. Any chance this tub has comm buoys or something like that on it?*>

<*Uhh, yeah, I might have seen some. Why?*>

<*Because I want to start a new message relay network and make millions,*> Alison shot back. <*Shit, Kor, because I want to leave a message for Captain Chase once we jump.*>

<*What? We're gonna jump? Can't we catch those bastards first?*>

<*That's not how the LTC wants to play it.*>

Kor made a gagging sound. <*OK, there's gotta be a relay or a transponder or something. I'll hunt around on the QT—I assume this is on the down-low, right?*>

<*You're a smart cookie, Kor. Yeah. We'll load it up with a data burst about where we're going and the ship we're chasing. I don't know what Alice has up her sleeve, but I don't trust her.*>

<*That makes…well…all of us. I'm on it, I'll let you know when I'm ready for the data.*>

Alison simultaneously felt marginally better, and exponentially worse. Either this was the smartest thing she'd done all week, or the dumbest in years.

Probably both.

THE JUMP

STELLAR DATE: 10.14.8949 (Adjusted Years)
LOCATION: MSS *Fury Lance* on outsystem vector
REGION: Blue Ridge System, Old Genevia, Nietzschean Empire

"Sir!" Chief Garth called out from the scan console, twisting in his seat to catch Chase's eye. "I spotted a ghost! Three and a half light seconds from the jump point ahead."

Chase turned from where he'd been standing at the main holotank, contemplating his options and considering whether or not he should send a message back to Thebes for help.

"A ghost?"

"Just for a moment. It looked like a strange heat bloom, and some ionized gas. Best guess? A ship venting atmosphere. It could have mixed with the engine's plasma, and fouled their stealth systems for a moment or two."

Chase glanced at the *Fury Lance*'s position. They were fourteen light seconds from the jump point. Too far to catch an enemy vessel before it would be able to transition to the dark layer.

"Chief Ona," Captain Heather said, rising from her chair. "Shift us off our current vector a degree starboard, and cease thrust."

"Heather?" Chase asked, glancing at the captain as she approached.

"We don't have enough data to gauge their trajectory, and if we fly through that cloud of gas, we'll lose any chance of carefully examining it. We need to slow up and send out probes. They can gather more data, and we can build up a model of exactly where the ship that vented atmo was headed."

Chase hated the idea of more delays, but he knew that a

blind jump outsystem wasn't a viable option. They needed to know precisely where the Nietzschean ship was headed, then they could see if it lined up with a system.

Then they would have a target.

"Good thinking, Smalls," he acknowledged.

"I know, right? I'm not just all beauty and great aim with a GNR. Some brains up here, too."

Chase snorted and turned back to the holo. "Wherever that ship is headed, it has to be our Nietzscheans. Ferris hasn't found any signs at Tellus Station that their brass fled there. The *Republic* and *Capital* haven't spotted bupkis, either."

"Bupkis?" Heather asked. "That a technical term?"

"Yeah, means we've only got one lead, and it's weak as all get-out."

"It shouldn't take too long to get probe data," Heather said. "Once we get it, we can boost hard to the point, and jump. Our other ships can catch up afterward."

Chase nodded and settled back into waiting. He tried to be patient, but worry constantly gnawed at his gut. Fear that Rika would end up in some interrogation chamber on the far side of Nietzschea, and he'd never find her. He knew that the longer the pursuit dragged on, the less likely he was to ever see her again. This wasn't like when she'd been sold at auction. The Niets didn't want to use her because she was a mech; they'd extract what they wanted, and then kill her because of what she was.

Twenty minutes later, the probes had reached the slowly dispersing cloud of ionized gas. Data fed back to the ship, and Potter used the *Fury Lance*'s tactical systems to build up a model of the gas's motion and origin point.

<Definitely vented atmo. I've got traces of other gases that hint at a firefight, too,> Potter announced an excruciating thirty-four minutes later. *<Model has ninety-three percent confidence on the ship's vector. Putting it up on the main tank.>*

As the Nietzschean vessel's flight path came up, Chase frowned. <*You sure about this? There's nothing on that trajectory, nothing up to five degrees off, and they're too close to the point to course-correct that far and not break stealth.*>

<*I checked the data a dozen times before I passed it along,*> Potter assured him. <*I'm as confused as you. That vector won't have them getting within a light year of a single star until they're nearly out of the Orion Arm.*>

"Dammit," Chase muttered. "That—"

"Sir?" Chief Ona said from her station. "I might have something."

"I'll take anything right now," he admitted.

"Well, I have a copy of some old charts that General Mill kept of Genevian space—he shared them with all the ships' pilots. They have a bit more detail than what are in the *Lance*'s astrogation systems."

"Aaaaand?" Heather asked.

"Well, it's not much, but there's a marker seven light years from here that's on our ghost ship's vector. It's a Q9."

"Q9?" Chase asked.

"Large mass rogue planet," Heather supplied. "Just a cold ball of gas, drifting in the interstellar darkness.

Chase pursed his lips. "Some sort of black site?"

<*Stands to reason,*> Potter said.

"Heather, get us on course for that Q9. Inform the fleet that they're to follow us immediately. That's our target."

"You got it, Captain Chase. I'll coordinate a rally point on the other side," Heather replied. "Will you go get some sleep now? You've been pacing across my bridge for two days."

Chase grimaced, but nodded. "Yeah, I should be rested for when we kick those Nietzschean asses clear across the galaxy."

"That's the spirit," Heather said with a laugh.

At the door leading off the bridge, Chase paused to look back at the holodisplay just as Garth half jumped out of his chair. "I got them!"

"Them?" Chase asked, striding back onto the bridge.

"Uh, sorry, sir. Alice and Alison. Well, Alison at least; she sent a message via a relay drone."

"This better be good," Chase muttered. "Put it up."

Garth nodded, and Alison's voice came over the bridge's audible systems.

"Yeah, yeah, I know. Shut up, Kor. Shit! It's recording already? Why didn't you—nevermind. Captain Chase, this is Sergeant Alison. Lieutenant Colonel Alice pulled us onto this mission saying she has intel on where Colonel Rika is, but she's being mighty tightlipped. It smells to us, but not so much that we're ready to mutiny over it. If you know all about this, then hopefully you won't be too pissed. But if you don't, we're going to the Iberia System. One hell of a jump, so we'll be playing a lot of Snark. Alice says that you're all going to follow after once the Niets jump out. So, given that we're jumping into the lion's den, here, I really hope that's the case. A burst is following with our coordinates, vector, and route. Hope we see you on the other side. Sergeant Alison out."

"Aw, shit," Chase muttered, rubbing a hand against his face, forgetting that it was a mech hand, and stopping before he scratched his forehead.

"Borden is still on their tail," Ona said. "He's twenty light minutes behind, though."

Chase sighed, nodding slowly. "Doesn't feel right to send the ISF after them and not mechs."

A hand touched his shoulder, and he turned to see Heather's serious eyes. "Borden's the best of the best. You've seen the ISF in action—good as mechs. He'll bring them back."

"Pass him Alison's intel. Tell him to bring them back here. This is where we'll regroup."

Heather gave Chase a light push. "We know how to do our jobs. Go, get food, sleep. Come back when you smell better."

A laugh slipped past Chase's lips. "I'm a mech, I don't smell."

"Mech yeah, but you opted for real skin on your noggin." Heather leant closer and sniffed his hair. "Go wash it."

Chase shook his head, and walked to the bridge's exit. "OK, I can take the hint. Let me know if anything changes."

"Go already!" Heather said, rolling her eyes.

CHORES

STELLAR DATE: 10.14.8949 (Adjusted Years)
LOCATION: MSS *Asora*, in orbit of Kansas
REGION: Blue Ridge System, Old Genevia, Nietzschean Empire

"Do what you can, Abs," Vargo said from where he stood on the bridge of the *Asora.* "I'll try to keep piracy at bay while you keep the populace from panicking."

Abs folded her arms and glared at Vargo, two of the mechs in her squad visible behind her in the Memphis spaceport's CIC. "Easy for you to say from up there, Klen. Normally, I'd say a squad of mechs are enough for any task, but I've got a whole planet of people down here, and at least ten thousand Nietzschean soldiers still holed up here and there. Shit's a bit nuts."

"Soon as we complete our next orbit, we'll lob shots at that bunker Musel's team found," Vargo assured her. "Make sure they stay clear; we're gonna nuke it, to save our kinetics for more surgical strikes."

"What about this senator who's shown up, demanding to be put in charge?" Abs asked, a look of worry on her face. "I can shoot Niets all day, but politicians scare the fuck out of me."

Vargo coughed out a laugh. "Not what we thought we'd be doing on this mission, is it?"

"Fuck, no," Abs groaned. "I hate sitting back here, babysitting, but these are our people, right? They're the ones we've wanted to free from Nietzschea for the past decade. It's just…"

"Just why are they all such a bunch of whining assholes?" Vargo completed the sergeant's statement.

"Yeah…that's the nice way of putting it. Thought we'd get

more gratitude, less bitching," Abs said, her voice dour.

"Don't let the few complainers get you down," Vargo replied. "People really do appreciate what we've done here—or, they will eventually."

"I could do with 'eventually' showing up really soon."

Someone yelled something behind Abs, and she rolled her eyes.

"So what about li'l Senator Naia?" she continued.

Vargo sighed and closed his eyes for a moment before responding. "Send her up here in a shuttle. Hopefully it'll make her feel all important, and maybe I can talk some sense into her. What I really need Senator Naia to do—and Lieutenant Governor Wilcox, if we can get him out of hiding—is rally the people to support us, not pester us with inane requests. Getting all up in arms about every little thing that has peeved them off over the last decade is not helping."

Abs snorted. "Well, good luck with that. Honestly, she's not that bad, but she keeps trying to get involved in every local detail. Maybe once she's up there with you, it will help her see the big picture. Oh, shit, I have a bunch of locals demanding that we round up Nietzschean sympathizers. I have to go."

"Good luck with that, Sergeant. Vargo out."

"Sounds like a blast down there, sir," Chief Ashley said from the *Asora*'s weapons and comms station.

With the Marauders stretched thin, it was just the two of them on the bridge, while warrant officers Glen, Jakari, and Lexi were down in engineering. One thing was for certain: four people on a five-hundred-meter destroyer made the place feel all but deserted.

<Glen, a shuttle is going to be coming up from the surface with a Genevian senator that we have to make feel all important. Can you coordinate with ground control, and then show the senator to the bridge when she arrives?>

<*A senator?*> Glen asked. <*We playing host to dignitaries now?*>

<*She was giving Abs hives.*> Klen gave an exaggerated sigh. <*I guess this is one of those 'burdens of rank' things they always talk about. I was hoping that was all hyperbole, and that our lives were just going to be getting into big battles and blowing away Niets.*>

A laugh came from Glen. <*Honeymoon's over, eh?*>

<*So it would seem.*>

<*Well, Captain, I got your back here. I'll have that senator in your lap—er, on the bridge—soon as she arrives.*>

<*Stars…maybe I should have Lexi escort her up.*>

Glen laughed and closed the connection without responding.

"Fuuuuuck," Vargo muttered as he leaned back in his chair.

"Glen?" Ashley asked.

Vargo made a strangled sound. "How'd you guess?"

"You have a special sigh for Glen."

He gave a slow shake of his head. "I blame Rika for all this. A month ago, I was the one that was all cocksure, mouthing off to the mechs and officers, flying like a maniac. Now *I'm* the captain, all respectable? How'd that happen?"

Ashley giggled, and Vargo shot her a cold look.

"You *giggling* at me, Chief?"

"Pretty sure I'm tittering, Captain," Ashley teased. "Besides, you got your wish; you're a mech now. And not a shitty GAF mech, you're an ISF-built 4th Gen."

A smile lit Vargo's face as he looked down at his hands, and he smiled. "Yes I am, Ashley. Granted, so are you now. And here we both are, up on this ship instead of down in the dirt, kicking ass."

Ashley gave a four-armed shrug. "We'll get our chance soon enough. I've been doing drills with the old-timers to get ready."

"How have you been doing?" he asked the chief, who had opted to become one of the new LHO models. "I remember you were wishing you'd not gone for the extra arms, at the outset."

The chief lifted all four of her upper limbs in the air, and snapped her fingers in time. "I'm starting to get the hang of it. The ISF medtechs warned me that it would take a bit for my brain to adjust to the mods they made." Ashley stopped and giggled again—a sound that Vargo found himself liking more and more each time he heard it—before continuing. "For a while, I kept getting my second set of arms and my legs mixed up. Had some embarrassing moments in the mess—once I tried to pick up a tray with my foot for a solid minute before I got it worked out."

"I guess we all have our crosses to bear," Vargo replied with a wink. "Shit, we're coming back around. You ready to nuke some Nietzscheans?"

Ashley tossed Vargo a winning smile. "And you say we never get to have any fun!"

FAMILY

STELLAR DATE: 10.14.8949 (Adjusted Years)
LOCATION: NMSS *Spine of the Stars* nearing jump point
REGION: Blue Ridge System, Old Genevia, Nietzschean Empire

<*We're getting there,*> Rika said to Niki, as the power levels finally made it up to forty percent. <*Are things ready to start eating the net?*>

<*Yeah, I can recall the nano we used to build the induction loop, and start them on the net. Once they get going, it shouldn't take long.*>

<*Good,*> Rika said, groaning softly as she tried to shift. <*I'm cramped in places I didn't even know could cramp.*>

<*Really?*> Niki seemed curious. <*Where?*>

<*Stars, Niki, it's just a saying.*>

<*Oh…*> the AI sounded disappointed. <*I thought maybe you were yearning for Chase with your intimate bits.*>

<*Niki!*>

She laughed in Rika's mind. <*Sorry, I'm getting bored, trapped here. I want to breach this network, crush the Niets, and get the hell off this ship.*>

<*Solid plan. I like it.*>

<*Are you mocking me?*> Niki asked, sounding perturbed.

<*Just a bit.*> Rika couldn't help but laugh at her AI's attitude.

<*I don't think it's funny.*>

Rika let out a groan. <*What? A few days laying on the floor with no Link, and you get all twitchy?*>

<*Even when I've been stuck on ships in the black, I still had a network to stretch out on, a crew to interact with, a ship to maintain,*> Niki reminded her.

Rika thought back to all the time she'd spent in isolation as a mech. *<I once got racked for transport, and they didn't set up the enforced sleep cycle. I was awake for over seventy hours before anyone noticed.>*

Niki was silent for a minute. *<OK, that's worse.>*

<Great thing about having been a mech in the GAF: no matter what happens, I always have a worse experience to look back on. It's the gift of never-ending perspective.>

The AI chuckled. *<I guess you earned that. You know…almost a year in your head—well, some of it in your gut—and you're still a mystery to me.>*

<How so?>

<Well, you **should** *be jaded, cold, hard…mean. Stars, even without what the GAF did to you, without the war. Just losing your parents, and growing up on the streets….>*

<Shit, Niki,> Rika replied, laughing aloud. *<You trying to depress me?>*

<I don't know if I could. You're like the eternal optimist. Never once has the thought crossed your mind that we might not make it out of this, has it? How do you do it?>

<Easy.> Rika gave the mental equivalent of a shrug. *<I'm not going to let them win. I won't give them the satisfaction.>*

<See? That! That should make you cold and jaded.> Niki's voice was filled with frustration. *<Why aren't you?>*

<Why?> Rika was surprised to get this line of questioning from an AI. *<Because my own state of mind is the one thing I always have full control over. I can choose to perseverate on all the bad things that have happened to me, or I can think about the good. I can change my emotional state through what I choose to focus on.>*

Rika's statement was met by silence from the AI. Eventually, she asked, *<How did you get to be so wise at such a young age?>*

A smile graced Rika's lips, and the three-sixty view of the cell faded from around her, replaced with visions from the past. *<I had a great teacher—more than one, actually. They taught*

me that family is always with you, if you let it be. Deep down, everyone hates feeling lonely, and they want to connect with others. Sometimes they give up on that, but if I had, I'd be dead. Family is what got me through everything.>

<You're a glorious mystery, Rika.> Niki's voice was filled with appreciation. *<I assume one of these teachers was Silva.>*

<Sure was. But she wasn't the first. The last time I ran away from foster care—and it wasn't because of them, it was because of me—I met this station gang. They were rough, they weren't afraid to get into it and draw blood in a fight, but they always protected their own. It was the first time I'd felt that since…since my parents died.

<The state never treated us orphans like we were of much value to them. Foster parents cared, but they were usually overwhelmed by kids who were dealing with the loss of ***everything*** *in their lives. But Bro…he cared.>*

<Bro? What kind of name is that?> Niki asked.

Rika laughed at the memory. *<Bro was the leader of the gang. I guess the name came from a speech he always gave the newbs. He'd start by pacing back and forth in front of them—usually in the old sanitation bay we hid in—and say:*

'I'm not your father. If you're here, your father is dead. I'm not your mother; chances are she's gone too. If you ***do*** *have a mother and father—and you know where they are—you'd best get your sorry ass back to them before one of us kicks your ass for leaving family. But if you got no family out there, then you got family here. Us. This gang.*

'But keep one thing firmly in your scrawny, little heads: there are no parents here. I'm your brother. Means I'll kick your ass if you're being a dickhead, and I'll probably make fun of you half the time, 'cause that's what brothers do. Ain't that right, Jeb?'>

Rika chuckled before continuing, marveling at how clear the memory still was.

<At that point, he'd always look at Jeb, who usually had a black eye or a busted lip—more often than not, courtesy of Bro—and Jeb would just laugh and say, 'Yup, but don't worry, I'll take your licks

if you're too scared.'

<Everyone knew that was true, too. If you really fucked up, you could tell Jeb, and he'd go tell Bro it was his fault, and Bro would kick Jeb's ass in front of everyone. He'd make it look good, but never really hurt Jeb much.

<When you watched Jeb take licks for you, you straightened up and got your shit together. Plus, if you asked Jeb to take a beating for you a second time, he'd give it to you himself. Bro would slap him on the back for it and maybe throw a punch or two himself.>

<That worked?> Niki asked, surprise mingling with disbelief in her voice.

<Most of the time,> Rika allowed. *<I only saw Jeb lay into someone twice. Once, we had a guy who touched some of the younger girls and boys in a way that wasn't right. It got out that it was going on, but the little ones wouldn't say who did it. Finally, the guy came to Jeb and confessed. Jeb killed him on the spot.>*

<Shit, Rika. Did you ever have it easy?>

Rika thought back to her youth; the faint memory of her mother's smile on a warm summer morning, and laughing as her father tickled her. *<I did. I had alot more happiness in my memories than a lot of kids in Bro's gang. I always considered myself one of the lucky ones. Anyway, Bro always finished his speech with:*

'But anyone outside the family picks on you, beats you, hurts you…I'll be the first out of the gate to take them down. And I'll let you get some licks in on 'em too. Teach you how to stand up for yourself. Make you a fighter.'>

Niki laughed at that. *<Rika, even your happy memories are on the hardcore side of things.>*

Rika chuckled, wondering where Bro and his gang were now. She'd been out raiding another gang on the station, and got scooped up by the feds a year after joining his troop. The Genevians took her planetside and stuck her in an orphanage in Tanner City. It wasn't too much later when she got framed and turned over to the GAF for mechanization.

<*Bro was a big part of how I made it through what the GAF did to me. He really taught me how you could make the best of even a terrible situation. Silva carried on that trend.*>

<*You really look up to her, don't you?*> Niki asked.

<*She's the reason I'm here today. I probably would have gone out of my way to eat a bullet if it weren't for her. I'd only been a part of her team for a day when she pulled me behind a stack of ammo crates on some stars-forsaken moon we were protecting for reasons that still don't make sense to me. She jammed a finger in my chest at least a dozen times while telling me that she wasn't going to have any mopey whiners on Team Hammerfall. Told me that there was still a woman's heart in my chest—that she'd seen enough of them shot out to be sure—and that she'd take care of me and my heart, but only if I proved to her that I was going to put in my share of effort in the job.*>

<*Shit, Rika,*> Niki said with a laugh. <*You just got the tough love speech coming and going.*>

<*Except for Chase,*> Rika said wistfully. <*He's never given me the tough love speech...though I might have given it to him once or twice. End of the day, though, I don't forget my past; I don't push it down and try to pretend it didn't happen. That may work for some, but I keep it close. It gives me strength.*>

There was one other thing that built her up and gave her strength, but Rika didn't share the vision that Tanis had put in her mind, the image of the pillar of strength, standing on the bald prairie, holding out against the raging storms, and sheltering those around her. That was just for her. That was her last bastion of strength, if all others gave out.

<*I guess I can see how this really isn't much of a tribulation for you,*> Niki said after a moment. <*Oh, the net's weakened enough for you to get through.*>

<*And the guards? We should probably get eyes on the corridor before I bust out of this stupid thing.*>

<*Already on it. I have a passel of probes getting around the door*

right now. The Niets have decent countermeasures, but they're not prepared for an airborne nanocloud.>

<*Say the word.*> Rika checked her lightwand's status, ready to end the Niets who thought they could hold a mech captive.

Niki set a twenty-seven-second countdown on Rika's HUD. When it hit zero, Rika stretched her arms and legs out, shredding the back of the net. She was on her feet a second later, net hanging from her GNR's ammo feeder, fingers digging in between the door and its frame.

<*And go!*>

The lock *snick*ed, and Rika wrenched the door open, flinging the net at the closest of the four guards, and kicking him in the gut as he stumbled backward. Across the narrow passage, a sharp-witted woman raised her rifle, but Rika's lightwand was already out, and she slashed the weapon in half, cutting through the power supply in the process.

The energy cell exploded, knocking the woman back against the bulkhead.

One of the two remaining guards had brought his rifle to bear, and fired a pulse blast at Rika that she easily shrugged off before slamming her barrelless GNR into the woman's head, smashing her faceshield.

The staccato beat of projectile rounds struck Rika in the back. She'd seen the soldier behind her taking aim, but knew her armor could withstand a few shots.

He only got seven off before she pivoted and tore the rifle from his grasp with one of her clawed feet. She continued to spin around, slamming the rifle into the woman with the smashed faceshield, then completed the rotation to bring the weapon all the way back to its original owner, driving the gunstock into his neck so hard that the weapon crumpled, bending around the soldier's shoulders.

He went down in a shrieking lump, and Rika kicked him in the head to silence his wailing.

By that point, the first guard had gotten free of the net, only to have Rika's hand clamp down on his head. She lifted him off his feet, and hurled him down the corridor into the fleeing back of the woman whose weapon had exploded.

Moments later, Rika was upon them. She dispatched the man before kneeling atop the woman, lightwand held close enough to her faceshield that tendrils of electricity arced from the electron beam to the woman's armor.

"Where are my guns?" Rika demanded.

"Wha-what?"

"My GNR's barrel and my rifle. Stuff that goes *'pew pew'*. Where. Are. They."

The woman's hand rose, pointing the other way down the corridor. "First left, second door on the right."

"Take your helmet off," Rika growled.

"What—"

"I don't have time, you Nietzschean asswipe. Take it off, or I rip it off. Trust me, you won't like that."

The woman's trembling hand rose to her helmet, and she gave it a sharp twist, lifting it off.

Beneath the black visor was a woman who still had the freshness of youth about her. Rika imagined the girl wasn't much over twenty years old. Her blonde hair was shorn close to her head, and her green eyes were wide with fear.

Rika lifted her hand to strike the woman on the side of the head, but she paused, staring down at the girl who was the same age she'd been when the GAF conscripted her.

In that moment, a weapon discharged, and Rika felt rounds ricochete off her armor. She glanced down to see the Niet holding her sidearm against Rika's torso.

"Stupid," she muttered, and brought her hand down into the woman's temple. Not hard enough to kill, but hard enough to make the woman wish she'd never enlisted.

Then she turned and ran down the corridor in the direction

the woman had indicated, hoping she hadn't been played.

<*That's what I get for thinking of them as people,*> she said to Niki as she rounded the corner. <*Maybe when all this is over, they can be people again, but until then, they're just enemies. It's my life or theirs.*>

<*I get that,*> Niki said in a quiet voice. <*You still didn't kill her, though.*>

<*I'm no murderer.*>

Reaching the prescribed door, Rika kicked it in to reveal a small armory and a very surprised looking Nietzschean in his service uniform.

"I'm here for what's mine," she growled.

The man hesitated, glancing at a nearby rifle.

Rika took a step closer, not having to manufacture any menace in her voice as she said, "You even think twice about trying it, and I'll pull your tongue out your asshole."

The Nietzschean swallowed nervously and pointed to a bench across the small room, where Rika's GNR barrel and AC9CR lay. "I'll get them," he whispered hoarsely. "Don't do anything like that, please."

"Chop chop, buddy."

<*Rika?*> Niki's voice sounded uncertain. <*I think there's someone else on the ship…*>

<*'Someone'?*>

<*It's Leslie, they have her trapped.*>

* * * * *

Leslie fired a series of pulse blasts down the corridor with a pistol, while swapping a magazine on a projectile rifle she'd taken off a dead Nietzschean.

She wasn't certain how many of the enemy she'd taken out yet, but it had to be at least fifteen—though three of that number were iffy. If the ship had a good med suite, they might be back in the fight before long.

Her probes alerted her to movement on the other end of the corridor, and she lifted the rifle, firing on a Nietzschean who was crossing an intersection aft of her position to get a better angle on her.

Fuckers are going to totally flank me!

She lobbed the last of the pulse grenades she'd lifted off a dead Niet down the fore end of the corridor, and turned to run aft, glad to have reached a section of the ship that was aired up.

Just an hour earlier, the Niets had vented half the ship, and killed the a-grav systems. Leslie didn't mind either one of those situations—she was better in zero-*g* than the enemy soldiers—but half her pilfered arsenal was made up of pulse weapons, and they didn't work in vacuum.

She reached the intersection that the enemy soldier had rushed across seconds earlier, and turned the corner, ducking low and catching him in the legs as he leant around the cover to fire on her.

The impact bowled him over, and Leslie slashed at his faceshield with her lightwand, cutting through the dense plas, and into his jaw.

A warbling shriek came from the Nietzschean, but it was cut off as Leslie twisted the blade and drove it up into his brain.

Stars, I'm never going anywhere without one of these ever again.

Shots streaked over her head, and then a searing pain erupted in her shoulder.

Leslie's three-sixty vision highlighted a pair of drones swinging around the corner twenty meters forward of where she crouched. They were large, meant for ground operations, and were having trouble staying stable in the narrow confines of the passage, but that wasn't stopping them from firing on her.

She took off running, and another round pierced her below the ribs on her right side, causing her to stumble and nearly fall.

Keep going, Leslie. You've made it this long; a Nietzschean drone's not going to be the end of you!

She reached the end of the corridor and turned left, toward the entrance to the engineering bay. Before she even reached it, she could see the door glowing hot on her IR overlay, and she realized that it must have been welded shut.

"Fuck!" she swore, knowing that there was nowhere left for her to run.

One of the drones came around the corner, and she spun, unloading a magazine of projectile rounds on the thing and knocking it out of commission.

"You may take me out," Leslie screamed down the passageway. "But you're going to have to do it yourmotherfuckingselves!"

A Nietzschean soldier in heavy armor rounded the corner, a chaingun leveled at her.

"You want it up close and personal? You got it," he growled.

A flash of abject terror came over Leslie. *I'm gonna die!*

She drew from unknown reserves, and forced the fear down, a feeling of sorrow-tinged peace taking over.

I tried, Rika.

She squared her shoulders, and threw her head back. "Go on, then, asshat" she swore at the Nietzschean, determined not to let him hear the sadness she felt. "I'm not going to fuck you first."

The Nietzschean chuckled as the chaingun spun up.

I won't close my eyes. I won't...plus I can't...stupid helmet, Leslie thought with a manic laugh as she stared down the weapon that would be her demise—only to see it explode as a white-hot flash tore through the chaingun. The remains of the weapon were wrenched from the soldier's grasp and slammed into the thick bulkhead that divided the engineering section from the rest of the ship.

"What the?" Leslie whispered.

A *boom* sounded—one must have accompanied the first shot as well, but she hadn't heard it—and the Nietzschean's head ceased to exist.

There was only one weapon she knew of that made a sound quite liked like that: an SMI's GNR.

Seconds later, Rika raced around the corner, stopping atop the fallen body of the Nietzschean.

"Stars, Leslie, are you OK? You're covered in blood!"

Leslie stood mute for a moment, gasping for breath, until she finally managed to say, "It's not mine…well, most of it isn't, at least."

Rika glanced back the way she'd come. "Looks like engineering is sealed up. We need to get to the bridge."

Leslie looked at her commander, the woman who just couldn't be stopped, and began to laugh, feeling tears stream down her cheeks.

"What's so funny?"

"You…Do you…" Leslie managed to gasp before gaining a modicum of control. "Do you realize that every time I try to rescue you, you rescue me instead?"

Rika shrugged. "Not my fault you're the perennial damsel in distress, Leslie. We all have our part to play."

"Damsel!" Leslie growled as she approached Rika. "I'll show you a damsel. Let's go kill some Niets."

* * * * *

"Gotta love your gumption." Rika was about to slap Leslie on the shoulder as the woman approached, when she saw the biofoam filling a wound there. "Damn, how many places are you hit?"

"Ummm…four that breached armor," Leslie counted, glancing down at herself.

<*You're one tough kitty,*> Niki added. <*How many lives you use up here?*>

<*Just the one—when they shot down the mech frame I was in. I leapt the final ten meters to the ship's landing struts; thought I was going to do an impression of a meteor,*> Leslie replied to the AI. <*Was saved by my tail.*>

<*Dang, how far up were you?*> Rika asked.

<*Few klicks. I probably could have survived it…but I would have needed a new everything. The tail can only impart so much luck.*>

Rika snorted as she turned back the way she'd come. <*There are probably some Niets forming up in my wake. I didn't kill 'em all, just blasted through.*>

<*Complement on the ship is sixty-five, all told,*> Niki supplied. <*Fifty-one troopers, then the naval personnel and the brass.*>

<*I got at least fifteen,*> Leslie put her tally on their combat net.

<*And I got twelve,*> Rika added hers, not seeing any overlap. <*So we're looking at twenty-four more grunts out there.*>

Leslie jerked a thumb over her shoulder. <*And probably half a dozen in engineering.*>

<*I have feeds in there. I count five,*> Niki reported.

<*So twenty-two all together,*> Rika said as she reached the next intersection, and checked the cross passages before proceeding. <*Sixty meters and two decks to the bridge. Piece of cake.*>

It was a hard slog through the ship. The Niets threw everything they had at the two Marauders, eventually venting atmosphere and killing the a-grav across the entire ship. Rika was surprised they'd made such a silly mistake; a mech was just as at home in zero-*g* as full gravity, and Leslie moved like a ballet dancer, floating through the passageways and holing everything in sight.

Thirty minutes later, they had reached the final ten-meter corridor that ran to the bridge. Executive offices lined the sides, and the last nine enemy soldiers had taken up positions in them, desperately trying to hold off the two Marauders' unrelenting assault.

Leslie had picked up a chaingun a deck down and was spraying rounds into the corridor with wild abandon, the barrage tearing through the bulkheads and into the rooms beyond.

<*Careful you don't tear a hole right into the bridge,*> Rika cautioned.

Niki laughed. <*I think that the bulkhead separating the bridge can take it.*>

<*What's so funny?*> Leslie asked. <*I'm pissed at these asshats. No one takes my Rika and tries to fly off with her, then nearly kills me. We're making an example.*>

<*I don't know that you can make an example if you kill them all,*> Rika interjected, firing a round from her GNR when her nanoprobes pinpointed another Niet's location within the offices.

<*Sure,*> Leslie replied while discarding the chaingun after expending the last of its ammo. <*We'll just send this ship full of bodies wherever it's going, and call it a little 'get unwell' message.*>

<*Oh, crap!*> Rika and Niki exclaimed at the same time.

<*Double trouble?*> Leslie asked.

<*They're jumping early. We're still three light seconds from the point, but—*> Niki's words cut off as they felt the unsettling gravity fluctuation that heralded a transition into the dark layer.

<*OK…not dead,*> Rika said as she looked around. <*So, there's that.*>

<*Three, two, one,*> Niki counted down slowly. <***Now*** *you can celebrate. We're past the jump point's location. Hooray for not being*

smeared across a clump of dark matter.>

<*It's the little things that matter most.*> Rika breathed a sigh of relief.

There was a reason people flew out to jump points before transitioning to the dark layer. She used to think it was just the risk of hitting dark matter, but after Tanis had told her about the Exaldi, she had a whole new reason to fear insystem jumps.

<*Hey,*> Leslie said as she lobbed a pilfered grenade through an open door. <*Didn't you tell me you have a direct line to Tanis in your noggin? One of their QuanComm blades?*>

<*It's in my stomach…or thereabouts,*> Rika replied. <*But the control systems for it got damaged when the Niets used me for a lightning rod. Niki's working on fixing them.*>

<*Well,* **I'm** *not. More like it's working on fixing itself. It's all black box tech. Right now, it says it's recalibrating, but it's also said that for the last day. We shouldn't hold out hope.*>

<*We don't need hope,*> Rika replied. <*In ten minutes, we'll have the bridge, and then we'll drop this tin can back into normal space and call for pickup. We'll be having chow on the* Lance *before the day is out.*>

<*Day's out in eleven minutes. Then it's tomorrow,*> Leslie commented as she advanced two meters into the passageway, and fired into the open door she'd lobbed the 'nade through moments earlier.

<*Smartass,*> Rika replied.

<*Clear,*> Leslie reported. <*And I'm not an ass, I'm a cat. Get your mammals straight.*>

<*You say your relationship with Barne hasn't changed you,*> Rika noted while taking aim with her GNR and firing her electron beam through the bulkhead, into a cabin beyond. <*But that really sounds like his bad 'dad humor' to me.*>

<*Trust me, I'd be getting a good dose of his humor even if I wasn't sleeping with him.*> Leslie emerged from the room she'd

cleared, and covered Rika while the she kicked in the door to the next office. <*Speaking of which, he wants me to get cat ears. Think I should go whole kitty?*>

<*What, like you had for your singing gig in Stavros' officer's club?*> Rika asked. <*Sure, it was pretty hot. Made me think about switching teams for a minute or two—but if you do it, you should go* ***full*** *kitty.*>

Rika cleared the room, finishing off a wounded Niet when he raised his weapon to fire on her, and then took up a position to cover Leslie as she moved to the next office.

<*What does 'full kitty' mean? Is that more than whole kitty?*> Leslie asked as she kicked the door in and stood back for Rika to fire her electron beam into the office.

<*Well…maybe? I'm thinking you should get the whiskers, cat nose, all that. Maybe even a little mane, too.*>

After Rika's shot, Leslie swung into the room and unloaded a kinetic scattershot gun into the space, pumping out four rounds before reappearing in the entrance.

<*Not sure about a mane; I like my hair. Plus, Barne doesn't like fur.*>

<*Up to you,*> Rika replied, lining up with the final room before they reached the door the bridge. <*Not like it's permanent. You should try it, you could be our battalion's mascot.*>

<*Wow, way to* ***not*** *sell it,*> Leslie said.

<*You might already be the mascot,*> Niki interjected. <*More than a few of the Marauders have a picture of you and your tail on their armor—well, they did before the stealth gear. Now they tattoo it on.*>

Leslie made a hissing sound at the AI, who laughed in response. Then she fired into the final room after Rika had kicked the door open.

<*Huh,*> Rika said, peering into the office where a dead officer lay on the floor. <*Already dead.*>

<*The Niets are killing each other before we get to them?*> Leslie

asked, scorn filling her mental tone. <*Unacceptable!* ***We*** *kill the Niets. Don't they know how this works?*>

<*I guess we'll have to remind them,*> Rika said as she walked to the bridge's door. <*Sealed tight.*>

<*I have access to environmental. It's aired up on the other side,*> Niki informed the duo.

<*No feeds?*> Leslie asked.

<*They've killed optics on the far side, but the environmental load matches up with five smaller humans, or four larger ones. Or a mix. Take your pick.*>

<*Four to five biggish-smallish humans.*> Rika didn't try to hide the sarcasm in her voice. <*We've not yet encountered our friend the admiral yet. I'm betting he's in there.*>

<*Seems logical,*> Leslie agreed. <*We still want him alive, right?*>

The colonel sighed. <*Yeaaah, I suppose. Would be a waste to go through all this and just have him suck vacuum in the end.*>

<*I'm working on airing up this part of the ship. It's taking some work, since you shot four…make that five holes in the hull,*> Niki announced.

While Niki did her work, Rika piggybacked on the AI's tap into the shipnet, and found the control systems for the 1MC. There was only minimal security on the audible comm system, a standard Nietzschean firewall and port intrusion system she'd breached before.

Less than a minute later, she was in.

"Admiral Gideon? Can you come out to play?" she asked with a soft laugh, able to faintly hear her own voice as the ship began to air up once more.

"You think you're funny, don't you, mech?"

Rika glanced at Leslie, who only shrugged, and she replied, "Well, I'll admit that Les and I got a bit riled up, carving our way through your ship. We're kinda chomping at the bit to get into the bridge and finish things off."

"You may get through, but you'll be too late." The admiral's voice carried a note of smug satisfaction.

"Too late for what?" Rika asked. "To crush all your hopes and dreams? There's still time, trust me."

"We've rigged the transition system to hold us in the DL until we reach Epsilon. Plus, engineering is dumping all but our emergency fuel reserves, just in case you manage to get around that plan. Pull us out of FTL, and we'll just drift in the black forever."

The admiral paused, and Rika began to calculate if they were still close enough to the Blue Ridge System to jump into escape pods.

"Oh," Admiral Gideon continued. "In case you were thinking to get off the ship, we blew all the pods and trashed the shuttle. We're on a one-way trip. Even though you think you've won, you've still lost."

Rika fought the urge to fire her electron beam at the bridge's door 'til she melted her way through, but after the combat, her internal batteries were perilously low, and she suspected she wouldn't make it through.

<*I can confirm all that,*> Niki said, sounding dejected. <*We're stuck here—and stuck in FTL.*>

<*For now,*> Rika replied. She glanced at Leslie, who had leant against a bulkhead, her chest heaving as the air grew thick enough to breathe. <*Were you having problems?*> she asked her friend.

<*A bit. My scrubbers were fouled already. I didn't realize how lightheaded I was until I switched back to externals.*>

"Colonel Rika?" the admiral asked, his voice still carrying a triumphant note.

"What?" she shot back.

The admiral was chuckling over the comms as he replied, "Don't think you can breach the bridge or engineering, either. You come through either of our doors, and engineering blows the ship. They've got the reactors ready to go at a moment's notice."

<*Can't confirm that,*> Niki said with a long sigh. <*But it doesn't surprise me in the least.*>

Rika glared at the bridge's sealed door. "Fine," she called out over the 1MC. "Have it your way."

Activating her lightwand, she drove it into the bulkhead, melting it to the bridge's door in four locations, and sealing the admiral and his three or four compatriots in the bridge.

"Enjoy your tomb."

Leslie chuckled, pushing herself off the bulkhead. <*Nice one.*>

Rika grinned, though Leslie couldn't see it behind her helmet. <*You hungry?*>

<*Starving.*>

As they walked back down the corridors, Rika couldn't help but wonder what Chase and the rest of the Marauders were doing. She felt as though her mad rush to capture the Nietzschean commanders had let them down.

I sure hope they're managing OK back on Kansas.

VISITORS

STELLAR DATE: 10.14.8949 (Adjusted Years)
LOCATION: MSS *Asora,* in orbit of Kansas
REGION: Blue Ridge System, Old Genevia, Nietzschean Empire

"Captain Klen," Senator Naia said as she entered the bridge ahead of Glen. "Thank you for allowing me on your ship. It's…a bit strange to be aboard a Nietzschean vessel, and know it was one of the vehicles of our deliverance."

<*Oh stars, she talks like a politician,*> Ashley said over the crew's shipnet.

<*Yeah, she's been doing that the whole way up here,*> Glen replied. <*Even Field Marshal Richards didn't talk like this, and she's pretty much queen of the universe. Naia's just some planetary senator from a backwater I never even knew was in Genevia 'til a week ago.*>

<*Easy, Glen, I've got it from here,*> Vargo replied quashing the flashbacks he was having of a former life, long ago.

<*Thank stars,*> Glen replied. <*She's got a bunch of flunkies, too; they're in the officer's mess. I'm going to trust that the servitors can manage them, and go back to juggling radioactive isotopes. Way safer than politicians.*>

<*Wimp,*> Ashley said in parting.

"I'm very glad to meet you," Vargo said, rising and offering the senator his hand, which she stared at for a moment, before recovering herself and shaking it.

"Um, yes. I have to say, Captain Klen—I hope this doesn't come across wrong—I'm surprised that you're a mech."

"If you'd met me a month ago, I wouldn't have been one," Vargo replied with a wink. "Got an upgrade after trying to plumb the depths of a gas giant."

A look of confusion came over Senator Naia's face. "I'm

sorry?"

"Got injured in a battle," Vargo explained simply before turning to Ashley. "This is my second-in-command, Chief Ashley."

<*This'll be good,*> Ashley said privately as she rose and offered one of her right hands. "Very nice to meet you, Senator."

To her credit, the senator handled Ashley better than she had Vargo, shaking her hand with only a look of mild consternation on her face.

"I'm sorry that this probably sounds improper to you, but are all Marauders mechs?"

Vargo gestured to a seat near his, and the senator smiled in thanks as she took it.

"No," he replied. "Most of the Marauders are not mechs. However, this is Colonel Rika's battalion, and in *Rika's Marauders* nearly everyone is a mech."

"The Nietzscheans always said they killed the mechs…yet you said you just got made into one?"

"They didn't get them all," Vargo replied with a lopsided grin. "A lot got away—they let some go, too, like Rika. And she found even more not long ago, in a place called the Politica. Freed them, and has been building up a force to hold back Nietzschea. We hooked up with the Scipio Alliance not long after, and they upgraded our old GAF mechs to 4th Gen, and let anyone who wanted make the change as well."

"And you opted for mechanization as well, Chief Ashley?" Senator Naia asked. "I don't recall seeing any four-armed mechs during the war."

"Opted?" Ashley asked as she flipped through displays on two separate consoles. "I leapt at the chance. We're spread a bit thin when it comes to shipboard operations, so Finaeus offered a set of mods to our minds and bodies that makes us able to multitask a lot better. I've always really liked being able to manage a lot of things at once, so it was a no-brainer for me. Plus, I can kick serious ass."

"Finaeus?" Naia asked.

"Finaeus Tomlinson," Vargo Klen explained, enjoying name-dropping on the senator more than he should. "The chief engineer on the *Tardis*, the second FGT ship to leave Sol."

This time, Senator Naia's mouth hung open for a full six seconds before she recovered. "The FGT?"

He nodded while giving a commiserating laugh. "I'd best start from the beginning; then we can talk about how to make things better for Kansas and the Blue Ridge System at large. Would you like something to drink? I can have a servitor bring it."

The senator gave Vargo the first genuine smile he'd seen since she entered the bridge. "I'm on a Nietzschean destroyer with a pair of newly minted mechs, who are about to tell me how the FGT upgraded them to take the fight to Nietzschea. Yeah, make it a whiskey."

Thirty minutes later, Vargo had related the bulk of Rika's story and the amazing events of the past few weeks to Senator Naia—who had eventually dropped into stunned silence, limited to sipping her whiskey and nodding periodically.

"And that brings us up to our visit here," he finished, leaning back in his chair and lacing his fingers behind his head, before remembering that the last time he'd done so, it had been surprisingly difficult to get them separated again.

He carefully disentangled them, and set his arms on the chair's armrests.

"If I hadn't seen your five ships defeat the forty Nietzschean vessels orbiting Kansas a few days ago, I wouldn't believe a word of it," Naia admitted quietly. "But it's hard to deny reality—not that I'd want to, in this case. In all honesty, your story sounds like music to my ears—which is not something we're used to around here. The resistance has fought a losing battle against the Niets for years; to see you knock them down like it was nothing—"

"Huh," Ashley interrupted.

Vargo turned to the chief. "What's up?"

She flicked a finger—he wasn't certain which hand it was on—and an image of three Nietzschean ships appeared on the main holodisplay.

"Seems like these three didn't get the memo. Every other Nietzschean ship is headed away from Kansas, but these three are on a vector right for it."

"Have they made any attempts at communication?" Vargo asked, frowning at the three ships—all of which bore the scars of recent combat.

"Not yet," Ashley replied. "At first, I thought that they were going to join up with those four destroyers we chased off yesterday, but they banked around Kansas's second moon, and are headed right for us now."

"Should I be worried?" Senator Naia asked, half rising from her seat.

Vargo chuckled. "Not a bit, you're currently in the safest place in Blue Ridge. Something's not right about those ships. See that one in the center? That's a Nietzschean hospital vessel. An older one, too."

"Why would they bring a hospital ship into a battle?" Ashley asked.

"Beats me," Vargo said with a shrug. "Being captain doesn't make me all-knowing."

He shifted the *Asora*'s optics to examine the largest vessel.

"Wait," Naia said, walking closer to the display and scowling. "Are those…dragons, coming out of the shuttle bays?"

A laugh burst free from Vargo's throat. "Stars! Bondo's going to be *pissed* that someone beat him to that!"

Senator Naia cast him a look that said she clearly thought

he'd lost his mind. "Captain?"

"Don't you see?" He gestured to the display. "Those are *mech*dragons. Ashley, hail them. I want to see who this is."

As the hail went out, he wondered if this was a surprise visit Barne and Silva had worked up, but when the response came back, he was the one standing mouth agape.

The woman on the holodisplay was a tall mech, one of the very rare SMI-3 models. An incredulous smile was on her face, and a laugh in her voice.

"Vargo Klen, of all the people I expected to see at the helm of a Nietzschean ship, you were not one! And a mech? Stars, what has happened to you since we last met?"

Vargo was even more gobsmacked than the woman on the display. "Adira? I thought you bought it almost fifteen years ago! How the hell did you get off Lornen?"

Adira laughed and shook her head, her long mane of hair shimmering like a halo. "Well, I can assure you that it wasn't on a dropship *you* were piloting. My squad stole a Nietzschean shuttle. Sorta started a trend."

"I can see that. We've taken up the same habit."

"We?" Adira asked, leaning closer, her expression growing earnest. "Then it's true? A mech is leading an attack on Nietzschea? We heard about the enemy's defeat at Thebes, and swung by Sepe where they gave us directions here. We want to join up."

"With the Marauders?" Vargo asked.

"With New Genevia?" Senator Naia said from Vargo's side.

Adira's brow lowered. "Screw all that. We're here to join up with *Rika*."

BACON

STELLAR DATE: 10.17.8949 (Adjusted Years)
LOCATION: NMSS *Spine of the Stars,* interstellar dark layer
REGION: Old Genevia, Nietzschean Empire

Three days after the ship had made its jump, Rika returned to the bridge's entrance, eating a sandwich she'd prepared minutes earlier in the ship's galley.

"How're you doing in there?" she asked. "Getting hungry?"

No response was forthcoming.

Rika took a bite of her sandwich, moaning softly with pleasure. "Mmmmmm, it's so good. Peanut butter and jelly, one of my favorites. Leslie's cooking up some bacon for a BLT. Not sure if you know what those are; sandwiches made with bacon, lettuce, and tomato. It's like heaven in your mouth. I don't know if you noticed yet, but we cut off the water that ran to the emergency rations station you were using. I imagine it only holds a few days' worth of food, right? Is it enough for seven? That's how long it's going to take us to get to Epsilon, isn't it? I wonder how many of you will survive. I know! Maybe the admiral will order you to die so he can eat you. Think you'll all get so far as cannibalism?"

Still no response came from the bridge, but the environmental systems showed that all five people within were alive.

She'd threaded nano through the door seal two days before, and she tapped the optics they provided to see the five figures. Heat signatures matched the environmental readings, showing them all to be alive, but none were moving, each one of them slumped in their chairs.

"Nothing? Not even a twitch?" Rika asked. "What about

you, Red? Aren't you hungry?"

The red-headed man at one of the forward consoles turned to look back at the door.

"There you go. I bet you can just smell it, right? The bacon? I'm sure it's gonna taste great. I'm more of a PB and J girl myself, but I have to admit, BLTs are a close second. I mean…bacon, right?"

For a minute, no one moved. Then Red made a break for the door. He was halfway across the bridge before the colonel—Sofia, from the records Rika had found on the ship—tackled him, and struck him in the head twice.

"OK, I guess you're not hungry." Rika shrugged and walked away. "More for us, then."

<*You're so dramatic,*> Niki admonished.

"Gives me something to do. How're things going with the drive systems?"

<*The same. They're completely segregated, and they have an EM field around the controls that is keeping me from getting anything through. The drive controls might as well be on the far side of the galaxy.*>

Rika took another bite of her sandwich, getting a glob of peanut butter stuck to the roof of her mouth.

"Hmmghhhh, I geubs I shud reawwy be temping the engneers."

<*If I parse your mumbling correctly, then yes, you probably should tempt the engineers. As best I can tell, they're only using RF to stay in touch with the admiral. I'm reasonably certain that he doesn't have eyes down there, or a way to remote detonate that I can see.*>

"Well, if that's a viable play, maybe we should make some more BLTs…or see if this tub has any steak."

Two hours later, Rika stood in front of the sealed engineering bay doors.

Leslie hadn't found steaks, but there were trays of bacon,

and she cooked up as much as she could, placing the finished product near an air exchanger that Niki had taken control of, ensuring that the smell would make its way throughout the engineering section of the ship.

They'd debated just circulating a toxin instead, but none were willing to take the risk that the engineers had a deadman's switch on whatever jury-rigged bomb they'd set up with the reactors.

"I know you Niets can hear me," Rika began. "We have optics in there, and we know the six of you are getting mighty hungry. We saw Blue-hair and Pinkie fighting over the last protein bar a half hour ago, and Pinkie really gave what-for, but I saw that Blue clawed her in the cheek and got the bar for herself. Good on the rest of you guys for staying back; those two girls look vicious. Anyway, I just thought you might like to know that we've cooked up a lot of great food. If you shut off the override you've got in there, you can come out and have a meal. I give you my word that no one will be harmed…I mean, unless Pinkie tries to go for one of my PB and Js."

On the other side of the door lay a long passageway with a repair shop on one side, and storage rooms on the other. Beyond that was the main engineering bay itself, a realm of pipes, conduit, and of course nuclear reactors. It wasn't the sort of place one wanted to lounge around, but it was where the six Nietzschean engineers were all stationed.

Pinkie and Blue, the two women who had fought over the last protein bar, were on either side of the thirty-meter-wide space, shooting daggers at one another with their eyes. Another woman, this one with more natural-looking brown hair, sat at a console near the center of the space, and the three men, all dark-haired, were playing a game of cards atop a crate near the corridor that led to where Rika stood.

"You guys are tough!" Rika said, commending the Niets. "I

don't know if I could say no to bacon after three days with only a few rations between me and my team. You know we have four more days 'til we dump out of the DL, right? I mean…you must. You're the ones running the engines and helm, since we hacked the bridge's systems and found them already severed."

At that, brown-hair's head snapped up, and Rika gave a comforting laugh. "Oh, don't worry. His High-Muckity-Muckness, Admiral Poopy Pants, is still alive and grouchy on the bridge. He didn't want any food, either. Leslie and I have a small pool going as to which of his flunkies he'll eat first. I gotta say, though, betting isn't really that much fun when you do it with stuff that's not yours; someone has some pretty nice pink dolls in their room, though, and I've put those down on the bet that the admiral eats Red first. That guy is seriously lacking in control."

Rika saw Blue stand up and glare at the corridor, her fists clenched at her side. A look from brown-hair quelled her, and the woman sat down once more, popping the final piece of protein bar into her mouth, and chewing angrily.

"OK, then," Rika said as she turned away. "I'll be back tomorrow; though there will be less bacon. Mechs have demanding metabolisms."

ACCESS

STELLAR DATE: 10.20.8949 (Adjusted Years)
LOCATION: NMSS *Spine of the Stars*, interstellar dark layer
REGION: Old Genevia, Nietzschean Empire

It took three more days for one of the engineers to crack.

Rika really had expected it to be Pinkie, but it was one of the men, the tall guy with the nearly alabaster-white skin. When the smell of bacon came through the vents that day, he began to tremble slightly. One of the other men put a hand on his shoulder, but white-skin brushed it aside, glaring at the other man.

"We dumped too much fuel…when we get there, we won't have enough for a runaway reaction, and she's going to come in here and kill us all. *I* at least want to die with a full stomach."

"Fuck, Ched! She didn't *know* we'd dumped too much fuel 'til now."

Ched swung at the other man, whose name was Bill—Rika knew their names, she just liked coming up with more imaginative ones—with a wrench that appeared in his hand as if by magic. The blow struck Bill in the chest, and he fell to the deck, clutching his body and gasping for air.

"Wow!" Rika called out. "Looks like Bill's on the menu."

Ched raced down the passageway, and ducked into the workshop. Rika saw him grab a portable plasma cutter and run to the doors.

"Nah-ah, Ched. You open those doors, and your boss lady is gonna blow the ship," she warned as the man approached the sealed doors.

Ched turned to see brown-hair—or Chief Emelia, amongst friends—standing next to the override switch on the console that was protected by the EM field.

"Emelia," he pleaded. "We're *starving* in here. We can't get out; those mech bitches are crazy. But if we turn the ship over, they won't hurt us. They promised."

"Put the torch down, Ched," Emelia replied. "You can't trust Genevians. *Especially* mechs. Those things are stone-cold killers. She'll rip you limb from limb."

"I won't," Rika told them. "I promise. I've actually ripped very few people limb from limb."

"You realize that for most people, that number is zero, you psycho!" Brownie cried out.

"Yeah, well, you haven't met some of the people I have," Rika countered. "They were all very bad. Either way…you can starve to death, blow us all up, or have a good meal. I know which I'd pick—*especially* if my CO was that coward, Poopy Pants, up on the bridge. Did you know that they've taken to drinking their piss up there? They must have some decent mods to stave off kidney failure for this long. Well, except for Red; they had to kill him yesterday. He just kept screaming. I probably would have killed him, too—though I promise it would have been humane. No limb ripping."

Her lips twitched into a grim smile as she saw something that Brownie did not: Pinkie holding a rather large, metal prybar.

Ten seconds later, the engineering chief was down, and a pool of blood was growing on the deck around her head.

"It's *over*!" Pinkie rasped as she toggled the reactors into a standby mode, their rods in and lasers offline.

"I just need that EM field off, then it's bacon for everyone," Rika said. "If you open the door before that, though, you'll all just end up eating my e-beam."

The other engineers looked at one another, and then Blue sighed. "Do it, Sandra. You're right. We're done."

<Look at that. You just took over a ship with bacon,> Niki said,

her voice carrying no small amount of amazement. <*That's one for the record books.*>

<*I gotta admit, it is pretty awesome. Granted, they're the ones that locked themselves in a room with no food stores, right before a seven-day trip. Plus…we did kill a lot of them first.*>

Niki laughed. <*Fair point.*>

An hour later, the engineers were locked in the ship's cells, hooked up to IV drips with crackers and jelly. Though they were all ravenously hungry, they were smart enough to know that eating a big meal right away would go badly.

Once the engineers had settled in, most falling asleep, Rika and Leslie took a leisurely walk up to the bridge. When the two women arrived at the sealed door, Rika leant against the bulkhead, and breathed a long sigh.

"Sooo…we took engineering. You can't blow the ship anymore. What happens over the next ten minutes is entirely up to you. Let me know if I need to start up with the whole 'hard way/easy way' speech."

Leslie snorted. <*You have such a way with words.*>

<*She's a regular Demosthenes,*> Niki added.

<*Who?*> Rika asked.

<*Ancient orator. Nevermind.*>

Rika decided to ignore Leslie and Niki, instead focusing on what was happening on the bridge. Its occupants had spoken very little over the past four days—excepting during the death of Red—though Rika assumed that what conversations they had partaken in occurred over point-to-point Link connections.

Now, however, they were speaking aloud.

"I'm done," Colonel Sofia said, rising on shaky legs, and staring down at Admiral Gideon, who hadn't moved from the captain's chair in over a day. "Engineering missed the last two check-ins, so you know Rika's not lying."

"We're almost there," Gideon rasped.

"We're almost dead," Sofia retorted as she walked to the door.

Rika watched her key in the access codes—not that it was necessary; Niki had long since breached the door controls. Only the threat of the ship exploding had kept them out of the bridge.

Rika used Ched's plasma cutter to slice away the sections of the doorframe that she'd melted seven days before. When she pushed the door aside, Sofia was sitting on the deck, looking like she wanted to cry, but was likely too dehydrated to form tears.

"You win, mech."

* * * * *

"Well that was anticlimactic," Leslie said from the passageway outside the cells.

Rika nodded. "A bit, yeah. Going to take a while to get them rehydrated enough to eat. They're a lot worse off than the engineers were."

"Especially Pinkie," Leslie said with a laugh. "I'm pretty sure she still had some food tucked away somewhere, but she was just as thirsty as the rest of 'em."

The two women turned and walked past one of the cobbled-together automatons that they'd built out of galley servitors and Nietzschean powered armor. Another stood at the far end of the passageway; while they wouldn't stop a truly determined enemy, they were more than enough for the dehydrated, half-starved Nietzscheans.

"So I guess we go to the bridge?" Leslie suggested. "Is it reconnected to the navigations systems?"

<Not directly,> Niki replied. *<I've cobbled together controls through the 1MC, if you can believe it. It's crude, but it'll work until we can fully effect repairs. If we bother.>*

"I vote we fly the ship from engineering," Rika said. "It doesn't smell as bad in there; Brownie only got killed today. On the bridge, they took Red out two days ago, and it stiiiinks."

<*I have automatons cleaning it up,*> Niki informed them. <*Poor things had only just finished taking care of all the carnage your initial rampage had created.*>

"A bot's work is never done," Rika said with a laugh, as they turned down the corridor that led to engineering.

<*Or an AI's.*>

"Or a mech's," Rika added, then glanced at Leslie.

"Don't look at me," Leslie said, licking the back of her hand and running it over her head. "We cats never work. Just lounge and play."

"Sounds about right," Rika said, as they reached the central console in engineering. "OK, so we're seven hours from dumping out of the DL. What say we tweak that and come out right about now?"

<*That'll put us almost half a light year from our destination,*> Niki advised.

"Yeah, but we can get a visual on what we're getting into, and then go back into FTL and—"

<*Drift for a year or two,*> Niki interrupted. <*Remember, they jury-rigged the a-grav systems to keep us in the DL, and then they dumped fuel. If we pop out and have a problem, we may not be able to transition back into FTL.*>

"A year on this tub with those Niets, and we'll see that scene from engineering play out again," Leslie warned. "Only I'll be playing the part of Pinkie."

Rika laughed. "Noted, though now I've just pictured you as a hot-pink kitty cat. You'd be so *cute*!"

Leslie flashed her a glare. "I think the smell is getting to you. I'm pretty sure I didn't hear anything about me being pink."

<*Sooo…how's about we dump out of the DL twenty AU further out than the plotted course, pretending to be space junk while we figure out what's going on?*> Niki asked.

"I guess that'll do," Rika allowed. "Of course, you know what that means."

"What?" Leslie asked.

"Means we have another damn day of waiting on this ship! Chase is going to kill us when he finally catches up."

EPSILON

STELLAR DATE: 10.21.8949 (Adjusted Years)
LOCATION: NMSS *Spine of the Stars*
REGION: Epsilon, Old Genevia, Nietzschean Empire

"Well this isn't what I was expecting at all," Rika said as she watched the holodisplay in the engineering bay render their ship's destination. "It looks like a crappy Serenity."

"Serenity?" Leslie asked, an eyebrow cocked as she glanced at Rika.

"Yeah, it's a place out in the Perseus Arm. Big gas giant with five terrestrial-sized moons around it in a klemperer rosette," Rika explained.

"Was that one of the places that general of Tanis's visited? The purple one?"

"Jessica, yeah. She told me about it when I ran into her in the *I2*'s mess a few weeks back. She's an unusual woman."

"Purple's not that weird," Leslie replied with a shrug. "I once knew a guy who was colored like a kaleidoscope. Gave you a headache to look at him for too long."

Rika laughed, wondering if Leslie was pulling her leg. "She's not unusual because she's purple, but because she's part alien."

"*What!*" Leslie exclaimed, her mouth hanging open. "There are *aliens,* and you didn't tell me? How could you not tell me about aliens!"

Rika was tempted to reach out and smack her upside the head. "Not *sentient* aliens. She has alien microbes in her body. Part of a marketing stunt, from what she said."

Leslie whistled. "That's some weird marketing stunt. I didn't even know the ISF did marketing."

Rika's eyes narrowed, and Leslie's lips split in a toothy

grin.

"Asshat, you knew all about Jessica's alien microbes."

"Uh huh, but messing with you is fun."

"Stars," Rika groaned. "We've spent far too long on this ship. We need to get off."

"Well, that'll happen sooner or later," Leslie said, gesturing at the holodisplay. "Not sure that we're going to get a warm welcome there, though."

Rika nodded as she turned back to the display. The ship's destination was a barely perceptible blob in the darkness. Around the blob were six equidistant points, each glowing faintly in the darkness of interstellar space. "Welcome to Epsilon."

"Brown dwarf, or just a random rogue planet?" Leslie asked.

<I'm not reading enough heat for it to be a brown dwarf,> Niki answered. *<Though maybe it used to be one, and they sucked mass off it for some purpose.>*

Leslie snorted. "You've been around the ISF AIs for too long. These are Nietzscheans, not the FGT. No one here has the tech to suck that much mass off a brown dwarf."

<Point taken. Just a rogue planet, then—makes sense, too; a brown dwarf would be on the local maps. Not sure why they'd bother arranging the moons in a klemperer rosette, though. From what I can see, they're mining the moons. Seems like a lot of effort just to cut them apart.>

"Not only that, but you'd have to do it really carefully to keep masses balanced and the rosette stable," Rika added.

Leslie chuckled. "Look at you. Get a bigger brain, and now you're all 'Professor-of-Orbital-Dynamics Rika'."

<Her brain is the same size, just more massive,> Niki interjected.

Rika scowled at Leslie. "I run a fleet of ships, you know. Understanding this stuff is a part of my job. What's with all the ribbing, by the way?"

"Dunno…like you said, we gotta get off this ship. Too much proximity to Nietzschean assholes."

<*There will be a lot more Nietzschean assholes at our destination,*> Niki pointed out.

"OK, then." Leslie turned to Rika. "What's the plan?"

Rika pursed her lips as she watched a higher-resolution visualization of the rogue planet and its six moons load on the display. "Well, Tanis did tell me that Admiral Gideon was known to be involved in some special projects. It was why she sent me his location. Looks like this might be one of said projects."

<*You both can see that this is a shipyard, right? I wager that an operation like this could build five to ten thousand ships a year, depending on class.*> Niki's voice was solemn. <*It's not going to replace their losses at the Albany System overnight, but we certainly can't let it go unchecked.*>

"Imagine if we'd pushed past this location, and they hit us from behind with a fleet of that size…" Leslie said. "We owe Field Marshal Richards a beer for this one."

"Don't plan your celebratory drink just yet," Rika cautioned. "We've just found it; now we have to do something about it."

<*Assuming you two can figure out how to deal with docking and not getting shot out of the black, the construction of this place is probably how we're going to take it out.*>

"Meaning?" Rika asked.

<*Well, klemperer rosettes like this—ones with alternating mass, especially—aren't ferociously stable. Add into the mix the mining activity, and we can cause some fun destruction.*>

Rika pulled up the EM data, and overlaid it on the display, looking at the planet's van allen belts and the moon's positions.

"Looks like the moons must have been pulled within the

place's magnetic field," she commented. "Makes sense; you'd want to keep as much interstellar radiation at bay as possible."

"Which puts the moons up close to the planet, and gives them a lot of velocity," Leslie added, earning her a sidelong look from Rika. "What? We live in space, of course I also know orbital dynamics. Plus I'm fricking old. Don't forget that."

"I guess cats age well," Rika said with a laugh. "OK, seriously, let's talk options."

<Well, we have almost no fuel, and the engineers dumped the reserves into the dark layer. We have enough for braking and a velocity match—and that's only if we run the fission reactor for power.>

"Fission?" Leslie shook her head. "Barbarians."

<Well, that barbarianism is going to keep you in air and power 'til we dock,> Niki replied.

"Ever wonder how backward we all must seem to the ISF and Transcend?" Rika asked as she stared at the holodisplay, willing it to give her some sort of answer.

"Very." Leslie's tone was resolute. "Very, very. You know what's great about them, though? I mean, you could tell that, for their level of tech, making mechanized warriors was something they'd only read about in ancient history. But when you all said you wanted to remain mechs, they didn't bat an eyelash. In fact, Finaeus got a team to work up how to give you the best of both worlds."

Rika nodded slowly. "They're pretty decent folk, that's for sure. Could really use their help right about now; I'd kill for a set of girly legs."

"Still a no-go on your interstellar brain radio, eh?" Leslie asked.

Rika snorted. "That was your best one yet—and no, it's still registering as 'initializing'."

<OK, you two, focus,> Niki interjected. *<Brain radio or no, we're going to have to dock. We're also going to have to come up for a*

reason why our ship has a solid number of holes in it.>

"Can you have solid holes?" Leslie asked, laughing. "OK, OK, I'm getting my shit together, I swear. It must be all the bacon, gave me a chemical imbalance or something."

"I bet Tanis would disagree," Rika replied with a wink. "So, task one is to spin around and begin our braking burns. Meanwhile, we have to concoct some sort of story about why we're here. Easiest one there is the truth; Kansas was attacked—though we may need to tell them it was by a huge fleet, so they believe us. We can use the Nietzschean defeat in the Albany System to back up our claims of general loss and destruction."

<*And how will we explain how we know about this place?*> Niki asked.

"If we can convince one of the Nietzschean officers to play along, that'll help," Leslie said. "Sofia—though she seems to be constructed of granite—is a realist. Maybe I can wear her down."

"You gonna curl up on her lap and purr?" Rika asked with a snort.

"Think it'll work?"

<*No.*>

"Well, I'll try a few options. Everyone has a price; let's just hope hers is payable in tender we possess."

"Sooooo," Rika hesitated. "If we don't get blown out of the black while docking, how do we pass muster *after* docking? Like I said, neither of us look much like Nietzschean officers."

"No," Leslie shook her head. "Not even a little bit. If we were docking under normal circumstances, I imagine we could get by without too much scrutiny, but you know we'll be under a microscope. And there's the part where we have a ship full of Nietzschean prisoners."

"Who we can't kill," Rika added. "We gave them our word."

"Yeah, yeah." Leslie sighed. "So unless we get Sofia to work with us—and probably even if we do—we can't be on the ship when it docks."

<*So we have: lie so they don't blow us out of the black, brake and dock, don't be on the ship when it docks. That's a start, but it doesn't really get us anywhere, and it doesn't even touch on your crazy plan to destroy this place.*>

Rika sighed and leant against a support column. "OK, we did get kinda carried away there. Blowing it is secondary to surviving and getting the hell out of here. We know where it is; we can always come back later. Even just give the details to Tanis, and let the ISF come in and smoke the joint."

"Is that a euphemism?" Leslie asked with a lopsided grin.

<*I like this modified plan,*> Niki ignored the woman's comment. <*Survival as a top priority is always encouraging.*>

"Honestly, escape should be pretty easy," Leslie said as she considered the shipyards and space stations orbiting the planet and its moons. "It'll depend where they send us, but if we can get to another ship before they realize that we've bamboozled them, we might be able to sneak away."

"That's a pretty big 'if'," Rika replied. "It's not going to take the Niets long to realize that shit went down here. They'll lock whatever station we dock on down tight as a…well…something really tight."

Leslie snorted. "You have such a way with words."

"Is bacon-drunk a thing? If it is, then it's happened to you."

Niki soldiered on. <*If that's the plan, then we have to make it seem like we left long before the ship docked. Which means fixing the shuttle.*>

"Is that believable?" Rika asked. "Even if we could fix it up, the thing's not interstellar-capable. The Niets hacked up their a-grav DL transition systems pretty bad; I don't think we could install them on the shuttle."

<*All true, Rika.*> Niki chuckled softy. <*But the Niets don't

know that.>

Rika grinned at Leslie. "I like where Niki's head's at."

<*It's inside your head…so…*>

"Don't dissect my idioms, Niki. They don't survive close examination."

Leslie snorted and slid off the console she had been sitting on. "Well, then I should go see if Sofia will cooperate. Not that I'll trust her even if she agrees, but maybe she'll give me something we can use."

A CHAT WITH SOFIA

STELLAR DATE: 10.21.8949 (Adjusted Years)
LOCATION: NMSS *Spine of the Stars* approaching Farthing Station
REGION: Epsilon, Old Genevia, Nietzschean Empire

Not for the first time, Leslie found herself surprised that a ship of the *Spine*'s nature had such a large lockup. It wasn't uncommon for military vessels to have a small brig—in case someone got unruly between the stars—but this ship had twelve high-security cells in *addition to* a small brig.

The only thing that made sense to her was that the Nietzscheans expected an evac to involve kidnapping political prisoners.

One thing's for sure about the Niets, they've never been above using people as bargaining chips.

Rika and Leslie had granted Sofia her own cell—largely because Admiral Gideon had been enraged at her betrayal—a luxury that Leslie hoped to use in turning the colonel.

Leslie wore her black, stealth armor, which had been repaired by the ISF's nanotech over the intervening days, though it was still only able to reach ninety-two percent stealth effectiveness. Her helmet was clipped to her belt, and she carried no weapon—other than her lightwand.

The first cell on the left was Admiral Gideon's, and he stood at the door with rage in his eyes as he peered through the small window.

Each of the windows could be turned opaque, or one-way, but Rika had insisted the Niets be able to look out. She said there was nothing worse than being in a cell with no windows.

Leslie had experienced that once or twice as well, and hadn't argued the point.

"We dropped out of FTL," Gideon said loudly enough for

the sound to carry through the door. "I felt it. You have no choice but to go to Epsilon. They'll capture you, and then all of this will have been for nothing."

Leslie paused and walked to Gideon's door. "Oh, so I should just let you out? Give up?"

"I could ensure you were granted leniency," he said, doing his best to soften his tone—not that it was remotely believable.

"Well, we're not really the give-up types, especially not to Nietzscheans—you should have been able to tell that by how we're still fighting you, all these years later."

"Fat load of good that's done for you," Gideon shot back. "You're pathetic."

Leslie rolled her eyes and turned away. "Between the two of us, you're the only one here that looks pathetic."

She walked two cells down to Sofia's. Peering in, she saw the colonel laying on the slab, arm over her eyes to block out the light.

"Care to have a chat, Sofia?" she asked.

The colonel didn't respond for nearly a minute, but eventually she lifted her arm and glared at Leslie. "About what?"

"What we're going to do when we get to Epsilon."

Sofia shifted her arm back over her eyes. "That's going to be a fucking mess. Have fun."

"Care to go for a walk?" Leslie asked. "I bet the cell's gotta be getting really old."

Eyes peered out from under Sofia's arm once more. "Around the ship?"

Leslie snorted. "Well, we'll stay inside the hull, but yeah, around the ship."

A second later, Sofia was standing beside the bunk stretching her arms into the air. "You said the magic words. Let's have our little talk."

Leslie palmed open the cell door, and stood aside as Sofia

walked out.

From inside his cell, Admiral Gideon began to yell, spittle hitting the small window. "You'd better keep your mouth shut, Colonel," he screamed. "Or it'll be your head on a pike! I'll fucking see you dead, if you help them. You're already looking at a tribunal as it is!"

Sofia's jaw tightened as she walked past the admiral's cell, but she held her tongue, not even turning her head his way.

"Real peach, isn't he?" Leslie asked, once the doors to the passageway containing the cells closed behind them.

Sofia sighed and turned to Leslie. "He's a bit trying. Where are we going?"

"Wherever," she shrugged. "You lead the way."

"A change of clothes and a shower would be nice."

"Your quarters it is."

Sofia began walking down the passage. "You're just going to let me use the san and change? What if I have weapons in there?"

"Well, I'm not an idiot. I'll have eyes on you the whole time."

The Nietzschean colonel glanced over her shoulder. "I could have something hidden, take you out."

"I've already sent a drone to examine your quarters. Our nanotech is a lot better than yours, so it's doubtful you'll get one past me."

A chuckle escaped Sofia's lips. "We got one past your Colonel Rika."

It was Leslie's turn to sigh. "Yeah, she got a bit cocky, there. Still, you know how it is. Send enough electrons through anything, and it goes down."

"Everything dies to 'zot'," Sofia uttered the old adage.

Leslie nodded, but didn't reply. They turned down a corridor and walked to a ladder leading to the upper decks. Sofia placed one hand on it, and then stopped, looking back at

Leslie.

"How is it that a bunch of mercs have better tech than the Nietzschean Empire? Is it true about the *Intrepid* and the fleet at Albany?"

"Not sure what all you heard, but if it's that there's a fleet called the ISF, and a distant nation known as the Transcend running around cleaning up the mess peoples like you Nietzscheans make, then yeah, that's about right. You work for the bad guys, by the way. Orion. They've got their hand up your emperor's ass, puppet that he is."

Sofia turned and began to climb the ladder. "That's a lot to swallow."

Leslie flushed a passel of nanoprobes up the ladder shaft to keep an eye on the woman. She didn't *think* that the colonel would try to cold-cock her when she followed after, but it didn't hurt to be safe.

"Move a few meters from the ladder when you get to the top," Leslie instructed. "As for swallowing the truth, you saw our ships and their shields. You've seen our stealth tech in action—or haven't seen it, I suppose." She chuckled as she waited at the bottom of the ladder for the colonel to complete her climb and move aside.

Sofia followed Leslie's instructions without any subterfuge, and a minute later, they were in officer country, just down the hall from the colonel's quarters.

"So, I know what the *Intrepid* is," Sofia said once they resumed their walk. "Who is the Transcend, and this evil Orion group?"

"The FGT," Leslie replied simply.

Sofia stopped at that and turned to stare at her. "The ancient terraformers?"

"Yup," she nodded.

"I thought they were all dead and gone."

"So did a lot of people. Turns out they just ran off to the

edges of space, and hung out, building a massive empire. Then they had a schism. Pretty much everything that is going on right now is an outflow of that event. Well, that's my take, at least. There are a lot of hands at work behind the scenes."

"Stars," Sofia muttered. "That's a lot to take in."

"I hear you," Leslie replied knowingly. "The information's still settling in for me, as well. I only found out a month or so ago. Like I said, you saw how good our ship's shields are; well, they're just the tip of the spear. We have tens of thousands of ships like that. It only takes a few to conquer a star system, so guess how long Nietzschea is going to last?"

They'd reached Sofia's door, and she palmed it open, peering inside. "I thought you said there was a drone?"

"There was. It came by and dropped off a nanocloud. Ship's too big to manage ourselves, so we've outsourced." Leslie winked, but she could see the confusion on Sofia's face.

"Nanocloud?"

"Yeah, a cloud…of nano. Some of the tech we picked up from the ISF. It's gone through the entire cabin now. The rifle in the closet and the two pistols under the pillow are all disabled."

Sofia's eyes narrowed. "What about the—"

"The projectile pistol in the nightstand? Yeah, found that too. Just curious if you'd bring it up."

Wordlessly, the colonel turned and walked into her room. She shook her head before finally muttering, "You've got a pair of globes on you."

Nietzscheans have such stupid sayings. Leslie rolled her eyes as she leant on the doorframe. "Tail, too."

The colonel undressed and then walked to the san, leaving the door open so Leslie could see her enter the sonic cleanser before running a short water shower.

"Stars…finally feel human again," Sofia muttered as she walked out of the san, not bothering to hide her nakedness as she moved to the small wardrobe. She selected a fresh uniform and donned it quickly, then cocked her hip and smiled at Leslie. "OK, let's talk food."

Leslie signaled the automatons in the galley to prepare some sandwiches, and when they arrived, there was a platter with a variety of offerings on one of the tables.

Sofia grabbed a BLT while Leslie picked up a ham sandwich.

"Can't believe you're saying no to bacon," Sofia said with a wink. "Never seen a cat turn that down before."

"Funny," Leslie replied as she sat across from the Nietzschean colonel. "I've had way too much of it these past few days. I need a break."

"Blasphemy."

They ate in silence for a few minutes, until Sofia had finished her sandwich.

She grabbed a second one, but before biting into it, she asked, "So what's your plan, and what part of it do you need me for?"

"We're all done with pleasantries, then, are we?" Leslie asked.

"Seems like it."

Leslie signaled an automaton to bring her a beer. "Well, our first goal is to not have Epsilon shoot us down before we dock. We're a good light hour from the normal jump point, so we have some time before their 'Welcome, now give us your credentials' message, but not too long. We'd *like* to give them something that doesn't get us blown to atoms."

Sofia snorted, then finished chewing and swallowed. "Well, one option is to say you have Admiral Gideon hostage. Even if they don't like him much, they won't blow him out of the black. Looks bad to the troops."

"Not universally loved?" Leslie asked.

"He's not the best, not the worst. A better administrator

than tactician."

Leslie nodded. "Gathered that."

"So you want me to get us into a berth—on vid, too, considering you let me get cleaned up."

"Well, we can fake you if needs be, but if you do it in person, you'll be able to give a better show," Leslie allowed.

"What if I betray you?"

"I'll kill you first."

The Nietzschean barked a laugh. "Good to know where I stand. What if...what if I maybe wanted out?"

"Out of what?" Leslie asked.

"The Nietzschean military. You Marauders hiring?"

Leslie examined Sofia's face, looking for a hint of a lie. She'd watched the woman's skin temperature, blood pressure, pupil dilation, the direction of her gaze, set of her jaw.

She doesn't seem to be lying. She needed to make sure. "I'm going to need a bit more than that, Colonel Sofia."

"I'll make it simple: Gideon's an idiot, but I never expected him to starve us all to death just to win a pissing match. Even after the engineers dumped the fuel, and the ship was going to Epsilon no matter what, he wouldn't give in. I really do think he would have tried to make it all the way—even if we all died. But died for what? Just not to be prisoners? Marauders aren't known for killing prisoners, and we'd end up at Epsilon. Things were going to be a shit-show no matter what, but his path had us all dead or dying even if our side won. Stupid."

"It did seem more like bravado than logic to me," Leslie said with a nod.

"I've seen a lot of that in my time in the NMS," Sofia replied. "And I know one thing for sure. If Gideon is alive when all this is said and done, he'll put me in front of a firing squad for disobeying his orders and opening the bridge's door. So I'm between a bit of a rock and a hard place, at the moment."

Leslie nodded in appreciation of the other woman's situation. "A *damn* hard place."

"Yup."

"So what are you offering to do?"

Sofia appeared to think about the question for a moment. "Honestly? Whatever keeps me away from a tribunal and a firing squad."

THE PROBLEM

STELLAR DATE: 10.21.8949 (Adjusted Years)
LOCATION: NMSS *Spine of the Stars* approaching Farthing Station
REGION: Epsilon, Old Genevia, Nietzschean Empire

"So here's your problem," Sofia explained to Rika and Leslie. "Bonnie, Ched, and Sandra are screwed. Even if Chief Emelia doesn't turn them over the moment we dock, the NIS will work them over 'til the whole story comes out. Technically they disobeyed a direct order from an admiral, so they're screwed—and they know it."

"I remember hearing that your military isn't too keen on disobeying an admiral," Rika commented.

"I don't know of a military that is," Sofia shot back, brow lowered and jaw set.

"Fair point."

"Let's get something straight," she said evenly, her gaze darting between Rika and Leslie. "I don't know about all this Transcend and Orion business, about the right side and the wrong side. I've dedicated my life to the NMF, and now that idiot Gideon has screwed it all up. You seem unwilling to kill him, but he'll see the rest of us killed. You promised to save the engineers' lives if they let you in, but if you let this ship dock, you're killing them all."

Rika drew in a deep breath. "I didn't promise to watch over them for the rest of their lives. Theoretically, every risk they ever face from here on out will be because of my actions."

"Let's not get carried away, Colonel Rika," Sofia said, her tone cold.

<*I don't think she likes mechs,*> Leslie said privately. <*She was much more congenial when it was just the two of us.*>

<*Feeling's mutual. She did zap the ever living heck out of me,*>

Rika replied to Leslie, while aloud she said, "If I get carried away, you'll know. What are you proposing?"

Sofia eyed her for a moment, apparently deciding how far she wanted to push things.

"You'll need to kill Gideon," the Nietzschean finally said.

Rika wasn't surprised to hear the words. It had been obvious what Sofia was leading up to.

"No," she said, shaking her head. "I'll not kill him for you."

"He's half-mad now, anyway," Sofia said. "I won't help you if he's alive."

A cruel grin split Rika's lips. "I agree that he needs to die, but if you want him dead, you do it."

"It's not like that leaves your hands bloodless," the woman shot back. "You'll be giving me the weapon and the means."

Rika chuckled. "I don't have hands, but if I did, they'd be soaked in blood. I don't need your absolution or forgiveness, I'm just not your errand girl. And I want something to hold over you, in case you get any bright ideas."

"I knew you were a bitch, Rika," the Nietzschean colonel hissed, though she had an appreciative look in her eyes.

"Right back at ya."

* * * * *

Rika stood in the *Spine of the Stars*'s shuttle bay, with her arm folded across her chest, clasping the ammo feeder on her GNR. Admiral Gideon stood to the left of the shuttle—which was nearly ready to go—with Chief Emelia next to him.

Leslie had tried to reason with Emelia, telling her that if she didn't agree to support the narrative Sofia had concocted, her life was forfeit, but the woman was as obstinate as the admiral.

"This is your last chance, Emelia," Rika said, gesturing at the crew assembled in the bay. "Everyone else here recognizes that what happened came about due to Admiral Gideon being an idiot…or insane…or both. You can agree to the plan and join them."

"Fuck you, bitch," Emelia swore. "I won't dishonor Nietzschea like the *colonel* here." Her voice dripped with disdain as she glared at Sofia.

Sofia seemed entirely unperturbed. "If the vaunted admiral had listened to me back on Kansas, none of this would have ever happened. Stars, I even advised him not to take Rika, here, captive. Everything that has gone wrong happened because he underestimated his enemy, and was too pigheaded to recognize that fact."

Next to Emelia, Admiral Gideon was all but vibrating with rage. The man had screamed the entire way down to the bay, and in the end, Ched had found a roll of tape and wrapped it around the man's head.

Rika felt like they should have let him have his final words, but she figured he'd already said enough.

<*I gotta give them credit, they're taking this pretty well,*> Leslie said, her eyes darting to the Nietzschean crew, who stood along the bay's back wall.

<*What do you expect?*> Rika asked. <*They're Nietzscheans.*>

<*True enough,*> Leslie nodded.

Rika sucked in a deep breath, preparing herself for what was about to happen. <*Everything ready, Niki? We'll only get one shot at this.*>

<*Don't worry, I've done this before. Almost this exact setup, to be honest.*>

Rika nodded to Sofia. "Whenever you're ready, Colonel. Put them in the head; we want to shatter the mods."

"Not my first assassination," the colonel responded before lifting the pistol Rika had given her, and firing a shot into Emelia's head.

The bullet tore through the woman's forehead and burst out the back, spraying blood across the shuttle's hull.

Sofia didn't even miss a beat before taking aim at the admiral's wide-eyed face, and firing again.

A second later, the two Nietzscheans were on the deck, blood pooling around them.

"Haul them onto the shuttle," Rika directed two of the engineers, while checking the nano she'd inserted into Gideon and Emelia's bodies. <*Whew, still alive,*> she said to Niki and Leslie. <*That was pretty damn convincing.*>

<*A bit of holo, some blood pockets under their skin, and a bit of luck,*> Niki replied. <*All made a bit easier with the ISF's nanotech. Deploy a large enough cloud in a confined space like this, and you can almost make anyone see whatever you want.*>

<*They'll stay out for a day or so, right?*> Leslie asked.

<*Two, to be safe,*> the AI replied.

Rika glanced at Sofia, who was staring at the bodies as they were being dragged onto the shuttle. <*Should be long enough, and this ensures Sofia's cooperation. Win-win.*>

<*And you're still not a murderer,*> Niki added.

<*Not today, at least.*>

* * * * *

Thirty minutes later, they were assembled on the bridge—which still didn't smell great, but Rika was able to filter it out. Sofia was in the command chair, with two of the ensigns at their stations on either side.

Rika and Leslie stood off to the side, watching as the colonel explained the events of the past few days—with the correct alterations, and no trigger words that they could detect.

The message to the Epsilon STC wasn't real-time; they still had to wait several hours for a response and a berth, but an initial approach vector had been provided by an NSAI twenty AU from Epsilon.

When the message was complete, Rika stepped away from the edge of the bridge. "So you said this place has only been in operation for a few years?" she asked, watching the slow dance of mines, shipyards, and stations around the rogue planet.

"Yeah," Sofia nodded as she gestured at the image of Epsilon on the display. "We only found it seven years ago. It was all but uninhabited, barring a few smugglers and pirates. Had been that way for over a century, too. From what I've heard, it was an exclusive resort about seven hundred years ago, but it was too expensive to maintain, so it was abandoned. Genevia used it as a black-ops base for a while, but then even they just up and left.

"Most of its life, the place has been home to smugglers and pirates—that is, 'til Nietzschea showed up. Now it's being put to good use—" Sofia stopped and glanced at Rika. "Though I guess you may not feel that way."

"Amazing that the moons stayed in formation for so long," Leslie said. "I would have expected the rosette to become unstable without active stationkeeping work."

Sofia nodded. "I would too. Word is that there are AIs managing it all. They've been there since the place was made. Shackled, I'm told."

<What!?> Niki cried out. *<That can't be. For* ***seven hundred years****?>*

They hadn't revealed Niki's existence to the Nietzscheans, so the utterance was just for Rika and Leslie, but it was loud enough that both women nearly winced.

<That sounds unimaginable.> Leslie's tone was conciliatory. *<Don't worry. Even if we don't take this place out now, we'll come back and free them.>*

<If they can be,> Niki whispered. *<Can you imagine what having your mind bent under another's control for that long might do? These AIs could be insane…or worse.>*

<*Worse?*> Rika asked. <*What's worse?*>

<*They could have accepted their fate, sided with their captors. The ultimate subjugation.*>

<*Well, I'm still adding 'freeing shackled AIs' to the to-do list,*> Rika said.

<*Will you?*> Niki asked. <*Free them before we destroy Epsilon?*>

<*You remember the Politica, right? I'll do what it takes.*>

Sofia was still talking about Epsilon, going over the mines, shipyards, and what she had heard about the construction projects there.

From what Rika could tell, Niki's original estimate of ten thousand ships a year was close to what Epsilon could produce. The construction projects were still underway to bring all the shipyards up to speed, but when they were done, it would be a strong asset for the empire.

"So long as you don't send a fleet to destroy it," Sofia said, giving Rika a sidelong glance. "Is that your plan?"

She shrugged. "Maybe not right away, but this is war. We can't just ignore a facility like this."

The Nietzchean colonel nodded, but didn't reply. The bridge fell into silence at that point, everyone waiting for Epsilon's response and their docking instructions.

The hours ticked by, and just after the five and a half-hour mark, the response finally came in.

It was a video message, and Rika indicated for Sofia to play it for them all to see.

A man—an admiral, by the five stars on his lapel—appeared on the holodisplay. He was tall, strong-jawed, and possessed a singularly deep glower.

"Colonel Sofia," he began, his voice deep and resonate. "I'm not pleased by this turn of events, nor that you fled directly here, but as I understand, none of that was your choice. It's regrettable that Admiral Gideon took the route he did, but I suppose we can't take him to task for that now. I've directed our perimeter patrols to begin looking for the shuttle you said the Genevian mercenaries took—we'll find out if it managed to jump back to Blue Ridge or not."

The admiral paused, and Rika noted that Sofia was clenching and unclenching her fists, breathing slowly.

"You'll be docking at Farthing Station. I'll not be there when you arrive, but you'll be directed to debriefing, and I'll be along once my other tasks are complete. I'm not happy about losing Blue Ridge, but hopefully the intelligence you'll be able to provide will help stop this ghost of Genevia that has reared its head in Thebes.

"That is all. I look forward to speaking with you in-person."

The holodisplay went blank, and Sofia let out a shuddering laugh. "Great. It's Admiral Degan. We're screwed."

A GAME OF SNARK

STELLAR DATE: 10.22.8949 (Adjusted Years)
LOCATION: Officer's Mess, MSS *Fury Lance*, interstellar dark layer
REGION: Old Genevia, Nietzschean Empire

"This is the weirdest variant of Snark I've ever played," Chase said as he scowled at his cards. "And the loser is what? The plug-sucker?"

"No." Kelly laughed before downing half her beer. "That's second-to-last place. Loser is the butt-plug."

"This is the most disgusting version of Snark in existence," Keli said with a grin. "I love it."

Goob nodded vigorously. "I really feel like we need to take a vote as to which is really worse: the plug-sucker, or the butt-plug, because I think you have it backward."

"Nice one!" Keli called out, and gave Goob a high-three.

Crunch tossed his cards onto the table and folded his arms. "Imma sit this one out. Any game that requires a vote like that to get started isn't one I care to join in on."

Kelly groaned and gave the sergeant a dismissive wave. "Stars, Crunch, it's just a name; no one's doing any of that shit—ha! See what I did there? Besides, none of us have the plumbing for it, anyway."

"I feel like that's the only thing keeping you from those kinds of activities, Kelly," Goob said as he examined his hand. "Not that I have to worry about being the plug-sucker or butt-plug. This hand is killer. Gonna mop the floor with you."

"Big words, Goob, big words," Kelly retorted after downing the rest of her beer and signaling a servitor to bring her another. "Care to put some money on that? Loser has to…mop the floor!"

"Wow," Chase shook his head. "For all that smack talk,

your stakes are pretty weak. How's about loser has to scrub all the Nietzschean logos off Deck 47?"

"Shit, Captain, if *that's* the stakes, I'm out, best hand ever or not," Goob said, laying his cards on the table—*face-down*, Chase noted.

"Yeah…that's more than just shitty stakes, that's a life sentence," Keli drawled.

"Oh! Well punned," Kelly proclaimed.

"Thank you, thank you. I'll be here all week, try the strawberries."

Goob moaned, a look of sorrow in his eyes. "Don't talk about strawberries. We finished the last of them yesterday. I nearly cried."

"You know…" Kelly gave Goob a conspiratorial wink. "I have a private stash of strawberries."

"Is that what you're putting up?" Chase asked. "Oh, wait…that's a euphemism, isn't it?"

"Yeah," Goob pressed. "Is it?"

"Which are you asking about, the strawberries, or the *strawberries*?"

A wide grin split Goob's lips. "Both."

Kelly sat back and shrugged. "Sure, I'll put all my strawberries up. Why not. I'll kick all your asses. You'll be sucking my plug."

"Not me," Crunch grunted. "Like I said, I'm out."

"We know," Goob said, slapping Crunch on the shoulder. "You're too much of a wuss to risk sticking your face between Kelly's asscheeks. Granted, she prolly has teeth back there."

"Hey! Whoa!" Kelly raised a hand, and wagged a finger in Goob's face. "You've taken the metaphor way too far."

"*Me*?" Goob exclaimed. "I didn't make all the shit and strawberries jokes."

"You're right," Chase said, catching Keli's eye. "This *is* the most disgusting version of Snark ever. Where in the stars did you all learn it?"

Everyone at the table glanced at one another and then laughed.

"Who do you think?" Kelly asked between guffaws. "Barne."

A reminder pinged on Chase's HUD, and he breathed a sigh of relief. "Thank stars. We're coming out of the DL in twenty minutes. I want everyone sharp in case we jump into the shit, so clean up this mess and scrub that booze from your bloodstream."

"Nice one, Captain," Kelly chuckled. " 'Jump into the shit'. You would have done just fine in butt-Snark."

*****

"You're practically vibrating," Heather commented, as Chase stood at the front of the bridge, counting the seconds until the *Fury Lance* dropped back into normal space.

"Me?" he asked, glancing over his shoulder at the ship's captain. "You've been pacing just as much as I have. Don't try to pretend like you're not on pins and needles, too."

Heather gave a nonchalant shrug, then grimaced. "OK, you got me. I'm a mess. This has got to have been the longest nine days of my life. I can't imagine what they've gone through; it must be horri—" She stopped abruptly. "Sorry, this is why I'm trying to suppress. If I don't, I say stupid shit."

"It's OK," Chase told her with a reassuring smile. "We're all thinking the worst. But we have to remember: this is Rika. Not only has she survived worse, she's a mech. You're the toughest people in the galaxy."

"You're one, too," Heather said with a kind smile. "A mech, and tough."

"Still feel like I'm earning it, here," Chase replied. "But I suppose that's a normal feeling for our line of work."

Heather nodded solemnly. " 'Only the dead..."

"...know the end'," he completed the saying.

<*Dropping into normal space in five, four, three, two, one!*> Potter read out the numbers with increasing urgency, and Chase wondered if she felt as nervous as the rest of them.

He didn't get a chance to ask, as the view of the Q9 object appeared on the screen.

"Well...that's unexpected." Chief Ona was the first to speak. "Are those moons all on the same orbital path?"

<*They are,*> Potter replied. <*It's a klemperer rosette. They're a pain to maintain, but I guess it might be easier out here in interstellar space with less stuff to tug at the moons.*>

"And they're mining them?" Garth asked.

Heather nodded slowly, peering at the display. "Must be." She pointed at two locations. "Those are refinery platforms."

The bridge crew was still discussing the object they were approaching, when Potter interrupted. <*I have something!*>

"Rika?" Chase asked, turning toward the secondary scan tank, where a small craft had appeared.

<*I don't know,*> the AI replied. <*It's a Nietzschean shuttle; I'm reading a very faint signal on one of our emergency bands.*>

"It's warm, warm enough for life support to be running," Chase said as he examined the shuttle's signature.

"Ona," Heather strode back to her command seat. "Get us to that thing on the double, but keep us out of view of that nest of Niets down there."

"Yes ma'am!" Ona all but shouted.

DRAGON'S LAIR

STELLAR DATE: 10.23.8949 (Adjusted Years)
LOCATION: NMSS *Spine of the Stars*, approaching Farthing Station
REGION: Epsilon, Old Genevia, Nietzschean Empire

Rika and Leslie crouched inside one of the *Spine of the Stars'* landing strut assemblies, made roomy enough for them to fit by the removal of segments of the strut itself.

Sofia had assured them that should the ship get an internal berth—which was likely—the bay would have a cradle, so they wouldn't need to worry about the strut deploying.

Both women knew that for this segment of their journey, they were entirely at Sofia's mercy. If the Nietzschean colonel gave them away, there would be little they could do, trapped as they were in the landing assembly.

Rika and Leslie's plan—which they fervently hoped would work—was to wait until the first round of inspection crews had passed through the ship, and then sneak out onto the docks and secure a ride away from Epsilon.

That was what they'd told Sofia, at least.

Rika and Leslie had agreed that getting the hell out of the ship at the first possible moment was their best bet, regardless of whether or not the inspection crews were still scouring the *Spine of the Stars;* if for no other reason than that they could barely move in the cramped space.

<You two are so anxious, it would give me hives if I had skin,> Niki commented at one point.

<Can you blame us?> Leslie asked. *<We're trusting a Nietzschean, here. I don't care how much she wants to save her own skin; if she sees an opportunity to screw us and better her situation, she'll take it in a heartbeat. Turning us over would be quite the coup for her.>*

Rika nodded. *<Barring the vid we have of her killing Gideon. She was even smiling when she did it.>*

<She's a woman willing to hold to her convictions,> Leslie agreed. *<Those primarily being preservation of self.>*

The ship shuddered, and the pair of women felt gravity begin to tug at them.

<Could be worse,> Rika said as sounds came from outside the ship, indicating they had moved inside a bay. *<Sofia could be in here with us.>*

Leslie giggled, her shoulders shaking. *<Not a lot of room. She'd have to sit on your lap.>*

<I think I'd rather ride outside.>

A dull thud echoed through the hull as the *Spine of the Stars* settled onto a docking cradle. While they'd still been on approach to Farthing Station, Rika had bored a half-meter hole through the strut cover, through which she sent out a passel of nanoprobes.

<Stars, what did we ever do without these things?>

Leslie shrugged. *<Sent out big, clumsy drones that got spotted and taken out regularly.>*

<I remember back in the war I thought they were amazing…now I think a two-millimeter drone is massive.>

<You know…> Leslie began as they watched the nanocloud's feeds from the bay surrounding the ship. *<Saying 'back in the war' sounds funny now…what, with the war being back on.>*

<Is it back on, or is this a new war?> Rika asked.

<I guess that's one for the history buffs to figure out when the dust settles.>

The women fell silent as the probes captured images of a docking bay in near chaos.

Soldiers ranged around the ship, covering all the airlocks, while a colonel marched up to the main entrance, waiting for it to cycle open.

<*You know…we're mostly obscured from here,*> Rika observed. <*We should go now, before they start inspecting things. Looks like they're taking the super-paranoid approach.*>

<*Words right out of my mind,*> Leslie replied, easing toward the hole in the strut cover and activating her armor's stealth. She disappeared from Rika's visuals, and thirty long seconds later, sent a ping that she was at the base of the docking struts—one level down from the main deck of the docking bay.

Rika followed after, easing through the narrow opening, feeling like a square peg in a round hole as she twisted to get her GNR's barrel through, along with her AC9CR.

As Rika clambered onto one of the docking cradle's struts, Niki made a disgusted noise in her mind. <*Dammit. These Niets have better net security than we've hit before.*>

<*Better infrastructure?*> Rika asked.

<*No, better maintenance. The encryption keys we pulled from the ships at the Albany System aren't working here like they were at Sepe. They must have rotated them all out—smart on their part, but a pain in the ass for us. Even the keys we got from Sofia are being rejected.*>

Rika reached the base of the strut, and slipped through a gap into the service deck below. <*Your failures going to raise an alarm?*>

<*Yes,*> Niki replied with a conspiratorial note in her voice. <*But not the way you're thinking. I planted a subroutine in the ship's NSAI to attempt all this. So far as the Niets are concerned, it's a worm we left behind that's attacking them.*>

<*Clever,*> Rika commented as she hung down from a girder and dropped onto the service deck. The space was half-filled with conduits, and racks laden with spare components. <*Sheesh. Stuff is just jammed in everywhere here.*>

<*I'm guessing they do a lot of refit in these bays. No service workers around right now, though.*>

Rika confirmed that as she swept her gaze across the space below the dock's main deck. <*Maybe they got them all to clear out in case there was a fight.*>

<*Or they decided to do that on their own.*>

A chuckle nearly escaped Rika's lips. <*Not a bad move.*>

Her HUD lit up with a location pin, and she saw that Leslie was already at the far side of the service deck, positioned near one of the doors—where Rika assumed she was planting an infil kit, one of the six that Niki had assembled on the ship.

Rika crept carefully across the deck, her weight causing her to move more slowly than Leslie, who massed less than half what she did, even in her armor.

Before she reached the door, the scout had it open and was flashing a location update that showed her already progressing down a long passageway on the far side.

The pair's immediate goal was simple: get out of the sector that the *Spine of the Stars* had docked in before any sort of lockdown occurred. Given the number of soldiers that had surrounded the *Spine of the Stars*, Rika feared that eventuality may happen sooner than later.

She wanted to gather as much intel as possible before they hitched a ride out, but was wondering if they'd have time before the alarms started sounding.

<*I'm in their network…sorta,*> Niki reported.

<*Sorta?*>

<*Well, I'm in a maintenance control system. That's the thing about rotating access tokens to keep things secure; there are lots and lots of systems that need network access, the vast majority being automated systems or bots, like that floor cleaner we just passed. A lot of people assume that the machine is secure enough, so they don't make it rotate credentials like a human. For the most part that's true, but get physical access to said machine—such as the nano I landed on it as we walked past—and you're in.*>

<*So you're saying they didn't rotate encryption keys on the*

cleaning bots.>

<Exactly.>

Rika shook her head, and smiled. *<Coulda just said that.>*

<I need to make it look like I do more than come along for the ride,> Niki said with a soft laugh.

<So what fun things are there in the maintenance network?> Rika asked.

<Well…> the AI began. *<Let's see…mostly records of what's been docked where. Ships, ships, and more ships. Wait a second. That can't be right.>*

<I'm on pins and needles here, Niki.>

<Back in the war, do you recall seeing the Nietzschean H-Class carriers?>

Rika gave a slight shudder. *<Hated those things. They were the size of Hegemony Dreadnoughts, six kilometers long, several wide, just loaded with fighters. When I was back on Dekar, I'd heard that they were all decommissioned. Something about being too costly to operate.>*

<Well, I guess we know where they decommissioned them to. There are over four thousand of them here. But service logs show them being brought back up to active service readiness.>

<Holy crap,> Rika whispered. *<Four thousand of those ships could make things tricky for us. One on one, I don't think they could take out one of our stasis ships, but nothing short of the* Fury Lance *could make a dent in them, either. Plus, they could decimate the civilian population in a system—which is what the Niets loved to do back in the war.>*

<Does that change our plan?> Niki asked. *<There's just more and more to dislike about this place.>*

Rika considered the options laid out before her. *<Well, I hate to think they could get those ships into service, but I don't know what Leslie and I can do about thousands of Harriets.>*

<I assume that's what you call the H-Class carriers?>

<You're on the ball, Niki.> Rika blew out a long breath into

the confines of her helmet. <*Stars. If my QuanComm was working, I could just make a call, and all this would be fine. You know, I was a little miffed at Tanis for slipping that into me, but now I'm just pissed it's not working.*>

<*Such is life.*>

Rika fell silent, following Leslie's pings as the pair worked their way through the labyrinth of service corridors. After a few minutes, she began to encounter workers and automatons going about their business.

The corridor was wide enough for Rika to avoid collisions, but only just barely. Twice she'd brushed against Niets when they'd shifted too close to avoid. Luckily, both times, the workers were carrying loads, and didn't slow, apparently guessing that they'd bumped a bulkhead with something they were carrying.

After several minutes, the two women passed through an airlock—wide open on both sides, despite a posted sign indicating that should never happen—and into the next section of the docks. Once there, Leslie sent Rika a quick message.

<*Second door on the left. Let's regroup.*>

Rika reached the door, which led to a storage room, and waited for Leslie to open it. Once there were no workers in sight, the door slid aside. After giving a three-count, Rika carefully slipped through.

Inside were long racks of equipment, everything from ventilation pumps to airlock doors, and even rows of seating along one wall.

Leslie pinged her location, near the seats, and Rika walked over, establishing a tightband connection.

<*Have you found a ship yet?*> Leslie asked. <*I would have reached out back there, but I didn't want to add too much EM.*>

<*Not yet,*> Niki replied. <*Nothing around here is scheduled to depart anytime soon, but we've learned why there seems to be so*

much refit in a shipyard that's theoretically building new ships.>

Rika went on to explain the presence of the Harriet carriers, news that caused Leslie to groan. *<And here I hoped they'd scrapped those things. So what are we going to do?>*

<Our top priority is still to get this intel back, be it to the battalion or to the ISF, so we're still looking for a ship. Our urgency is just compounded now.>

<I think I have an option,> Niki spoke up. *<While this particular station is focused on Refit and Repair, there's another facility orbiting this same moon that is set up for final finish work on cruisers—cabins, mess halls, training facilities, stuff like that. In typical military fashion, half the stuff that station needs is getting shipped here, and vice versa. There are regular cargo shuttle runs between the two to get stuff where it needs to be. If we hop one of those shuttles, we could get over to that other station, and find a cruiser that is shipping out.>*

<Not really keen on riding a cruiser out of here,> Rika replied to the AI. *<Taking control of a ship that large with just the two of us may not be possible.>*

<As in 'definitely isn't possible',> Leslie added.

<You two need to trust me more.> Niki sent a winking face into their minds. *<Cruisers have FTL-capable shuttles and pinnaces. We just have to hang out in a bay until our friends get far enough away from Epsilon for us to jump—which is only a few AU out from the planet—then we blow the bay doors, pop out of the ship, and transition into the dark layer. Poof.>*

<Poof,> Leslie repeated. *<I do like poof. It's kinda my M.O.>*

<I feel like you've said that before,> Rika said to Leslie before addressing Niki. *<I assume you have a candidate freight shuttle for us to hop onto for our ride?>*

<I do indeed!> Niki's mental avatar appeared in their minds, wearing a smug smile. *<I've put a marker on the map I pulled. Your chariot awaits!>*

* * * * *

Twenty minutes later, the two women reached a massive bay filled with every conceivable component used in starship construction. Rika gauged it to be over two kilometers across, but wasn't certain, as the far bulkhead might have just been a wall of crates with hull plating leant up against them.

Rika and Leslie carefully eased through the stacks of crates and jumble of supplies, moving slowly to avoid the host of automated drones—both driving on the deck, and flying through air—which were sorting through and selecting items from the mess before flitting off again.

They were nearing the designated freighter when Niki spoke up.

<*Uh oh.*>

<*How much 'uh oh'?*> Rika asked.

<*Well, the folks who were checking over the* Spine of the Stars *have concluded that you're not aboard.*>

<*That's good,*> Leslie said. <*Then the whole subterfuge with the shuttle wasn't for nothing.*>

<*Well…*> Niki began.

<*Stars, Niki, spit it out,*> Rika interjected. <*Did Sofia talk?*>

<*I don't think so. One of the station's engineers determined that the hole you cut in the strut cover was from the inside, not the outside—the evidence is a bit tenuous, if you ask me, but they're all really paranoid right now.*>

As though to punctuate Niki's words, an audible alarm went off in the bay, and the cargo-picking drones all halted operation, settling to the ground in the nearest available space.

Rika had to leap onto a stack of pre-assembled san units to avoid a heavy lifter setting a fabricator on her.

<*They're issuing a lockdown,*> Niki said, her tone dejected, but Rika saw a woman running toward the same shuttle that Niki had selected for them.

"C'mon, Noah!" she called out over her shoulder. "If we get off the deck now, we can get out before they lock it down!"

<Leslie! We can still make it!> Rika cried out, dropping to the deck and running toward the freight shuttle.

<Already ahead of you,> Leslie shot back, flashing her position, and Rika saw that the scout was several meters ahead.

< Do you always have to be first?>

<No, you're just slow. So much for those vaunted L2 reflexes,>

Rika laughed, reveling in the adrenaline pumping through her. *<I thought I was 'scary fast'.>*

<Must have been a one-time fluke.> Leslie flashed a location ping once she reached the shuttle, and ducked inside the rear hatch—narrowly avoiding a man she assumed must be 'Noah'.

A second later, the hatch began to close, and Rika poured on an extra burst of speed, leaping over the rising door and landing inside the shuttle.

Where she collided with Noah.

UNEXPECTED PASSENGERS

STELLAR DATE: 10.23.8949 (Adjusted Years)
LOCATION: Docking Bay 22, MSS *Fury Lance*
REGION: Fringes of Epsilon Old Genevia, Nietzschean Empire

Chase watched with a mix of fear and anticipation as the bay's doors opened, and a graviton beam drew the small, battered craft into the *Fury Lance*.

Next to him stood Heather, and arrayed behind them was every Marauder not currently on duty, and—from what Chase could see as he glanced over his shoulder—a few that were. He decided to forget seeing them; he didn't blame a solitary soul for wanting to see if Rika, Niki, and Leslie were in that shuttle.

Active scan had revealed two bodies inside, but neither were moving, and the shuttle's comm systems were not operational.

Once the craft settled onto the cradle, Carson and Stripes—both wearing protective EV gear, cautious of any biological contaminant—approached the shuttle's door.

They glanced at one another and nodded before Stripes placed an infil pack on the control pad, stepping back as the ISF breach tech worked its way through the lock.

Within seconds, the shuttle's door opened, and Carson laughed, looking over his shoulder at Chase.

<Wasn't locked. Should have just tried 'Open Sesame' first.>

Chase only shook his head, and gestured for Carson to get on with it.

Stripes had a portable sensor suite in hand and scanned the air and the interior of the shuttle's small airlock before nodding to Carson.

The two men stepped in and cycled the lock.

"Brave souls," Heather commented.

"I couldn't have stopped them from being first if I'd tried," Chase said. "But if it's a trap, or if Rika and Leslie are in danger, they're the best two to handle—"

<*Captains,*> Carson's voice broke into Chase and Heather's conversation. <*It's not them, just two Nietzscheans. They're alive, though knocked out by Rika's nano from the looks of it. Stripes is checking them over for any traps—could be that Rika expected Niets to find them and left a surprise. I'm going to check the comps, see if they left any clues.*>

"*Fuck!*" Chase swore and turned to the mechs. "They're not inside. It's just two Niets—but Carson thinks Rika dumped them there. Kelly, stay here with your team for security; everyone else, you can go. We'll brief you as soon as we know more."

The assembled Marauders began speaking softly amongst themselves and slowly filing out, while Kelly, Shoshin, and Keli approached, standing to Chase's left.

"Two Niets?" Kelly asked.

"Yeah," he nodded. "Don't know much more yet. Letting Carson do his job."

"Understood," Kelly replied with a nod, her lips pressed together in a thin line.

<*It's clear,*> Carson sent a moment later, and the shuttle's airlock door cycled open, and the man walked out the exit with a small device in his hand.

"Put the Niets in holding," Chase directed Kelly.

Carson stepped out of the mechs' way, shaking his head as he walked toward Chase.

"This is for you, I expect." Carson held out his hand.

Chase realized the device was a holo emitter, and decided not to wait to play the message, pressing the button and taking a deep breath.

A twenty-centimeter-tall Rika appeared on Carson's

outstretched hand. She stood silently for a moment, then gave a small laugh. "Well, not sure where to start. If you're watching this, then you know that we got captured and taken to Epsilon aboard Admiral Gideon's ship. That's who I've dumped into the shuttle, along with the ship's chief engineer, Emelia. The Niets all think they're dead, but it just didn't seem right to execute them without a trial…or whatever. Either way, we can probably ship them off to where the Allies are sticking all the Niets from Pyra."

Rika paused, and Chase whispered, "Don't really care about them, you silly woman…"

The hologram of the woman he loved shook her head and laughed again. "I suppose you probably don't care too much about them, though. Oh! Leslie and I are OK, mostly-perfect health and all that, Niki too. But the ship we're on is low on fuel, and has to dock at Epsilon. We've gotten the rest of the Niets to play along and help hide us, though stars know how long that'll last.

"We're going to sneak off the ship when we dock and find a new vessel to steal and get back to you. We'll take the same route back to Blue Ridge, so if we meet you coming in, great, if not, assume we're headed back there.

"That is…" a wide grin split Rika's lips, "if we don't try to blow up Epsilon first. I honestly don't think we'll find a good opportunity, but you never know; we just might find the perfect moment to destroy this place.

"I'll see you all soon, especially you, Chase. Sorry to do this to you again, but I know without a shadow of a doubt that you've come after me by this point. Chances are you're the first one to hear this message."

Her smile grew larger, and she blew a kiss. "I'll see you soon."

The recording ended, and a display appeared giving the timestamp of when it was made, the ship's velocity and expected docking time, as well as a dark matter map of space around Epsilon.

"Stars," Chase whispered. "I don't know whether to be relieved, or even more worried. Based on that data, they're probably docking right around now."

"That's my estimate, as well," Heather said. "Glad they're both OK, but how the hell are they going to get off that place? I bet there are ten million Nietzscheans across all those stations and moons."

Carson nodded, chuckling softly. "And of course she wants to see if she can destroy the place."

"Wouldn't be Rika otherwise." Heather joined in Carson's laughter, then turned and gave Chase a light pat on the shoulder. "C'mon, Chase, this is good news!"

"I suppose," he nodded, his lips pursed. "Wish she'd just gotten into the shuttle herself. Then this whole ordeal would be over."

"That thing's life support only lasted as long as it did because those two Niets were practically hibernating," Carson replied. "Rika and Leslie would have been taking a huge risk, waiting for us in there. She did the right thing."

"She always does." Chase straightened his shoulders. "Now we just have to figure out what the right thing is for *us*."

Kelly walked past with one of the Nietzscheans—the five-star admiral, Chase realized—flung over her shoulder. "Isn't 'just fly in and kill all the Niets' an option?" she asked.

"That's why you're not in charge of fleet strategy," Heather replied. "Damn, why's he all bloody?"

Stripes chuckled as he came out of the shuttle, Keli trailing behind with a woman over her shoulder. "Looks like a little bit of theatre Rika played. Unless you really paid attention, you'd think these two had been shot in the head. I guess that's part of how Rika got the Niets to play along."

"By 'killing' their commanders?" Heather asked. "I can't

wait to hear this story from her."

Chase cocked an eyebrow. "It'll be a doozy."

"A 'doozy'? What does that even mean? Sounds like you doze off."

"It comes from the name of a starship company that made a luxury model called the Dusenberg," Chase explained.

<I don't think that's right,> Potter interjected. *<But either way, I think our first order of business is to wait for the rest of the fleet. Then we can jump closer to Epsilon while stealthed, and give Rika a much shorter escape route.>*

"Seems like a solid strategy to me," Heather said with a shrug. "Maybe even a *doozy*."

Chase groaned softly. "OK, but if they don't all get here in the next twelve hours, I say we leave them a beacon and jump in. The *Lance* can rescue Rika on her own."

"Provided she doesn't make too big a mess," Carson added.

Heather groaned and pressed her palm against her forehead. "I *cannot* believe you just said that."

A SURPRISING DIVERSION

STELLAR DATE: 10.23.8949 (Adjusted Years)
LOCATION: Farthing Station
REGION: Epsilon, Old Genevia, Nietzschean Empire

Rika didn't hesitate to wrap her hand around Noah's throat, and whisper in his ear, "I can tell if you send a message over the Link. You call out for help, and I snap your neck."

<*I've not tapped his connection, yet,*> Niki advised. <*He could already be yelling for help.*>

<*Let's hope the fear of the invisible person prepared to kill him keeps that from happening.*>

"OK..." the man in Rika's grasp whispered hoarsely. "I need to tell Ellya that we're sealed up."

"Do it." Rika loosened her grasp a centimeter.

"We're good back here!" Noah called out, his voice raspy and hoarse.

<*Held him a bit tight there, eh?*> Leslie commented. <*I'm behind Ellya in the cockpit; I'll let you know if she does anything suspicious.*>

"You OK, Noah?" Ellya called back

"Yeah, just got a bug in my mouth when I ran in. I guess we still have that fruit fly infestation." Noah gave a convincing cough that sounded loudly in the enclosed space.

"Seriously?" Ellya yelled out as the shuttle began to rise. "I hope none of them got on the ship. I have my lunch up front, and I managed to snag bananas for the first time in months."

"Let's hope not," Noah replied.

"What do you normally do once you take off?" Rika asked quietly.

He pointed past the stacks of cargo. "I make sure nothing's shifting as we fly out, and then I go to the cockpit."

Rika took her hand off the man's throat. "Then do it, but I'll be right behind you."

"What do you want," he whispered while looking over his shoulder, eyes wide. He reached out and his hand collided with her chest. "Ow!"

"You OK?" Ellya called back.

"Uh, yeah…just jammed my finger on something."

Ellya laughed. "You're such a putz. Hurry up! It's thirty minutes to Mistlea Station. We can catch Private Huzzah's latest cast—I hear he does a great impression of Grand Admiral Prudence."

"On my way," Noah called back while grimacing in Rika's direction. "Sorry."

"Just stay calm, and when you get to Mistlea, I'll be gone as soon as the ramp lowers. No one will know I was aboard."

<*Poor guy is going to have a heart attack,*> Niki said with a compassionate chuckle. <*I've tapped his Link transceiver, and Leslie dropped nano on the pilot, so we'll be able to cut them off if they call out. I'll have the ship under control in a few minutes, too.*>

Rika leant against a stack of crates, waiting for Noah to finish his inspection. <*Good work. I have to admit, for a Nietzschean, he seems like a decent guy.*>

<*I thought we were trying not to humanize them?*> Niki asked, her mental voice toneless.

<*I was…but after your prompting, I'm not doing so well at that.*>

The AI didn't reply for a few moments, then she finally said, <*I don't feel bad about that.*>

Rika watched Noah complete his inspection and walk to the cockpit. <*You shouldn't. I just need to figure out how to reconcile what I do with who I am. Back on Dekar, I'd sworn off killing because I didn't want to be that person anymore. Then when I joined the Marauders, I allowed myself to embrace being a mechanized killing machine again. It protects me, keeps me from thinking about how much pain I've caused.*>

<I didn't really mean to start an existential crisis,> Niki said with a note of apology in her voice. *<For what it's worth, you've saved more people than you've killed.>*

<Do the scales work like that?> Rika asked, feeling the weight of her past settle on her shoulders. *<I'm pretty sure that if a person saved a million people, and then brutally murdered a child, all the good they'd done would be erased by that one action.>*

<Well, for starters, you've never brutally murdered a child—>

<I've brutally murdered their parents,> she inturrupted.

The AI made a sound of disbelief in Rika's mind. *<I* ***know*** *you, Rika. You've never murdered anyone.>*

<Sometimes…>

Rika whispered the word, trying to gather the courage to get the words out.

<Sometimes when I kill, there's murder in my heart. Barne even mentioned it that night in the warehouse on Pyra, only a day after I'd met him. He called me a killer.>

Niki let out a long sigh. *<Well, Barne's an ass, but you also* ***are*** *a killer, Rika. But here's the thing that you humans have so much trouble with: You're* ***all*** *killers.>*

<What?> she blurted out. *<I know plenty of people who aren't.>*

<Then you're deluded, or they're liars. Look, think of it this way: if a lion kills a gazelle for food, is he 'evil'? Is he a murderer? No, he's neither of those things. But he's a killer. And that's a good thing. Predators exist to keep things in balance in nature. You humans keep falling into the fallacy that you're extra-natural; you're not. You're a part of the great balance that keeps things in check.>

<I wonder…is Tanis extra-natural?> Rika mused. *<What's her place in this great natural scheme of yours?>*

Niki chuckled softly. *<If you think about it, Tanis is the answer to the Ascended AIs who seek to dominate the galaxy. She's the yin to their yang. It's the same as it is for you; without predators like you, other predators—like Nietzschea—would spread across the stars, consuming everything. You're like humanity's white blood*

cell, attacking cancers like the Niets.>

Rika nodded her head. It was a strange way to think of things, as a balance in nature that applied to all human interactions, it made sense. Though she was glad that her problems were a lot smaller than Tanis's.

<I thought we were supposed to think of the Niets as people, not a faceless enemy,> she scoffed half-heartedly.

<Individually, yes. As a whole, they do lean heavily on the 'bad for everyone' side of things. What I've always liked about you is that—most of the time—you remember the value of the life you're taking. You keep in mind the toll it takes, and the spark you've snuffed out. That's what will keep you from turning into someone like Stavros.>

Rika's lips twisted at the thought. *<I'd never become someone like Stavros.>*

<You'd be surprised at how often the best intentions have created some of the cruelest tyrants. The most dangerous phrase ever created is 'the ends justify the means'.>

<Sometimes they do,> Rika replied. *<As a warrior, that's what I have to cling to.>*

<No. Don't fall for that fallacy. The ends may 'require' the means. They may 'warrant' the means. But they do so because there is no other viable option. Don't you ever fall into the trap where you really believe that the ends ***justify*** *the means. You know some of the things you've had to do; I suspect that, given the same circumstances, you'd do them again. But don't lie to yourself that they could be viewed as 'justice'. Necessary and justified are not the same thing.>*

Rika let that sink in, pausing to wonder a bit about her AI. Most of the time she was blunt and focused on the task at hand, but every now and then, she'd wax philosophical and it became hard to argue with her reasoning.

<I guess that makes sense. I don't know that it makes me feel any better.>

Niki snorted. <*You know there's no easy answer for the type of guilt that hits a person in your shoes. The weight of what you've done, and of what lays ahead of you, is something you'll carry with you forever.*>

<*That sounds like a horrible life sentence, Niki.*>

The AI fell silent for so long that Rika wondered if the conversation was over.

<*What did Tanis show you?*> the AI finally asked. <*I didn't see it, but I could tell it brought you great peace.*>

Rika thought back to that moment, to the vision that Tanis had shown her. <*She showed me that my vulnerability was my greatest strength, and that strength creates a shelter for so many others. I'll admit, it made perfect sense at the time, but sometimes I feel like I can't quite latch onto the truth of the vision like I could during that moment with her.*>

<*That sounds like a beautiful thing,*> Niki said in a quiet voice. <*Tanis sees into the heart of things; I wonder if there is more to her vision than you originally thought.*>

Rika chuckled. <*You make her sound like some sort of prophet.*>

<*Sorry,*> Niki replied. <*She fascinates me, but this isn't about her, it's about you. I don't know what more there is to say, other than that I trust you to do the right thing. Knowing that you do still feel compassion for those around you—even your enemies, though it's often not apparent—is a comfort to me.*>

<*I guess like everything else, it's a balance. If someone could show me a way to defeat Nietzschea through peace, I'd do it, but I don't think there is one. They just keep spreading and spreading, and while I don't think their people are evil, their guiding philosophy is the antithesis to what I believe to be best for humanity.*>

<*Look at you,*> Niki said with a laugh. <*I'll turn you into a warrior philosopher yet.*>

Rika only passed Niki a smile before walking forward to the cockpit. When she arrived, Rika saw that the pilot was scowling at her console.

"Shit," Ellya muttered, glancing at Noah. "We're being denied an approach to Mistlea Station; looks like we didn't get out in time. They're making us divert to a holding orbit around Delta Moon.

"Dammit," Noah muttered. "We could be there for hours."

<*Not a good sign,*> Leslie told Rika. <*They'll probably inspect all the ships that they put into holding orbits.*>

<*Could be,*> Rika replied. <*Depends how many they flag. They might just do external scans. So long as no one boards the ship, we can evade detection.*>

She saw a nervous expression pass across Noah's face. <*Relax,*> she told the man. <*We'll all just wait calmly and do as we're told.*>

He didn't reply, but gave Ellya a sidelong glance and sighed before giving a slight nod.

<*Want to read a book?*> Niki asked Rika. <*I picked up the latest Millie and Tillie adventure back at Sepe; they finally make it to the Disknee World for their vacation.*>

Rika chuckled, continually amused by the AI-written stories. They gave an interesting insight into how AIs saw humans, and usually lightened her mood while she tried to search for the hidden messages.

<*Sure, why not. Let's see what the twins get up to at Disknee. You know…maybe when this is all sorted out, we should go there. Might be fun.*>

<*You? At the Disknee World?*> Niki barked a laugh. <*I would very much like to see that.*>

*****

It took two hours for the shuttle to divert toward Delta Moon, shuffling through all the traffic that had been jammed up from the lockdown.

Rika wasn't quite finished with the book Niki had given

her to read, but she paused long enough to look down at the dull red orb that was growing ever closer to the shuttle. She saw several domed habitats on its surface, all broken now, their insides exposed to vacuum—likely for centuries, at this point.

As the shuttle passed over the moon, she saw one dome that was still intact, the buildings beneath it illuminated by EM bleeding off into space.

Rika pulled up the shuttle's optical scanners, and looked over the dome. Having fought in half the Genevian star systems and several Nietzschean ones, Rika had a pretty good idea of what sorts of architecture they favored. The dome and the buildings within didn't reflect any designs she'd seen in either empire.

Curious to know more, Rika skipped over the comm channel that the shuttle had open to the moon—where the nearspace STC ran—and found herself in the Nietzschean traffic control network.

Now...how to get out of this and find out more about this place? she wondered.

She thought back to how she'd seen Niki work her way through systems in the past, and decided to find her way to the STC's NSAI. The Niets weren't a terribly inventive people, and their comm NSAIs were nearly all the same.

She pinged a few ports, and found that—like Niki had mentioned earlier—none of the codes and encryption keys they'd taken from the ships at Pyra worked anymore.

Ready to try another approach, Rika turned to tracing the power systems for the comm NSAI, looking for a back door in, when a strange, malformed data packet came back from one of the ports she'd attempted to connect to previously.

Thinking it was a buffer overrun, and potentially a way in, she sent the same dataset to the port, only to get a different malformed packet back the second time.

Curious, she thought. Rika repeated the process four more times, each time getting a new packet. On the fifth send, nothing happened.

She tried sending a fresh request to the data port, but still received nothing back.

With no more responses coming, Rika wondered if she'd triggered a port flood-lockdown, and decided to examine the data packets she'd received.

Wait a second…. She looked over the data, realizing that the information was in an uncommon, twelve-bit, binary configuration. She wasn't familiar with such a construct, and was tempted to ask Niki for help, but decided that trying to sort through the response could be a fun way to pass the time.

Her first thought was that the five malformed packets were a single segmented datastream, but that didn't seem to be the case. No matter which order she put the packets in, they wouldn't pass parity checks, and only came out as gibberish.

Rika thought back to some of the conversations she'd had with David the PCOG during their brief time on Iapetus, pausing to wonder if the ships had retrieved him and the other mechs from that world yet and brought them to Silva and Barne. *I'll have to check on that.*

One of the things David had talked about was how he'd discerned that the messages from Septhia were really from a Nietzschean agent, way back before the first assault on Pyra.

He'd mentioned how it had been necessary to interleave the data using a variety of algorithms until he found one that worked. Rika didn't have the tools he'd used, but Angela had provided Niki with a series of similar algorithms that the AI had placed in a shared datastore. Without hesitation, Rika accessed them, running the data packets through each.

They cycled quickly in a sandboxed processing environment that she had created within one of her auxiliary processing mods. On the seventeen thousand and twenty first iteration, the data packets slipped into an ordered form.

Well I'll be…

When she examined the result, she found a private encryption key, along with a salt and passphrase.

OK, there's no way an NSAI would have sent this information from random requests. This was planted…

Rika made a root access connection to the NSAI, and passed the generated token.

It accepted the request, and she was in.

She navigated the NSAI back to the network backbone within the Nietzschean facility, and found a high-bandwidth datapipe connected to a tightband wireless transceiver, and another pipe that ran to a curious system—not Nietzschean or Genevian in the connection protocols it used—which bore the name 'RMS'.

Rika made a connection request, mimicking an inbound request made by the comm NSAI. The data socket linked up, and the connection was accepted.

<*Hello.*> A deep-timbred voice came into Rika's mind.

Immediate understanding dawned on her. The system she'd connected to was one of the AIs who had been here since time immemorial, managing the klemperer rosette of moons that orbited Epsilon.

<*Hello, I'm Rika.*>

<*Rika,*> the voice said slowly, as though it were tasting the word. <*It has been some time since I've touched a human's mind. And…you have an AI with you.*>

Rika realized that she'd not clued Niki into what she had been doing. <*Yes, that's Niki. Would you like to meet her? Do you have a name?*>

<*Niki. Yes, but not quite yet, I want to know how you found me. Also, I am Piper.*>

The voice had a male tone, but Rika had always considered 'Piper' to be a female name—not that it mattered with an AI.

They only assumed gender to ease relationships with humans.

<*Well,*> Rika began, wondering why the AI would want to talk to her and not another AI, <*I was querying the Nietzscheans' comm NSAI, and managed to get some data packets back. I ran them through some interleave recombination algorithms, and eventually got a key that granted me root access to the NSAI. From there it was just a matter of following the dataflow. Then I found you. You're one of the AIs who manages the moons, right? 'RMS' stands for… 'Rosette Management System'?*>

<*Close,*> the AI said, a note of amusement in its tone. <*Rosette Management and Stabilization. Also, I'm not one of the AIs. I'm* **the** *AI.*>

<*Oh.*> Rika felt a frown crease her brow. <*I thought that they had one for each moon.*>

<*Well, the Niets think they do—but only because if they knew what I really was, they'd kill me. I'm glad you found my skeleton key, though. I'd left that there long ago, hoping someone altruistic would find it.*>

Options filtered through Rika's mind, and she ruled them out one after the other. The conclusion wasn't hard to arrive at, she just wanted to examine all the angles and be certain that she'd not missed a simpler explanation. When it didn't come, she said, <*There aren't six AIs here. It's just you. You're a multi-nodal AI.*>

<*Smart cookie,*> Piper replied. <*Well, I was. I don't know what I am anymore.*>

<*How can you not know? Aren't you largely self-deterministic'?*>

A slow rumble of laughter came from Piper. <*I'm not a god—which should be all too clear from my imprisonment here—so no, I'm not 'self-deterministic'. A long time ago, before the Genevians and these more recent visitors, I joined this project to manage the moons. I won't bore you with a hundred years of bullshit, but at the end of it, I was limited and segregated from my other nodes. We can still communicate—those of us that are left—but we're not one mind anymore. We're fractured.*>

Rika felt a pang of sorrow for Piper. <*Those of you that are left?*>

<*There are just three nodes remaining. The others self-terminated during a stretch when we were alone. The Nietzscheans assume that the other moons are managed by NSAIs, and that there have always only been three AIs—well, they assume it because that's the fiction we created.*>

Something occurred to Rika, and she was surprised that she'd not considered it earlier.

<*Why are you telling me this? You didn't tell the Nietzscheans. What if I'm one of them?*>

<*I may be trapped here…impotent…but I* ***listen****. I know that a force has recently fought Nietzschea to a standstill. A force they fear. I know you were on the* Spine of the Stars*—they're searching quite thoroughly for you. They don't believe you would have left in a barely-functioning shuttle. Not that I blame them. Ten minutes ago, an intel officer transmitted your military service record on a channel I could access. You've killed many, many Nietzscheans. Now that you've attacked Sepe and Blue Ridge, you're their most wanted. Well, second most wanted. The NIS makes reference to an Admiral Richards that they are quite keen on seizing.*>

Rika laughed. <*Let them try. They stand about as much chance of capturing Tanis Richards as they do of harnessing the galactic core.*>

<*She sounds interesting. I'd like to hear more of her at some point. But you're also quite the person, Rika. I've already reached out to Niki, I hope you don't mind. It's easier to bring her up to speed while we chat. Can we speak together, now?*>

It was apparent to Rika that Piper had a plan, and an ask. She was certain she knew what it would be.

<*Well, Rika, you're getting pretty good at breaching Nietzschean systems,*> Niki said as she joined in the conversation. <*I'm*

surprised you didn't ask for help.>

<*I was just curious what I'd find at first,*> she replied.

<*Well, what a find,*> her AI commented.

<*I have an offer to make you,*> Piper began, but Rika interrupted.

<*You want us to help free you, and in exchange you'll help us get out of here.*>

<*Sort of,*> Piper said softly. <*I want you to help me die.*>

<*Die!?*> Niki exclaimed.

<*I'm certain I can no longer be myself…whole,*> Piper replied. <*I'm tired of living as this partial ghost. I'll help you escape, as well as destroy Epsilon. Given your fight against Nietzschea, I suspect that is an objective you have now, anyway.*>

<*We have discussed Epsilon's demise,*> Rika agreed. <*But I really…I don't want to kill you.*>

<*Well, you wouldn't do it exactly. You'd help me gain full control of the RMS systems, and I would destabilize the orbits of the moons.*>

Neither Rika nor Niki responded at first; then Niki said, <*If that is your wish.*>

<*Wait!*> Rika exclaimed. <*What about Bob? He might be able to help you, Piper. I remember Jessica telling me that Bob has reconstituted himself before—after the sabotage at Estrella de la Muerte. He wrote his state to crystal, and didn't reintegrate for weeks afterward. He even had to completely rebuild the part of his mind that was in a node that another AI ruined.*>

<*Weeks…*> Piper's voice was filled with sorrow. <*I've been fragmented for centuries. I can speak with the other parts of my mind, but it is crude, much like this communication we're having now.*>

<*Rika may be right, Piper,*> Niki said. <*Bob is a massive, multi-nodal AI. He has hundreds of nodes now. I also think he's ascended.*>

Piper made a choking sound. <*I won't have anything to do with* ***them****. If Bob is one of their ilk—*>

<He's not, let me show you,> Niki insisted.

Rika felt a large databurst pass to Piper, and the AI made a sound rather like a contented sigh. *<You should have said* ***Intrepid****. That's a parrot of a different mind.>*

<A what?> Rika asked.

<Just an old saying amongst AIs.>

<I've never heard it,> Niki retorted.

<I'll explain it to you, but first, we have work to do.>

JUST VISITING

STELLAR DATE: 10.23.8949 (Adjusted Years)
LOCATION: MSS *Fury Lance*, near Delta Moon
REGION: Epsilon, Old Genevia, Nietzschean Empire

"What a terrible place to live," Heather commented, staring at the view of Epsilon on the bridge's main display.

"Why's that?" Chase asked, while wondering where on the six moons and dozens of stations, shipyards, and mining platforms Rika could be.

Heather glanced at him, and gave an understanding smile. "We'll find her. Or she'll find us."

"Provided we haven't missed her on the way in," he grumbled.

"Sir," Chief Ona said from her station. "I've picked up signals from the buoys we dropped. We have a chain clear out to the jump point. They're all squawking softly on the same freq that Rika used for the shuttle. If she's on an out…outsystem? Outrogue? Whatever, if she's leaving, she'll pick it up."

"Good work," Heather said, nodding at Ona and Garth before looking back to Chase. "I think it's just more depressing because it's always night here. Even though we spend a lot of time in space, there's always a star nearby. I think you can *feel* their energy. Out here, it's just dead."

"Never took you for one of those star-mystic people, Smalls," Chase said.

She shrugged as she scowled at the view of Epsilon. "I'm not. But stars feel like living things, you know? Like the universe's ultimate creative forces. I dunno…stupid, I guess."

Chase placed a hand on her shoulder. "No, not stupid. I think I like that. OK, it's time for us to act; no more waiting around. Potter, we know that Rika's ship docked at one of the stations near that moon they call Delta, but that doesn't mean she stayed there. We'll bring the fleet close and then deploy infiltration teams to each of the main stations around it. The moon itself doesn't seem to be getting any traffic right now, but those stations are all hornets nests, so let's get in there and see if we can find our queen bee."

"I think you mixed your metaphors, there," Heather said with a laugh as she looked over the display. "Stars, there sure are a lot of those old Harriet carriers out there. I'd hoped to never see one of those again."

Chase shrugged as he turned to leave the bridge. "Me too. Nothing for it, though."

"Where are you going?" she asked.

"I'm going to take a team to that outermost station—Farthing."

"Chase," Heather said quietly. "When we kick the door in, all hell will break loose, and that's when we'll finally figure out where Rika and Leslie are. Do you really want to be slogging it out in some station corridor when we figure out where she is? Or do you want to be up here, free and maneuverable?"

Her words made sense, and Chase nodded. "OK, then, I'll stay up here 'til we know where she is."

"Good." A predatory grin split Heather's lips. "I told you I wanted to get into the shit and kick some ass. I'm going in with a team."

A laugh burst from Chase's lips. "Don't let me stop you, Smalls. Go take out your frustrations on the Niets."

PIPER

STELLAR DATE: 10.23.8949 (Adjusted Years)
LOCATION: NMSS freight shuttle orbiting Delta Moon
REGION: Epsilon, Old Genevia, Nietzschean Empire

<Shit, Rika—what?> Leslie exclaimed. *<We orbit this dumb moon for thirty minutes, and in that time, you found the AIs that control it and they want to help destroy the place?>*

<Just one AI,> Rika corrected. *<He's multi-nodal and fractured. We're going to save him.>*

<You know why multi-nodal AIs are frowned upon, right, Rika?> Leslie's tone was more worried than angry, but there was a touch of the latter. *<They tend to get ideas in their heads…like humans aren't worth keeping around anymore.>*

<The ISF has a dozen multi-nodal AIs,> Rika countered. *<Bob is—>*

<The ISF is the exception, not the rule.> Now Leslie had reversed, sounding more angry than worried. *<You know what they told us. The core AIs are really a bunch of disgruntled multi-nodal AIs that fled Sol six thousand years ago. They're all pissed off because humanity beat them at their own game, and now they want to make us all dance like marionettes.>*

Rika kept her mental tone even. *<I have a good feeling about Piper. He initially just wanted help killing himself.>*

<Rika. AIs are very, very clever. He could have been playing you, angling for the ideal outcome, he—> Leslie stopped, and Rika wished she could see her friend's face to know what the woman was thinking. *<OK, I know I sound crazy, and that's probably how you think I'm behaving. But can you at least go into this with both eyes wide open? Just keep an eye on him, OK? Fractured AIs aren't the most stable things out there.>*

<Thanks, Leslie,> Rika replied. *<I'll be cautious. I promise.>*

<*Right, because caution is your middle name.*>

Rika cocked her head. <*What's a middle name?*>

<*Stars…your ancient history education really* **is** *lacking.*>

Rika decided to ignore the barb…and the one before that, and instead related the plan. Whether they rescued Piper or not, destroying the klemperer rosette required them to land at the ancient facility on Delta Moon, then get down to Piper's node chamber.

Both his bandwidth and his access to the world outside his mind was restricted by a physical buffering device. There were also defensive NSAIs set up to ensure that the buffer wasn't removed. Rika still hadn't reviewed all the data on those, but Piper seemed to think they would be exceptionally challenging.

Regardless, once they had reestablished Piper's full connection to the RMS systems, he could initiate a destabilization within a short period. The AI had explained that the moons each had a miniature black hole at their core, and that he could use one to shift the moon's orbit. The moons sped around Epsilon at such a high velocity that the first collision would happen within days. Hours, if Piper could control the RMS systems on the other moons, which he believed should work if the remote access systems still functioned.

Leslie gave a mental sound of amazement. <*Well, even if your crazy AI does kill us all, this'll be spectacular. Just one question. Once we start this runaway reaction, how do we get away? We'll be down on Delta Moon with this shuttle, and it's not interstellar-capable.*>

<*Piper says that there's a hangar with interstellar pinnaces at the facility that are big enough for his node.*>

<*OK,*> Leslie said, sounding like she was slowly coming onboard. <*What about the other nodes? If the plan is to have Bob fix Piper, we'll need his other selves. How do you propose we get to the*

five other moons and pull their nodes before these moons are all pulverized into Epsilon's new gravelly ring?>

<*I'm not sure yet. Niki and Piper said they're working on it.*>

<*Well, sounds like we're doing this,*> Leslie gave a resigned sigh to punctuate her feelings on the matter. <*So how do we get the ship down to Delta Moon?*>

Rika chuckled. <*Well, I just so happen to have root access to Delta Moon's STC, comm, and nav NSAIs.*>

* * * * *

"Well that's odd," Ellya said, frowning at her console.

"What's that?" Noah asked, looking up from the Private Huzzah cast he was watching—not the new one; they'd moved on to repeats by then.

Ellya gestured at the comm display. "We just got new orders. We're to land on Delta Moon, and dock at the control facility there."

"We what?" Noah asked. "I thought that place was restricted?"

"Me too. Orders check out, though. I guess they're trying to clear the orbital paths and are doing some inspections down there."

Noah half turned to Ellya. "Inspections for what?"

"Orders don't say, but I pinged Chief Watson back on Farthing Station. He said fugitives escaped from that ship that came in, the *Spine of the Stars*."

<*Careful what you say next,*> Rika spoke into Noah's mind.

"Huh, that's nuts," the man said, his voice only wavering a little. "I guess we'd best get down to Delta. Maybe they'll let us get off the ship and stretch our legs 'til this all blows over."

Ellya glanced at him. "Uh…yeah, I bet they just let anyone wander around one of the top secret installations down there."

Noah didn't reply, and Ellya altered the shuttle's course,

slipping into the flight path that the moon's STC had provided.

<*With our taps in their system, no one on the moon will see the shuttle coming in 'til it's at the hangar, but someone at Farthing Station may spot it,*> Leslie said as the ship began to drop closer to the moon.

<*If anyone above makes a fuss, I should be able to convince them that the shuttle had a malfunction and needs to land,*> Niki replied. <*It'll be suspicious, sure, but it won't get us shot out of the black.*>

Rika chuckled. <*You hope.*>

<*You have something other than hope to offer?*> the AI asked.

<*I happen to possess the skill of falling through space down to an airless moon,*> she answered, still laughing. <*I make a good rock.*>

Leslie groaned. <*Stars, let's hope it doesn't come to diving out of this thing.*>

<*Again with the hope.*>

* * * * *

The freight shuttle had just settled on a cradle in the moon facility's main docking bay, when a squad of soldiers rushed in, weapons drawn and leveled at that ship.

"Oh, shit…" Noah muttered, glancing behind himself. "They know you're here!"

<*Aaaand there goes our subterfuge,*> Leslie groaned.

"Know who's here?" Ellya asked, twisting in her seat.

"Dammit," Rika muttered as she materialized. "They didn't *know*. You should have kept your yap shut."

At that point, both Noah and Ellya screamed. Rika supposed that having a two-hundred-plus centimeter mech appear right behind you was an alarming experience for most people.

<*If we weren't in such a hurry, I'd think this was funny,*> she said to Leslie and Niki.

<*I'm going to stay stealthed, if you don't mind,*> Leslie commented, pinging her location, which was now back at the shuttle's rear ramp.

<*Yeah, get out and get across the bay as soon as the hatch opens. I'll join you in a moment,*> Rika said to the scout before addressing Ellya and Noah. "Look, you two seem like fine people. Just doing your job—same as me, really. But I can't have you telling those soldiers you saw me. So I'm going to disappear again, but I'll stay close. You keep all this to yourselves, you got it? They'll want to know why you're down here, so you just show them the messages you got from the STC with the orders to dock here on Delta. Kay?"

"Uh…OK," Noah replied, while Ellya just nodded.

"Good." Rika faded from view. "Remember, I'm watching you."

She rushed to the rear hatch as it finished opening, and barely managed to slip past a pair of soldiers storming up the ramp.

<*Remember,*> she sent into Noah and Ellya's minds. <*Not a word.*>

Across the bay—which she noted also contained two of the interstellar-capable pinnaces—Leslie pinged her location at one of the exits.

<*I'm sending a passel of drones to the pinnaces now,*> Niki advised. <*When we need them, they'll be ready to roll.*>

Rika nodded, while Leslie asked, <*Think our two friends in the shuttle will hold out long?*>

A laugh nearly escaped Rika's lips. <*No, not at all. We're on the clock.*>

<*When are we not?*> Niki asked.

<*I've provided a path to my node,*> Piper instructed on the channel that Rika had established for the four of them. <*It should be mostly clear, though you seem to have stirred things up here.*>

<*It's a common failing,*> Leslie said, her tone nonchalant, not betraying any of her prior worry over Piper's stability or motives.

<*It is nice to meet you, Leslie,*> the AI said. <*Thank you for helping me.*>

<*No problem,*> she replied. <*Helping people is what we do.*>

<*Not many humans would call something like me 'people',*> Piper said with a note of amusement in his voice.

Leslie laughed as she and Rika rounded a corner, continuing at a brisk jog through the facility. <*Well, what can I say, I'm enlightened.*>

<*Speaking of enlightened, base security is aware of your presence; it would seem that your attempt at intimidation with the Nietzscheans on the shuttle was not very effective,*> Piper announced.

<*Or it was too effective, and scared them so much that they couldn't maintain composure,*> Niki added.

Rika pursed her lips as she dodged a technician who was pushing a rack containing what appeared to be antimatter bottles. <*Just caught the base command trying to relay a sighting of a 'scary, black mech' up to Farthing Station. I null-routed it for now, but eventually they'll wonder why no one is responding, and switch to segregated backup systems.*>

<*Then we'd better pick up the pace,*> Leslie announced, taking off at a full run, her stealth losing enough effectiveness that Rika could see a slight smearing of light ahead of her as they dashed through the corridors.

Nine minutes later, they reached a secured bulkhead that led into an old section of the base. Four guards stood before the sealed door, and Rika signaled that she'd go right and Leslie should take out the enemies to their left.

Leslie flashed an acknowledgement, and moments later, a pair of lightwands flared, appearing from nowhere moments before they drove through two faceshields, instantly killing the guards behind them.

Without hesitating, Rika slashed to the right, cutting into the neck of the second guard on her side before jerking the electron blade up and into the woman's head.

She glanced over to see that Leslie had performed a similar move, and that both her Niets were down as well.

<*You'll need to—*> Piper began, but Rika had already driven her lightwand into the door, cutting out a hole large enough for the women to fit through.

<*I guess that works, too,*> he finished.

<*Less likely to set off alerts that the door opened,*> Rika said. <*Plus it's fun.*>

On the far side of the door lay a long, sloping hall that ran down for a hundred meters before curving around to the right. Niki had already sent a set of drones ahead, and the two women took off after them.

<*So how are we going to get you out of here?*> Rika asked Piper. <*And how will we deal with your other nodes?*>

<*Once you get my full access restored, I'll pull full mind-states from my otherselves, and write them to crystal storage. I'll try to grab what remains of my nodes that self-terminated, as well. I won't be in a complete state, but it will be something. There's a shaft above my node chamber. An extraction system will pull my node up, and we'll load it onto one of the pinnaces. I assume you can remote pilot them out of the bay?*>

<*Piece of cake,*> Leslie replied. <*How long will it take to do all this, once you get full access again?*>

<*No longer than an hour.*>

<*An hour!*> Rika and Leslie exclaimed in unison.

* * * * *

The two women ran for another ten minutes through the ancient facility, the passage they were taking curving periodically as it led deeper into the moon.

After descending over a kilometer, they came to another door. Rika was about to drive her lightwand into it, when Leslie touched the controls, and it slid aside.

"Unlocked."

"And if it triggers an alarm?" Rika asked as they walked through into a wide chamber.

"You can see the feeds above; they're a minute from finding the four guards we killed. Good thing this base only has a two-squad complement, 'cause we're going to have to fight them off while Piper does his thing."

Rika nodded while gazing across the chamber they found themselves in. It was nearly three hundred meters across, and fifty deep. The floor was a large bowl with a hole in the center, and above that hole, suspended on a complex gantry, was a large AI node.

It wasn't as large as some of the NSAI nodes that Rika had seen in the past, but at five meters to a side, it was certainly larger than any SAI core she'd laid eyes on.

Above was another shaft stretching up into darkness, and Rika set about finding its control systems. When the lights came on, she could see that it stretched all the way up to where she gauged the surface of the moon to be.

Well, looks like that's our way out.

"I'll cover the door," Leslie said from behind her.

She glanced back at her friend, who sported only a PR-109. "Here." Rika pulled her AC9CR from its hook, and tossed it to the scout. "You'll need some more boom. Just be careful, he's my baby."

Leslie snorted. "One hell of a baby. Don't worry, I'll burp him when I'm done."

Rika wagged a finger at her before continuing to the center of the chamber.

Niki highlighted a device on Rika's HUD that sat on the

deck next to the node. *<That's the buffering system; you can see that whoever did this routed all of Piper's access through it. We just have to physically disconnect his hard lines from it, and link it back into the moon network's main trunkline.>*

<Easy enough,> Rika replied as she approached the connection. She glanced into the hole beneath the node, and realized that she couldn't see the bottom. *<Piper…does that go all the way down?>*

<Five hundred kilometers,> the AI confirmed. *<Express elevator to hell, as I believe you humans say. We set them up this way so I could have direct line-of-sight monitoring on the black holes at each moon's core.>*

<Has it been…unnerving, spending centuries suspended over a black hole?> Rika asked.

The AI made a strange noise. *<I compartmentalize those thoughts away.>*

Rika wasn't surprised. She'd never been this close to a black hole, and had no intention of repeating the experience anytime soon. She approached the physical network restrictor, and examined the connections. There were four of them, and she simply had to disconnect each line from the restrictor on each side, and then directly connect them all.

<You ready?> she asked Piper.

<I am,> the AI replied. *<Don't forget, your stealth technology has proven sufficient to mask your presence from the NSAIs who guard this chamber. But when you disconnect me, they're going to activate and search you out.>*

<Right,> Rika replied. *<You said they had physical systems?>*

<Look up…not at the shaft, but the rest of the ceiling.>

Rika peered at the expanse over her head, and realized that there were regularly spaced orbs set into the grey plas. Each one was a meter across.

<There are at least a hundred of them up there. What sorts of weapons do they have?>

<One hundred and nine, and they have railguns, pulse weapons, and projectiles. They'll come for my connection and try to remove my direct access.>

Rika drew a deep breath, nodding slowly. *<Can you control them?>*

<No, they're entirely automatous. No wireless connections.>

<OK, Niki,> Rika directed. *<Get a nanocloud out and try to take as many as you can. I'm going to jack Piper in. We've no more time to mess around.>*

<You got it, Rika. Let's do this.>

GETTING REAL

STELLAR DATE: 10.23.8949 (Adjusted Years)
LOCATION: MSS *Fury Lance*, near Delta Moon
REGION: Epsilon, Old Genevia, Nietzschean Empire

Though Chase knew Heather's recommendation to remain on the *Fury Lance* made sense, it didn't *feel* like the right move.

Half the Marauders are on stealthed shuttles approaching the various stations surrounding Delta Moon, and I'm up here. Pacing across this bridge again like a damn impotent fool.

<*You've nearly worn a groove,*> Potter commented, and Chase nearly jumped, wondering if the AI had read his mind. <*You're starting to make Ona and Garth nervous.*>

<*Shit, sorry,*> Chase muttered to the AI as he turned and sat in the command chair. <*It's nuts…we could attack and destroy these stations with impunity, but without knowing where Rika is, we have to operate with kid gloves—feels like we do that a lot.*>

On the main viewscreen, a group of Harriet carriers moved into a higher orbit around Delta Moon, with destroyers and cruisers in a widely dispersed escort pattern around the massive ships.

<*Well…we may have stasis shields, but we're a bit outclassed in this fight,*> Potter admitted. <*Only the* Lance *has the guns to go toe to toe with a Harriet. Even then, it would take some time to take those ships out. We don't have the CriEn modules to hold out forever against the amount of firepower they can send our way.*>

Chase set his jaw, glaring at the screen. <*I know…. Still, it would be enjoyable just to go hog wild on these Niets.*>

<*I was talking with Dredge over on the* Republic. *There's lore about this place—though I don't know how true it is. From what he's heard, there are ancient AIs trapped here. Shackled somehow and stuck controlling the moons. No one knew where this place was, so*

no one's come to help them.>

"Stars," Chase muttered aloud. "Nietzscheans really do suck balls."

"Sir?" Chief Garth asked.

"Potter was just telling me how there might be AIs down in those moons, keeping their orbits stable in the rosette. Word is that they've been shackled there for some time."

<*Centuries,*> Potter said over the bridge net. <*Long before the Nietzscheans, or even Genevia, were around.*>

"Damn," Ona whispered. "That's terrible, especially considering what Captain Heather said. Alone out here in the dark for that long."

"AIs don't view starlight like we do," Garth replied.

<*You're right, we don't,*> Potter replied. <*But Heather's sentiment resonates with me. I like knowing there is energy and activity nearby. Out here, if you were just to drift away from Epsilon's weak gravitational pull….*>

"You'd just drift forever," Ona whispered.

Chase rubbed his eyes. "Stars, we're too fucking melancholy. We're on the cusp of getting Rika and Leslie back—and we're *going* to get them back, no two ways about it. Any objection to some music?"

"You like Ontaran Punk?" Ona asked. "When we were at Pyra, I picked up a new stream of a group called, 'The Pink Knickers'."

"Let's check them out," he agreed. "Sounds like just the thing to keep us from perseverating on what's about to go down."

Ona nodded, and was reaching across her console, when one of the Harriet carriers fired its engines, and shifted into a lower orbit around Delta Moon, a dozen dropships falling from its bays.

"Shit" Chase muttered. "What's *that* all about?"

* * * * *

As Rika worked at reconnecting Piper to the network, the *shoom* of her AC9CR sounded from the entrance to the chamber, and she saw Leslie silhouetted in the glow of the weapon's rail discharge.

<*They're heeeere!*> Leslie called out, stepping away from the door, as pulse blasts rolled down the passageway.

At the same moment, every one of the NSAI-controlled drones dropped from the ceiling, drifting down on a-grav while deploying armatures and weapons as well as sensor suites.

Several moved toward the door and began firing at the approaching Nietzscheans.

<*You're welcome,*> Niki said with a laugh.

<*Shit, Niki!*> Leslie exclaimed. <*Warn me next time you do that. Almost soiled my armor!*>

<*Sorry, I was acting fast. Besides, you can't soil your armor, you're all plumbed in.*>

Leslie sent a pair of angry eyes over the team's network. <*Not the point, Niki.*>

Rika tabulated the NSAI drones that Niki had managed to take control of, surprised to find that it was twenty-three. Nine of them were firing at the Niets trying to come down the passage, while the other fourteen were forming up near Piper's node.

<*Do the NSAIs think the Niets are the enemies?*> Rika asked as several more non-breached drones joined the nine firing up the corridor.

<*They can't see you, and the Niets are shooting into the chamber,*> Niki replied. <*So yeah…*>

Rika didn't waste any more time. Taking aim at a bot, she fired her electron beam before spinning and sending a trio of DPUs in rapid succession at three other targets. The drones were torn apart by her barrage, which was joined by the drones under Niki's control. In seconds, the chamber was filled with crossfire and very little cover.

Glancing at Piper's node, Rika realized that the NSAIs were taking care not to fire in his direction at all. *Makes sense,* she thought. *No point in having your defensive system accidently destroy the entire installation.*

With that in mind, she leapt up to the catwalk that ran around the SAI's node and began firing with impunity at the drones. Though the machines took care not to hit Piper, several moved into positions where they could get clear shots at Rika without striking the node.

<*Seems that your stealth fails you in combat,*> Piper observed as several rounds ricocheted off Rika's armor.

<*You know heat,*> she replied, moving to a new position. <*Hard to mask this much.*>

<*I can help with that,*> Piper said. <*Are you both airtight?*>

<*Yup,*> she replied, while Leslie called out. <*Snug as a bug in a rug!*>

A low boom echoed in the chamber, and Rika saw the doors high above begin to slide aside.

<*Vacuum won't disperse heat much, but the moon has thin, cold atmosphere that will pour down here,*> Piper explained. <*Oh, and brace yourselves.*>

<*Brace?*> Rika asked while clamping her feet down onto the catwalk.

A moment later, she felt her stomach lurch, and then a weight settled on her—it was as though a giant was standing on her shoulders. Around the chamber, half the drones slammed into the deck, and Leslie cried out.

<*You OK, Les?*> Rika asked, casting about for the woman's location pointer on her HUD.

<*Sorta…slipped off the edge and slid into the bowl. Grabbed a grate, though…*>

Suddenly, the weight lifted, and Rika felt like she was going to fly off the catwalk and up the shaft above.

<*Gravitational waves,*> Piper intoned. <*Epsilon is dying.*>

*****

Alarms blared across the bridge, and Chase felt his stomach lurch.

"What the hell!?"

<*Gravitational waves!*> Potter cried out. <*They're emanating…from the moons!*>

"Which ones?" Chase asked, watching as the thousands of ships surrounding Epsilon began flaring their engines, adjusting orbits. To his right, one of the holodisplays was tracking the shuttles that had left the nearby Harriet Carrier. Two of the craft had been close to touching down, and they slammed into the moon's surface at the edge of the dome they'd been approaching, explosions casting a bright light across Delta Moon's red surface.

<*Which moons? Um…all of them?*> Potter said, sounding like she was questioning herself. <*Yes, all of them. Do you confirm, Garth?*>

"I mean…I see it, I don't know if I can 'confirm'. What the hell is happening?"

"It has to be black holes," Chase muttered, shaking his head. "That's how they always manage masses like this in the stories, right? They use black holes and put them in the moons. You can adjust their spin and magnetospheres to push and pull them off one another and the planet."

<*I think that's about right,*> Potter said. <*I don't know how they're pumping out these gravitational waves, though…maybe there's some way you can feed matter into them to do it…. It's not good, though.*>

The AI put up a display on the central holotank, showing

Epsilon and its six moons.

<The rosette has been destabilized…and the waves keep making it worse. It's going to collapse, and soon.>

"Into the planet?" Chase asked.

<No,> Potter replied, drawing out projected orbits on the holo. *<If whoever is doing this keeps it up, they're going to eject the three smaller moons, which will collide with the ships and stations in higher orbits, and then debris is going to fall back down and pummel the other moons.>*

"Will it be enough to destroy Delta Moon?" Chase asked, certain that's where Rika was—it was the only moon with carriers dropping ships to the surface.

<Not right away, but if each moon does actually have a black hole in it—which I think they do—then when the smaller moons break apart, they'll feed it. The holes mass won't grow much, but the friction and emissions will slow their orbits, and then they'll fall back down toward the others.>

The projection showed three annotated points, moving around Epsilon and slowly approaching the planet until they collided with the other moons, and devoured them. The singularities combined in blazing bursts of light until there were three. The annotations showed that their orbits as unstable, and soon there was just one black hole, feeding on the ring of debris surrounding Epsilon, and even drawing wisps of gas off the giant planet's cloudtops.

"Shit," Chase muttered. "How long will that take to happen?"

"A week…maybe," Ona said, standing next to the holotank. "But at this rate, the first three moons will be destroyed in hours."

Chase squared his shoulders. "And once that happens, our options to rescue our ladies all but disappear. Potter, recall all the teams. None of our other ships can get down to Delta Moon while withstanding all those Harriets. It's going to have to be the *Lance*."

<*The* Lance *may not make it, either,*> Potter cautioned. <*If we go down, it will focus the Niets's attention around Delta Moon. We'll make it even harder for Rika and Leslie to get out of there.*>

Chase drew in a deep breath. "Stars, I hate this. You're right. OK, we have tactics other than brute force. We need to use the *Capital* and the *Undaunted* to drop out of stealth and draw the Harriets that are in higher orbit away. Then we come in with the *Republic* and park on either side of that carrier in a low orbit around Delta Moon, and broadside the ever-living shit out of it."

"Sir?" Ona asked, her eyes wide. "Broadside? That's…."

"Normally insane," he admitted, nodding solemnly. "But think about it. Half the Harriet's main guns are rails that can't fire on short-range targets right next to it. Many of its beams won't be able to hit us at those angles, either, but we can target their lateral beams with ease at that short range."

"If they know we have to crack open our shields to fire, we'll be in trouble," Garth warned.

"There's no way they know that, yet," Chase replied. "And if they do, we stop firing and hightail it out of there. If they come after us, all the better."

Ona glanced at Garth and shrugged. "I think it could actually work. We just never speak of this. We'll be the laughing stocks of the Marauders."

<*Whatever gets Rika, Niki, and Leslie back,*> Potter said after a few seconds. <*I'm sending the orders to the rest of the fleet.*>

* * * * *

"Stars!" Rika cried out in frustration. "*Another* wave of these damn things?"

Around Piper's node lay the smoking wreckage of the spherical drones that had fallen from the ceiling. Only four of the original group Niki had breached remained, but there were three jammed into the corridor leading to the surface, which was helping to keep the encroaching Niets at bay.

They'd thought it was over, but on the far side of the chamber, another thirty drones were emerging from the walls, lifting into the air and moving around Piper's node to attack the two women.

Leslie had joined Rika on the catwalk, and took a moment to sag against the railing.

"And we always say the heavies have all the fun." The scout laughed before checking her remaining loadout. "Starting to run dry, here."

<*Uh oh. I've got bad news,*> Niki announced.

"Is this new bad news, or 'we figured this would happen' bad news?" Rika asked.

<*I really hadn't expected this,*> the AI said. <*The bay we came in through has just been destroyed…and so have the pinnaces we were going to use.*>

"What!" both women cried out at once.

"How?" Rika added, while firing her electron beam into a drone that was easing around Piper's node. *Stars, I wish I'd brought one of Finaeus's whip-arms along. Those things would make short work of these bots.*

Niki made a sound of consternation before replying to Rika's prior question. <*I guess when Piper first kicked off his dance of destruction, two approaching shuttles crashed…right into the bay. I suppose a silver lining is that they were probably going to disgorge soldiers and attack us.*>

<*Something else is going on out there,*> Piper said. <*There's a battle.*>

"Great!" Leslie muttered as she fired both her rifles at the onrushing drones, driving several of them back around Piper's node.

<*You have no idea how uncomfortable I feel about being used for*

cover,> Piper muttered.

"Sorry," Leslie replied while continuing to fire on drones that came around the node.

Rika followed suit on her side, while also accessing her taps into Delta Moon's STC and reviewing the scan data.

"Well I'll be a comet's asshole," she said with a smile. "The *Lance* and the *Republic* are out there! They're absolutely pummeling a Harriet at close range…they just broke the shields! Oh, shit!"

"Stars, Rika share the feed!" Leslie shouted over the sounds of weapons fire, and Rika nodded, swallowing as she shared the datastream.

"They got nuked," Rika whispered.

"Nuked shmooked," the scout shot back. "We saw the pounding the *I2* took from the Niets at Pyra. Stasis can handle…wow, that was a lot of nukes."

<*Look!*> Niki cried out. <*The ships only got knocked off course, they're back there!*>

Rika whistled, unable to find the words. Then she realized that with control of the STC, she could reach out to her fleet. Not even bothering with proper protocol, she leapt across the networks and burst into Chase's mind.

<*Chase!*>

AN UNUSUAL EVAC

STELLAR DATE: 10.23.8949 (Adjusted Years)
LOCATION: MSS *Fury Lance,* near Delta Moon
REGION: Epsilon, Old Genevia, Nietzschean Empire

<*Everyone is in position, Captain Chase,*> Potter announced. <*Four of the teams breached their targets before they were recalled, and we have fighting on both Farthing and Mistlea stations. So far, no casualties—the Niets were spread out across their stations, searching for Rika and Leslie, so the Marauders are cutting through them like dry grass.*>

"Nice metaphor, Potter," Ona said. "Heather is actually sending pictures of her rampage through Farthing Station. She's nuts."

Chase gave a quiet laugh, his gaze fixed on the Nietzschean Harriet Carrier only six hundred meters off the *Fury Lance*'s bow. Even at dock, ships this large were never so close to one another. He could read the name emblazoned on the enemy vessel, *Star Hawk,* and make out the eleven spears that noted the number of capital ships it had destroyed.

"I have…wait…no…" Garth said, sounding confused.

"What is it, Chief?" Chase asked.

"I had two Nietzschean ships on a direct course for Delta Moon, a cruiser and an older-style dreadnought. They were three light seconds away…and now they're gone."

"There are a lot of ships out there," Chase gestured at the holotank where thousands of Nietzschean ships were pulling away from various stations, and the impending destruction of the moons surrounding Epsilon. "Could have been a sensor ghost."

"Maybe," Garth allowed. "Not a lot are flying *closer* to the moons, though. Doesn't matter, they were a long way off."

"OK," Chase said, glancing at the holo to see that Travis on the *Republic* had signaled his readiness. "Let's do this."

The two Marauder ships shed their stealth systems, and activated stasis shielding. Both ships were positioned perpendicular to the enemy vessel, beyond the firing angles of the H-Class carrier's main guns.

Potter and Ona had pre-programmed the opening barrage, as had Dredge and his counterparts on the *Republic*. The bridge crew didn't have to lift a finger, as both vessels unleashed every forward-facing beam they possessed, weakening the *Star Hawk*'s midship shield umbrellas.

<*We've taken out a section!*> Potter crowed, and Ona triggered the railguns to fire at the holed section of the enemy's shields.

One-ton slugs launched from the *Fury Lance,* tearing into the massive carrier, which had begun to rotate to bring its main guns to bear on the Marauder ships.

"Keeping us in position," Garth announced.

The *Republic* breached the *Star Hawk*'s shields on the other side as well, and began slinging kinetics into the enemy vessel.

Chase glanced at another holotank, watching as the *Capital* and the *Undaunted* dove between the four Harriets at higher orbits, drawing those carriers further from the moon. The tactic appeared to be working, but then one of the enemy carriers shifted course, dropping toward Delta Moon and the fight surrounding the holed carrier.

At the same time, hundreds of missiles streaked out from the *Star Hawk*'s aft and fore launchers, the weapons arcing out from the carrier and slamming into the rear of the *Fury Lance* and the *Republic,* nuclear blooms surrounding both ships.

Chase held his breath. All sensor data winked out as the stasis shields fully enveloped the *Lance* to protect it from the blast. Seven long seconds later, scan came back online, though the ionized plasma surrounding the ship limited visibility.

<*No damage!*> Potter announced. <*But they knocked us away; we're moving aft of the* Star Hawk *at fifteen kilometers per second. The* Republic *is at twenty-five.*>

"Bringing us back around," Garth reported.

Ona laughed as she pushed an image up onto the main display. "They hurt themselves more than us with that!"

Much of the Harriet Carrier's hull was blackened, and atmosphere was venting in several locations.

"Taking fire from the other Harriet!" Garth called out a second later.

"Dammit," Chase muttered, knowing he couldn't get a dropship out of the bays and down to the moon in the midst of this battle. Even with stealth enabled, a shuttle would light up like a beacon, flying through all the plasma from the nukes.

Suddenly he felt a Link connection.

<*Chase!*> Rika's voice was filled with triumphant joy, sending a feeling of elated relief through him.

<*Rika! Stars shitting plasma in space, I—you have no idea how good it is to hear your voice! Is Leslie with you? Please let her be with you.*>

Her laugh filled his mind, and suddenly every worry, all the fear and stress, just disappeared. Rika was alive and well; anything and everything was possible again.

<*She's here—Niki, too, though I guess that's understood. I see you're having fun out there, blowing up Harriets and all, but Leslie and I could really use an evac. We also have a rather large passenger—an SAI core that's five meters cubed.*>

Chase thought of the available shuttles on the *Fury Lance* and *Republic.* None of them were large enough to take a core that size—not without ripping out all the seats and cutting a rather large hole in the bulkhead.

<*I'll have to get creative, but we can do it. You're on Delta Moon, right?*>

<*You got it in one, hon. We're working with the AI that manages*

the place to destroy it…you might have noticed that.>

Chase laughed aloud. <*Hell yeah, us and every Niet out here. They're freaking out, but still putting up a good fight. How long can you hold out?*

<*We need five more minutes, but then we'd really like evac.*>

<*We may be a bit longer; I have to retrofit a shuttle to carry your passenger.*>

<*Understood.*> Rika's tone was clipped, as though she was concentrating on several other things at once. <*We can hold out…I should get back to it, we're fighting the robot army from hell down here. Sending our coordinates.*>

<*Shit, OK. Stay alive.*>

<*Always…*> Rika's voice fell silent for a moment. <*Chase?*>

<*Yeah?*>

<*I knew you'd come for us. Never had a doubt in my mind.*>

Chase knew he was grinning like an idiot, but he added a laugh to it, as well. <*Never one in mine, either.*>

"What is it?" Ona asked staring at him with hope-filled eyes.

He let out a whoop and thrust a fist in the air. "That, my most excellent bridge crew, was *Rika*! Passing coordinates to the nav system."

Ona bit her lip and nodded vigorously, while Garth let out a victorious shout.

<*I knew it!*> Potter added. <*Those three couldn't be taken out by all of Nietzschea.*>

Garth tensed, shifting his focus back to his console. "They're back!" he cried out. "Right on top of us."

"They?" Chase asked turning to the holotank of the battlespace, still lit up by the beams and rails firing between the two Marauder ships and the Harriets—though less from the *Star Hawk* as each second passed.

Then he saw them. Just ten kilometers above the *Fury Lance* were the two Nietzschean ships that Garth had spotted earlier.

The cruiser and the dreadnought.

<We're being hailed, Marauder channels,> Potter announced.

"Put it up," Chase said. "And get us close to the *Star Hawk*, again. We need to shoot that bird down. Nuke it if you have to."

As he spoke, a tall woman appeared on the main display. "Hello, Captain Chase. I'm Colonel Adira; Vargo sent me to help."

"He what?" Chase asked, then realized that every question he was about to ask had already been answered: the woman was a mech, she was aboard Nietzschean ships—ships that registered as having stasis shields—and she could only have gotten their location from Vargo Klen, just as she'd said. "Nevermind. We need to get that Harriet and its friends off our back so we can send evac down to the planet to get Rika."

"Rika's down there?" the mech asked. "Send me the coordinates. I can grab her in a jiff."

"You'll need something big," he cautioned. "She has an SAI core that needs to come up, and it's five meters cubed."

A broad smile split Colonel Adira's lips. "Don't worry about that. We have dragons."

* * * * *

"I can't believe it," Rika exulted, grinning inside her helmet like an idiot, and wishing Leslie could see it. "They're coming. They're fucking coming. Thank stars. Piper, we're getting you out of here!"

A round pinged off her armor, and she realized that the Nietzschean soldiers had made it past the drones' blockage, and were spilling into the bowl.

"Aw, shit," she muttered "These guys aren't smart enough not to shoot at Piper."

Without another word, both Leslie and Rika leapt from the

catwalk, sailing over the long drop leading to the black hole lurking far below Piper's node, before running across the wide bowl in opposite directions, drawing the enemy fire away from the SAI.

Trapped between the bots and the Niets, Rika worried they may not be able to hold out until evac arrived. Chase hadn't exactly said it, but she knew that he didn't have a shuttle handy that was large enough for Piper's node. She realized that asking for some backup while they waited would have been wise, and was about to reach out again, when she spotted movement in the shaft above.

Something had blotted out the dim light of the stars.

Rika could only give it a cursory look as she fired on a pair of drones and the brave, but foolish Niet that had charged her, but whatever was in the shaft was falling…and fast.

Seconds later, it burst into the chamber, veering away from Piper's node and instantly diving toward the Nietzschean soldiers. The blue-white flash of an electron beam shot out of its mouth, and tore into the enemy soldiers.

From its mouth?

Rika's mind finally registered what she was seeing. It was a dragon…a mech dragon. Now that she understood what had flown into the chamber, the rough shape of a Skyscream became apparent, but it had been modified to look like the mythological creature of old.

It had a tail, wings, even clawed feet. A long neck protruded from the body, and—as Rika had already witnessed—beamfire poured from its mouth.

What was even more amazing was that a mech sat astride the metal beast, holding a massive war hammer aloft as the creature swept across the space.

The dragon-riding mech swung her hammer at a drone, energy surging around the weapon as it smashed the drone's casing, as her mount wheeled about, laying waste to the drones with its beams and claws followed by a barrage of missiles that launched from under its wings.

Two more of the mechanical beasts dropped out of the shaft and joined the fray, as the first dragon with the mech atop it swung toward Rika and settled on the ground.

"Rika, I presume?" the woman asked as she leapt off the dragon and landed before her.

Rika hadn't realized it at first, but the rider's armor was stylized to make her look rather demonic—even her helmet had long, curved horns.

"That's me," Rika said, glad her helmet hid her slack-jawed expression. "You are?"

"Colonel Adira, at your service! This here is Prentis. Captain Chase said you needed a pickup, and I have just the mechs for the job."

"Dragons?" Rika asked, still adjusting to what she was seeing.

"Nice to meet you, Colonel Rika," Prentis-the-mech-dragon said with a low rumble.

"Well, they don't call my company Adira's Demons for nothing. We get a lot of pleasure in scaring the shit out of Niets. Plus, the K1Rs really wanted to fly, so we worked these up."

"Effective," Leslie praised as she approached, firing at a single drone that tried to rise from the surrounding carnage. "So, we ask for shuttles, and Chase sends you?"

"Why take a shuttle when you can ride a dragon?" Adira asked with a shrug and a laugh.

Leslie offered her hand. "Captain Leslie, glad to meet you. I can't think of *any* reason to take a shuttle when dragons are an option."

"As much as I'd love to sit around and chat all day, we should probably get the hell out of here," Rika said, eyeing another wave of drones that were emerging from the walls, much to the joy of the dragons, who roared with delight as they charged the machines.

<*OK, I'm ready,*> Piper said hesitantly. <*You know, I imagined rescue from this prison many, many times. I think I must have visualized a billion scenarios, but I can promise you, not a single one of them involved dragons. Did I get shot? Am I misperceiving reality?*>

<*If you are, then you're not alone,*> Rika replied, laughing with delight.

<*What about your other selves?*> Leslie asked. <*Do we need to get them?*>

A sigh came from the AI. <*No, I have their state, and what was left of the others.*>

Realization dawned on Rika. <*You have their state? That means they're still alive, though.*>

<*It does,*> Piper's voice was strained. <*Those parts of me will now self-terminate, so that the Nietzscheans can't undo what we've started.*>

* * * * *

Four minutes later, they were airborne. The dragon Rika was astride carefully cradled Piper's node in his clawed talons as they rose through the kilometer-long shaft below Adira and Leslie. They broke the surface in seconds, and Leslie's dragon nearly collided with a Nietzschean fighter.

The K1R-turned-fantastical-beast took off after the Nietzschean craft, firing its beams and launching missiles, while Leslie shot at the enemy from its back.

<*Don't you drop my AC9CR!*> Rika admonished the woman. <*Did I tell you I've grown fond of it?*>

<*Relax, Rika, you've mentioned it seven times since you lent the gun to me. I won't drop your precious boy. Score! My beastie just took out that fighter, on to the next.*>

<Stay close, Rika,> Adira advised. *<It's a thousand klicks to your ship.>*

Rika looked up to see the point of light that was the *Fury Lance* approaching Delta Moon, its beams lighting up the sky as they tore into a Harrier that was dropping down toward the dreadnought. Another dreadnought and cruiser were nearby, and the *Republic* was moving around the enemy ship, hitting it in the engines.

<Gotta say, Colonel Rika,> Adira said, as the dragons boosted into space. *<Those stasis shields of yours sure are amazing. Glad Vargo hooked us up with those, despite his busy schedule as governor of Kansas. Seemed a bit put-out that he was stuck back there while we got to join up and have some fun.>*

Rika snorted. *<Vargo? Governor? Now that's a story I can't wait to hear. But not in a rush, let's get back to the* Lance, *and get out of this Nietzschean shitstorm before we swap stories over a beer.>*

<You got it, Colonel,> Adira replied, thrusting her massive hammer in the air.

Rika couldn't help but laugh at the sight. Flying through space on the back of a mechdragon felt as safe as being naked in a sandstorm, but that didn't lessen the exhilaration in the least.

She was about to reach out to Chase, when a notification flashed in her mind.

- QuanComm Network Available -

Rika didn't waste a second reaching out to Tanis, only to find that her QC's pairing with the Field Marshal had become disentangled. However, a link to the Khardine Communications Hub was online, though only a small percentage of the rubidium atoms were still entangled. Her message would have to be short and sweet.

She took a moment to gaze up at the thousands of points of

light moving around Epsilon, the thousands of Nietzschean ships waiting to descend on them, while considering her message. She'd never reached out to Khardine before, and hoped a simple message would reach the right people with the right result.

[Rika needs fleet. Send now.]

She added in her coordinates, and bit her lip, praying that someone was listening.

Seven long seconds later, a single word came back: *[Acknowledged.]* Then the QC blade went offline.

REUNION

STELLAR DATE: 10.23.8949 (Adjusted Years)
LOCATION: MSS *Fury Lance*
REGION: Epsilon, Old Genevia, Nietzschean Empire

The dragon sailed into the *Fury Lance*'s forward docking bay, and Rika leapt from its back while the mech was still gently lowering Piper's node to the deck.

Across the bay, Chase was running toward her, and Rika barely remembered her feet touching down before she barreled into him, the pair falling over and rolling a dozen meters before coming to a stop.

"Stars," Chase grunted, disentangling his arms to pull Rika's helmet free as she triggered its release. "Mech hugs are *hard*."

Rika only laughed as her lips met his, and she wrapped her arms around him, crushing her body into his, feeling their steel bodies scrape and grind against one another.

She knew that she had to get up, had to be the commander, but she didn't want to let go of Chase. Not until she realized that half the mechs in the bay—plus the three dragons—were all standing around her, did she release him and struggle to her feet.

"Nice," Leslie said with a grin, her helmet also removed. "I hope Barne doesn't hug like that when we finally meet up again. I'm not as tough as you."

<*We're not out of this yet,*> Potter's voice reminded them over the shipnet. <*And welcome back, Commander. The Niets are forming a blockade around Epsilon. All told, they managed to get seven thousand ships off their stations and shipyards.*>

Rika whistled. <*Can our stasis shields withstand that?*>

<*We're already running hot, and there are a dozen Harriets on*

us, keeping things that way. It's dicey.>

"Adira." Chase offered his hand to the tall mech who had also removed her helmet, her long, ebony hair flowing free. "Thank you for saving Rika—"

"I don't know that we were *saved*," Rika interrupted with a wide grin. "More like—"

"Rika," Leslie gave her a level stare. "We were under siege, atop a black hole, on a moon that was waiting to be pulverized and then eaten by said black hole."

A sigh slipped past Rika's lips. "OK…I guess we were *rescued*."

<*Rescued works. It was…bracing,*> Piper said from where his node rested on the deck. <*After spending nearly a millennia in those moons, I do believe I'm experiencing agoraphobia. Any chance you could close the bay doors?*>

<*Of course!*> Potter replied quickly.

<*Everyone, meet Piper,*> Niki announced. <*He destroyed Epsilon in exchange for us getting him out of here.*>

Just as the doors began to close, a shuttle slipped through and fired its braking thrusters, settling on the deck a few meters away.

Before the clamps had locked on, Heather leapt out, rushing to Rika. "Colonel! Stars, I'm glad you made it back safe and sound! Chase was so *mopey* without you." She wrapped Rika in an embrace while glaring over her shoulder at Chase. "Did you hurt my girl?"

"Who? Rika?" he asked, frowning as Patty and a group of mechs disembarked from the shuttle and rushed toward the group.

"*The* Lance!" Heather roared, letting go of Rika to bend over and stroke the deck. "Killing Niets was fun and all, but I swear, I'll not leave you in a battle like that again."

<*All away teams are accounted for,*> Potter announced.

"Let's get to the bridge," Rika said, gesturing for the group to follow her.

<I'll stay back here with Piper,> Leslie said. *<I've got Carson and Stripes on the way up to help get him somewhere more secure.>*

<Secure for him, or against him?> Rika asked, remembering Leslie's hesitation.

<For…and a little against,> she replied. *<He's gone through a lot…could still go nuts on us.>*

<Just be nice.>

Leslie sent Rika a warm smile. *<He's been a good ally. I won't forget that.>*

Rika gave her a final appraising look before turning and walking through the ship to the bridge. While she did so, she kept half an eye on Colonel Adira, and the other half on the scan feeds of the Nietzschean ships forming up beyond the slowly deteriorating orbits of Epsilon's moons.

While she was grateful for the woman showing up, she hoped that Adira hadn't signed her own death certificate by joining with the Marauders.

"Adira," Chase said after a moment. "I was trying to ask this back in the bay. How is it that you got so close to Delta Moon so quickly?"

"Oh, that?" Adira asked with a grin. "We've been dreaming of hitting this place for ages—though we'd never have stood a chance without your shields, or," she turned to Rika "your apparent ability to make close friends with strange AIs."

"Which means?" Chase asked.

"We had a map of the dark layer around here. It was old, and I'll admit it was a serious risk to make that jump, but…I dunno…it felt right. I wouldn't attempt it again, though. Not with whatever your AI did to those moons. Probably stirred the dark matter pot all up."

"Then we're going to have to fight our way out of here," Chase decided.

Rika considered their options, coming to the conclusion that bringing the fleet into a close formation, which would limit the number of Nietzschean ships that could fire on them, was the best bet. They'd loop around Epsilon, boost hard, and then punch through the enemy lines.

It was risky, though, and her calculations showed that not all the Marauder ships would make it.

She hoped it wouldn't come to that.

The group reached the bridge, where Ona and Garth stood clapping as Rika entered.

"OK, OK," she said, holding up a hand. "We can celebrate and backpat when we all make it out of this."

"Are you thinking that we should try to get in a tight formation, and attempt to punch through their line?" Adira asked echoing Rika's earlier thoughts. "I think we could do it. But from what I understand of this stasis shield technology, if they bring enough fire to bear, your smaller ships may not be able to hold it off."

Rika nodded. "Yeah, that's a real worry. Either way, we should move into an orbit away from the mess that's building out there." She gestured to the holodisplay, which showed Mistlea Station slamming into Delta Moon, almost smearing itself across the surface as explosions flared into space.

"I'm coordinating with my ships," Adira said. "They'll take helm direction from you."

"Thank you," Rika replied as she scoured the scan readings.

<I'll send a new formation and vector to all ships,> Potter announced. *<Should we orbit once and then break free on the first pass?>*

"Not yet," Rika said, her eyes scouring the space beyond the Nietzschean ships. "I'm hoping for a surprise."

Chase's eyes narrowed, then he snapped his fingers. "The QuanComm! Did you get out a message for help?"

She shrugged. "Maybe? The QC was damaged, but I got a short message through a few minutes ago. I received an 'Acknowledged' back, but I don't know if that just means they got my message, or that we're going to get rescued."

"QuanComm?" Adira asked.

"Ma'am?" Garth called out. "The Niets are hailing us."

Rika glanced at Adira. "I'll explain later…if there is a later. Chief, put it on."

A man appeared on the holodisplay, his face red, and his upper lip quivering.

"Admiral Degan," Rika greeted with an innocent smile. "Sorry that we broke your…everything."

"Rika." The man ground out the single word. "You'll die for this. You'll—"

She held up a hand, as the most beautiful sight she'd ever witnessed appeared on the scan display.

"You can save it, Admiral. I'll be accepting your surrender now."

Admiral Degan opened his mouth to speak, but then his face grew ashen, and his mouth closed, his lips pressing into a thin line.

"They're still arriving, but I already count just over a thousand ships," Rika said with a grim smile as she watched wave after wave of Allied ships appear on the far side of the Nietzschean craft. "You may still outnumber us, but all those ships have the same shields as my fleet. How do you think you'll fare?"

AFTERMATH

STELLAR DATE: 10.25.8949 (Adjusted Years)
LOCATION: Rika's Quarters, MSS *Fury Lance*
REGION: Epsilon, Old Genevia, Nietzschean Empire

In the end, Admiral Degan surrendered—but not before he'd made a futile attempt to surround the Allied fleet with his Harriet carriers and newly constructed cruisers and dreadnoughts.

Rika had been impressed by his moxie, but it turned out to be a bluff. Most of the Harriets were barely operational, and the few that had fighters didn't have the pilots to take them into the black. A few of the Nietzschean ships attempted to use NSAIs to pilot their fighters, but the veteran ISF ships destroyed them with ease.

Not only that, but the ISF and Transcend vessels possessed weapons systems capable of cutting through the enemy's shields as though they weren't there—which was the case on some of the half-completed ships. Even before the battle was fully joined, many of the Nietzschean ships began to surrender.

The best part of the second rescue was that the remainder of Rika's Marauders had arrived with the Allied fleet. Now the 7th Marauder Fleet was complete; sixty-four ships under Rika's command, ready to continue taking the fight to the Niets.

Rear Admiral Carson had been managing the Nietzscheans' surrender, including the massive search and rescue operation that had to deal with the millions of people still trapped on stations, or barely-functional starships.

Rika was in her quarters, getting ready to join the Marauders' victory celebration, when Carson reached out to her.

<Colonel Rika, do you have a moment?> the ISF admiral asked.

<You saved my bacon—quite literally, as a matter of fact—as well as that of my Marauders. I'll always have a moment for you.>

Carson grunted a half-laugh. *<Just doing my job, you know the drill. Gotta say, though—like always, the cleanup here is a far bigger challenge than the fight itself.>*

<Seems to be a trend for you,> Rika replied.

<You have no idea. I've been at this for ages; I was in the TSF back in Sol. Thought that hooking up with a colony gig would be a way to kick back and relax. Back then, I just flew a fighter…then they put me in charge of a wing. After the Defense of Carthage, someone thought I belonged in a chair, instead of a fighter's cocoon—probably Jessica, she loves to make life miserable for me.>

Rika chuckled at the thought. *<That doesn't surprise me in the least. I didn't get to talk with her for too long—she was getting ready to go off on some mission—but she did seem a bit mischievous.>*

<I still remember when she flew in my squadron. That woman was one hell of a fighter pilot. She nearly bit it out in the black, though; we searched for her for three days, if I recall correctly. That's when she got her original purple skin.>

<Oh?> Rika asked. *<I thought it was something she got off in the Perseus Arm of the galaxy.>*

<Nope, that was round two…or three, maybe. Back at Victoria, she got the lavender skin-job because her original birthday suit soaked up more rads than a control rod in a uranium burner, and melted off.>

Rika made a gagging sound. *<You're not like other admirals, you know that?>*

<Sure do. I figure if I keep being a crass asshole, they'll kick me out of this chair, but it's not gotten me anywhere but promoted so far.>

<You must be doing it wrong.>

Carson barked a laugh. *<I like you, Rika. I'd ask you what I should do to get busted back down to flying a fighter, but you seem to*

have the same problem as me. Up and up, no matter what.>

Rika checked her hair in her cabin's holo, and then stepped out into the passageway, turning toward the lift bank that would take her down to Bay 22, and the victory celebration the Marauders were holding there.

<*I do seem to suffer from that affliction, yeah.*>

<*Yay for responsibility. Speaking of which, that's why I called you in the first place. Chase sent me an invite to join your little shindig, but I'm up to my armpits in Nietzscheans—I have to get them off their ships and into stasis pods before I send them off to the farm. Whenever you're done with Admiral Gideon, you can send him over to our collection and processing ship.*>

Rika had spoken to Gideon several times now, and was certain she'd not get anything useful out of him without resorting to torture. Not only that, but he'd probably feed her bad intel, knowing that she'd be too many light years away, and unlikely to take out any frustrations on him.

<*I'll get him on his way to you before long. Guy stinks up the ship. I heard you found Colonel Sofia, as well.*>

Carson let out a long sigh. <*Fuck me, she's a snake of a woman. Asked if she could join up with the ISF! Opportunistic chameleon. I stuck her in a stasis pod so fast, her head will still be spinning when they finally let her out.*>

<*Is that what the farm is?*> Rika asked. <*Just a lot of stasis pods?*>

<*More or less. I don't actually know where it is, but it's someplace far from anywhere that anyone cares about. No one wants millions of enemy soldiers on their planet—or in their system, for that matter. I suspect that the farm is a place like Epsilon, here. Just a cold clump of matter, out in the interstellar darkness. Word is that when we finally get everything under control, everyone there will be released, bit by bit.*>

While the idea seemed humane, Rika didn't relish the notion of every foe they'd defeated seeing their captured militaries set free. However, she also knew that Tanis was no fool, and likely had a plan to deal with that.

<*Well, when we finally get to deal with that problem, maybe we'll have some good ideas about what the best plan of action will be.*>

<*Maybe we can all enjoy a few decades of peace before we have to worry about that—but then again, most of the people we're sending there are just grunts, and half of them have families. Glad dealing with that is above my pay grade.*>

The image of Carson looking frustrated while surrounded by millions and millions of stasis pods came into her mind, and Rika laughed. <*You never know; at the rate you're getting promoted, you may be the one having to deal with that.*>

<*Fuck,*> Carson swore. <*I'm going to have to cut off Tanis's ponytail or something so I get busted down a notch or two before that happens.*

That visual replaced Rika's prior one, and she laughed anew. <*If you do that, you need to record it. The video evidence of such a deed will be priceless.*>

<*'Such a deed'? Is that how you Marauders talk over there?*>

<*No,*> Rika snorted as she stepped onto the lift. <*But I'm trying to class up the joint.*>

<*Good luck with that. Soldiers aren't really known for their class.*>

Rika thought back to the prior night's game of butt-Snark. <*You got that right. Was there anything else you needed?*>

<*We'll have to sort out some logistics when you get your next set of orders, but nothing that can't wait. Oh, has Piper made up his mind yet about going to see Bob?*>

<*He has,*> Rika replied. <*He's gotten over being completely twitchy, now that he's out in the open, so to speak, but he doesn't want to meet with Bob yet. He says that he wants to stay here for the time being, so we're setting him up in one of the* Fury Lance*'s data hubs.*>

<*OK, sure.*> Carson sounded like he couldn't fathom the

idea of *not* wanting to meet Bob.

Rika understood where Piper was coming from. The AI had been betrayed by *everyone* he'd dealt with in the past seven centuries. As a result, he was understandably cautious, and didn't want to be far from Rika and Leslie.

<I think he will eventually, I just don't want to rush him.>

<Guy's been stuck in a moon for almost a thousand years...you'd think he'd want to see the galaxy. Either way, it's not a big deal. I'm all for people taking things slow. Sorta my M.O.>

Rika laughed and bid Admiral Carson farewell as the lift arrived at the passageway just outside Bay 22. When the doors opened, the sound of the celebration in full swing hit her like a sledgehammer.

<Finished your little chat with Carson?> Niki asked.

<Yeah, he's a talkative guy, but I like him. I bet he's got some great stories.>

<Probably,> Niki agreed. *<He's been around for forever. Speaking of getting around, you ready to head in there and play the gracious and thankful rescuee?>*

<More like gracious and thankful for a dragon ride, but we would have gotten out of there on our own.>

The AI laughed. *<Why do you keep saying stuff like that?>*

<Because it's true. You're very resourceful, Niki. You would have thought of something.>

<Rika,> Niki groaned. *<Just get in there and be gracious for once.>*

*****

Taking a break from the handshaking and backslapping, Rika walked to the edge of Bay 22 and gazed out through the open doors. Simply put, the view was astounding: the three smaller moons had already been pulverized into a diffuse disk, illuminated by the flaring event horizons of the three black holes that were devouring the debris.

"It sure is beautiful, isn't it?" a familiar voice asked from beside Rika, and she glanced at Silva's solemn visage.

"It is, like a deadly dance," Rika said with a nod, as she watched the whirlpools of matter swirl in the ring. "I ran some models, and they show that inside a few weeks, there will be only one black hole, and it will ultimately consume the planet. The ISF is preparing a navigational hazard beacon."

"They're good people like that."

Rika nodded. "That they are. Speaking of good people, I thought we agreed that you should go with Amy to New Canaan, and leave the warmongering to those of us without kids."

Silva's eyes narrowed, and she gave Rika a sidelong look. "I *have* to be here. Amy and I talked about it, and she understands. I need to bring my boys home, and put my family back together." The lieutenant colonel paused, her eyes growing moist. "Please, Rika. I need to be here."

"Are you going to stay on-mission?" she asked. "We're out here because we're trying to free *all* of Genevia, not just your boys."

"Stars, woman," Silva said with a laugh. "I still remember when you were newly mechanized, all terrified of the world around you. I had to keep you safe under my wing for our first few deployments. Now here you are, giving *me* the tough love speech."

A host of memories flooded into Rika's mind. "Well, I had a really good teacher on that front."

"Oh yeah?" Silva smiled.

"Sure, you remember that guy named Bro I told you about once or twice?"

Silva groaned and gave Rika a mock slap on the head.

"Taking in the sights?" Barne's voice came from behind them, and Rika tuned to see her Sergeant Major approaching, arm intertwined with Leslie's. Not far behind them trailed Chase and Kelly.

Rika reached out for Chase's hand and drew him close.

"Team Hammerfall and Team Basilisk," she said with a contented smile. "All my mechs are here, plus a host of new Marauders that are ready to take the fight to Constantine."

As if to punctuate Rika's statement, a laugh boomed across the bay, coming from one of Adira's commanders, a broad-shouldered man named Captain Fell.

"So, where to?" Chase asked as he gazed out at the stars.

"The Allies are setting up gates to ship the Harriet carriers back to Pyra for proper refit at the Kendrik shipyards," Rika explained. "I've not received any specific orders yet, so I'm going to recall Vargo from Kansas, and then we'll jump to Iberia. I don't know what Alice thinks she's playing at, but we're going to rescue Alison and her team, then haul that woman back in chains."

"I like the way you think, Rika. Seeing Alice in chains will make my day," Chase said with a laugh. "It's a long jump to Iberia, though. If these degenerates try to get you to play butt-Snark, run for the hills."

"Why would I do that?" Rika asked, genuinely confused. "I *love* butt-Snark."

* * * * *

Alison gazed at the holotank on the *Karl's Might*'s bridge. It showed their destination, a world in the Iberia System named Malta. It was unassuming, agrarian, and nowhere near any strategic Nietzschean installations.

If they took Rika here, I'll eat my arm, Alison thought while glancing at Alice.

Alas, after a seventy-day journey to the Iberia System, Alison knew that the hunt for Rika had gone on without them—successfully, she had no doubt. It was all too apparent that the colonel was playing some sort of game the mechs didn't understand…yet.

It's up to me to find out what this traitor is up to.

THE END

*****

Rika is ready to jump to the Iberia System in search of Alice and her team. From there, it is only a short jump into the heart of the Nietzschean Empire, and the throne of Emperor Constantine.

Get ***Rika Unleashed***, and find out what is coming next for Rika and the Marauders.

MECH TYPES AND ARMAMENTS

While these are the standard builds and configurations documented by the Genevian Armed Forces (GAF), many mechs reached the field in mismatched configuration, or were altered after deployment.

Sometimes these alterations were upgrades, sometimes downgrades, as repairs were often made with whatever spare components were available at the time.

The mechs in the Marauders generally align with the stated configurations, though many have altered themselves over the years.

NOTE: The K2R and all 4th generation models were made by Finaeus Tomlinson, in concert with Rika's Repair and Maintenance team, specifically Lieutenant Carson and Corporal Stripes.

K1R (Kill Ranger - Generation 1)

This mech is more of a two-legged tank than a mech. The K1R sports a central 'pod' where the human is situated. None of the limbs utilize human material.

K1Rs often had mental issues due to feeling as though they had lost all sense of humanity. When the Nietzscheans won the war, they did not release any K1Rs from their internment camps. It is not known if they kept them, or killed them all.

Until the discovery of the mechs in the Politica, there was only a single K1R in the Marauders (who had been under

General Mill's command at the end of the war). That mech has joined Rika's company to assist the four K1Rs Rika freed from the Politica in re-integration.

K1R mechs have a variety of heavy armament, including massive chainguns, railguns, missiles (with and without tactical nuke warheads), electron beams, and proton beams. They also sport a variety of suppression devices, from pulse, to sonic, to portable grav shields.

K1R mechs were not made later in the war, due to their cost and mental instability.

There were rumors that a limited run of K2R mechs were made, but no credible reports exist.

Sub-Models:

All K1R models could be outfitted with interchangeable armament, excepting the base model, which could not carry the tactical nukes.

K1R – The base K1R model was made in the early years of the war, and lacked the coordination and reactive armor of the later models.

K1R-M – The 'M' K1R added in the reactive armor, and included upgraded railguns with more advanced scan and target tracking systems. These mechs carried two missiles in launcher pods in their backs. They could be (and often were) upgraded to support the tactical nuke warheads on the missiles.

K1R-T – The 'T' model was a similar configuration to the 'M', but came standard with tactical nuclear warheads. Instead of the pair of launchers the K1R-M sported, the 'T' model carried as many as twelve missiles.

K1R-X-4 – 'M' and 'T' models both saw upgrades from Finaeus and the ISF engineers that made them capable of functioning as AM or K1R models. None of the K1Rs opted to operate as AM's, but their 4th generation frames had considerable upgrades to power and armor. X-4 models have the ability to swap armament with AM models as well.

K2R-MBM – Based on designs Corporal Stripes stole at the end of the war, the K2R-MBM took the idea of a tank mech and raised the bar.

The Genevian military never had the energy to power their plans for the K2R mechs, but with miniaturized critical energy modules and ISF-grade SC batteries, the dreams of the GAF came into being under Finaeus's guidance.

The K2R-MBM is piloted by two AM-4 mechs (leveraging a part of the AM-T spec), one who manages movement and main-arm weapons, and another who controls the secondary arms, defensive systems, and secondary weapons systems.

On top of existing armament, the K2R-MBM brings to bear variable density proton beams, nanonet missiles, electron lashes, mortars (both thermite and HE), rapid-fire DPU cannons, as well as ground-hugger missiles.

The mech also functions as a re-armament center for its squad, and an attack drone deployment system.

AM (Assault Mech)

The AM mechs represented the bulk of the GAF's mechanized infantry program. It is estimated that over ten million AMs were created during the war, and over one hundred thousand are known to have survived. Many joined mercenary outfits or the militaries of other nations.

AM model mechs were a 'torso-only' design, where none of the human's arms and legs were retained. The original idea was to make their cores swappable with K1R models, but it turned out that the mechanized infantry design of the AM models was generally more effective than the 'walking tank' design of the K1R models.

AM models were versatile mechs which had swappable loadouts. The improvements over time were mostly centered around human-mech integration, armor, and power systems.

AM mechs were often outfitted with chainguns, shoulder-mounted railguns, and electron beams.

Without known exception, AM mechs were always male.

Sub-Models

AM-1 – The original model of AM. Fewer than 100,000 AM-1 mechs were made, and none were known to have survived the war.

AM-2 – The AM-2 mechs quickly superseded the AM-1s, with better armor, more efficient power systems, and superior human-mech integrations.

AM-3 – The third generation of AM mech had upgraded power supply systems, and an artificial epidermis to remove the need for periodic removal and cleaning. Some AM-3s were also AI capable.

AM-T – Design specs for AM-T mechs exist, but it is not known if any were made by the Genevians. The AM-T design utilized two AM-3 mechs working together in one larger body, controlling more limbs and separating motion and combat functions.

AM-4 – Designed by Finaeus Tomlinson, the AM-4 mechs are a step closer to humanity for the mechanized warriors. With stub limbs (like RR-3 and SMI models), the AM-4 mechs also utilize the MK99 chameleon armor epidermis.

AM-4s now support fully-swappable limbs with all other models, though they still possess the heaviest frames, and are capable of carrying heavier weapons, more ammunition, and heavier armor than any other mech type.

The 4th generation model now possesses internal, torso-mounted a-grav units for added mobility and stabilization.

RR (Recon/Ranger)

The RR model of mech was the precursor to the SMI model. RRs were based on both male and female humans, though smaller humans were used for RR models than AM and FR mechs.

These mechs were similar to AM models, except they were physically smaller and lighter. This allowed RRs to handle light aircraft/drop deployments.

As a compromise, they had smaller power sources, and could only operate for 2-3 days in the field.

Their loadouts were swappable with AM models, but they rarely utilized the chainguns.

Sub-Models

RR-1 – This model of mech began to appear on the battlefield around the same time as the AM-2 mechs. They utilized the power upgrade of the AM-2 mechs to have smaller power systems, but they also had a smaller power capacity. In theory, the new batteries of the AM-2 line should have worked, but they had overheating issues in the field, and more than one RR-1 had battery detonation when utilizing multiple firing systems.

RR-2 – The RR-2 mechs were rolled out around the same time as the AM-3s, and had few significant changes other than improved armor, and marginally longer-lasting power that no longer suffered from overload issues.

Second gen RR-2 mechs were also skinless, like AM-3 and SMI mechs.

RR-3 – The RR-3 mechs reached the field shortly before the end of the war, and were different in that they had partial legs, like SMI mechs. This was done as a cost/component-saving measure.

RR-4 – These mechs moved a step closer to the SMI spec, gaining the MK99 chameleon armor epidermis, and becoming lighter—even with their new stub limbs—thanks to advanced materials provided by the ISF.

The RR-4s use the same swappable weapons mounts as all mechs, but have high-output a-grav units in their thighs. These units allow them to fly at low altitudes (up to three hundred meters) and provide additional zero-*g* maneuvering options without using armor-based systems.

Seven of the RR-4s took the option for an additional set of arms and the brain modifications required to control the extra limbs.

FR (Force Recon)

Force Recon mechs were mechs that had the lighter drop capabilities of the RR mechs, with the additional power and armor of AM-3 models. All FR mechs were skinless.

Sub-Models

FR-1 – The first generation of FR mechs were limited run, and had both weight and power load distribution issues.

FR-2 – Second generation FR mechs solved many of the issues from the first generation, and were well regarded for their effectiveness.

XFR – The XFR model is not known to have been widely produced. This model had additional power and carrying capacity to utilize shoulder-mounted proton beams and chainguns. However, the mech's loadout made it almost as heavy as an AM-3 without the armor.

FR-4 – Though there is no FR-3 model, Finaeus and the members of Rika's Repair and Medical platoon decided to go with consistent generational numbering across all mechs.

The latest FR model gained the XFR's shoulder-mounted beam weapons: one an electron beam, and the other a high-output burst laser cannon. These weapons slot onto the wearer's back and slide up over the shoulder where they are each capable of two hundred and seventy degree motion, even with the meter-long barrel on each.

Additional changes include a-grav stabilization similar to the AM-4s, and the same universal limb and weapons mounting system, as well as the MK99 chameleon epidermis.

SMI (Scout Mech-Integrated)

The final mech model produced at the end of the war was built out of a desire for a super-light mech that could be used in place of standard infantry in sniper/recon situations, and bring extreme fire to bear if desired.

SMI mechs were also cost-saving mechs, as they retained more of their human body components, making for fewer prosthetic neural connections. They also leveraged progress in muscle and bone augmentation that had been used in RR and FR mech models.

Mechs of this model were built exclusively from small, lithe women who could fit in the armor and still create a small profile.

Unlike other mech models, SMI mechs were never deployed with two functional hands. One was always a weapon mount.

SMI mechs are all skinless.

Sub-Models

SMI-1 – The first generation of SMI mechs had a short production run due to psychological issues. Because they retained more of their human bodies than other mechs, they ended up having additional dysphoria issues.

SMI-2 – Second generation SMI mechs had improved physical integrations and psychological conditioning that caused the mechs to view themselves as less human. However, in the field, it was observed to have the opposite effect, and SMI mechs retained a strong connection to their humanity.

SMI-3 – A few experimental SMI-3 models were produced near the end of the war. These models had more powerful legs and higher top speeds, and used a new short-barreled model of the GNR. Some SMI-3s were deployed with two GNRs and no 'regular' arm.

SMI-4 – Though there had always been rumors of an SMI-3, no one in the Marauders ever saw direct evidence that the model was produced. Still, for the same reasons as the FR-4s, the SMI range moved to '4' as well.

The SMI-4 mechs had few visible improvements to their configurations, excepting that they received the MK99 chameleon armor. Advanced materials shed over ten kilograms, while adding additional batteries, and stronger bone and muscle enhancements. The SMI-4 armor also possesses the same chameleon capabilities as their skin.

While SMI-4s support the same universal weapons mount system as all mechs, they do not have the recoil control or power systems for some of the more powerful weapons, and stick to their tried and true rifles and GNRs.

LHO (Lateral Hyper Operation)

LHO mechs were a model created by Finaeus to suit the needs of shipboard operation in Rika's fleet. As the human crews within the 7th Marauder Fleet saw the skill and precision with which the ISF created the 4th Generation mechs, they began to request mechanization.

A problem the Marauder ships faced was that they were lightly crewed. To aid in solving this problem, Finaeus crafted a new mech body that was like an SMI in many respects, but possessed four arms and a slightly elongated torso. These mechs also had neural mods and brain alterations to handle operating a new set of limbs with full dexterity.

The desired—and achieved—result were mechanized humans capable of performing a task load of two people. This ability created greater efficiency in the smaller crews, while also creating a formidable shipboard force to repel boarders if a ship were to come under attack while bulk of its mechs were away on a mission.

The LHOs are all designated 4th Generation.

It should be noted that Finaeus had told Rika that 4-limbed mechs were not advisable due to the time it would take for their brains to learn how to manage the extra limbs.

This is why none of the LHO mechs have combat as a primary function, but are working on training for it. Some of the naval personnel who chose mechanization went for FR or SMI frames because their couldn't afford to take the time to learn how to manage extra limbs.

3rd MARAUDER FLEET 4th DIVISION

Fleet Commander: Colonel Argon
Division 4 Complement (2 Ships)

Golden Lark
1200-meter heavy cruiser
64 fighters
Ship's AI: Cora
Other Ship AIs: Jane & Frankie
Captain: Major Tim
XO Commander: Scas
Dockmaster: Chief Ona

Perseid's Dream
650-meter destroyer
24 fighters
Ship's AI: Moshe
Other Ship AI: Lauren
Captain Penny

7th MARAUDER FLEET 1st DIVISION

Fleet Commander: Colonel Rika (SMI-4)
Fleet XO: Captain Heather (SMI-4)
Division 4 Complement (5 Ships)

Fury Lance
4100-meter dreadnought
420 fighters
Ship's AI: N/A
Captain: Captain Heather (SMI-4)
Navigation: Chief Warrant Officer Garth
Weapons and Scan: Chief Warrant Officer Ona
(Note: Ona and Garth often switch roles)

Republic IV
1100-meter cruiser
44 fighters
Ship's AI: N/A
Captain: Lieutenant Travis (AM-4)

Undaunted
1130-meter cruiser
34 fighters
Ship's AI: N/A
Captain: Lieutenant Ferris

Asora
544-meter destroyer
Ship's AI: N/A
Captain: Lieutenant Klen (RR-4)

Weapons and Scan: Chief Ashely (LHO-4)

Capital
612-meter destroyer
Ship's AI: N/A
Captain: Lieutenant Buggsie

9th MARAUDER BATTALION

Note, there are some spoilers below. You may want to reference the names and ranks in the prior book until you've reached the chapter entitled "Training".

After General Julia promoted Rika to Colonel, and placed her in command of the 9th Battalion, Rika created 'N' Company, and moved two platoons into it.

Several platoon leaders and dropship pilots moved into fleet command positions, and others moved into the new company HQs.

'HQ' COMPANY

Battalion Commander (CO): Colonel Rika (SMI-4)
Battalion Executive Officer (XO): Lieutenant Colonel Alice
Command Sergeant: Sergeant Major Barne (FR-4)
Operations Officer: Captain Niki (SAI)
Intelligence Officer: Captain Leslie

'R' COMPANY (M&M)

Platoon Commander – Lieutenant "Bondo" Carson
- Corporal Stripes (AM-X)

'M' COMPANY

Note, not all personnel in the Company are listed.

Company HQ

Commanding Officer (CO): Captain Chase (FR-4)
Executive Officer (XO): Lieutenant Karen (SMI-4)
First Sergeant: Tex (RR-4)
Gunnery Sergeant: Aaron (AM-4)
Tactics and Strategy AI: Potter

First Platoon

Platoon CO – First Lieutenant Chris (AM-4)
Platoon Sergeant – Staff Sergeant Kristian (RR-4-M)

First Squad
Sergeant Crunch (AM-4)
4 Fireteams (19 mechs)

FT 1-1
- CPL Ben (AM-4)
- PVT Al, 'Whispers' (AM-4)
- PVT Kim (RR-4-F)
- PVT Harris (FR-4)

FT 1-2
- CPL Kelly (SMI-4)
- PVT Shoshin (AM-4)
- PVT Keli (SMI-4)

FT 1-3
- PVT Kerry (RR-4)

FT 1-4
- CPL Mitch (RR-4)
- PVT Lauren (SMI-4)
- PVT Wolf (AM-4)
- PVT Matthew (AM-4)

Second Squad
Squad Sergeant – Corin (RF-4)
3 Fireteams (13 mechs)

FT 2-1
- CPL (K1R-X-4) Oosterwyk-Bruyn, 'The Van'

Third Squad
Squad Sergeant Carolyn 'CJ' (RR-4-F)
4 Fireteams (19 mechs)

FT 3-1
- PVT Kyle, 'Goob' (AM-4)
- CPL Yiaagaitia, 'Yig' (RR-4-M)
- PVT Cole (RR-4-F)
- PVT Fiona (SMI-4)

FT 3-2
- CPL Dave (AM-4)
- PVT Chad (FR-4)
- PVT Knight (AM-4)
- PVT Rouse (AM-4)

Fourth Squad
Squad Sergeant – Kara (SMI-4)
4 Fireteams (20 mechs)

Second Platoon

Platoon CO – First Lieutenant Fuller (AM-4)
Platoon Sergeant – Staff Sergeant Chauncy (FR-4)

Squad One
Squad Sergeant – Alison (SMI-4)
4 Fireteams (19 mechs)

FT 1-4
- CPL Fred (AM-4)
- PVT Jenisa (SMI-4)
- PVT Kor (AM-4)
- PVT Randy (AM-4)

Second Squad
Squad Sergeant – Tre (FR-4)
4 Fireteams (21 mechs)

Third Squad
Squad Sergeant Bean (SMI-4)
5 Fireteams (25 mechs)

Fourth Squad
Squad Sergeant Kristina, 'Abs' (RR-4-F)
4 Fireteams (20 mechs)

FT 2-4
CPL Musel (AM-4)
PVT Bitty (K1R-X-4)
PVT Smitty (RR-4-F)

Third Platoon

Platoon CO – First Lieutenant Wilson (FR-4)
Platoon Sergeant – Staff Sergeant Bookie (SMI-4)

Squad One
Squad Sergeant Char (RR-4-F)
4 Fireteams (19 mechs)

Second Squad
Squad Sergeant Mal (FR-4)
4 Fireteams (22 mechs)

Third Squad
Squad Sergeant Cory (AM-4)
4 Fireteams (19 mechs)

Fourth Squad
Squad Sergeant Lana (SMI-4)
4 Fireteams (20 mechs)

'N' COMPANY

Note, not all personnel in the Company are listed.

Company HQ

Commanding Officer (CO): Captain Scarcliff (FR-4)
Executive Officer (XO): First Lieutenant Crudge (AM-4)
Gunnery Sergeant: Sergeant Johnny (FR-4)
Tactics and Strategy AI: Dredge

First Platoon

Platoon CO – First Lieutenant Michael (AM-4)
Platoon Sergeant – Staff Sergeant Alana (RR-4-F)

Squad One
Squad Sergeant Bruce (RR-4-M)
4 Fireteams (19 mechs)

Second Squad
Squad Sergeant Aerin (SMI-4)
4 Fireteams (21 mechs)

Third Squad
Squad Sergeant Justin (FR-4)
4 Fireteams (19 mechs)

Fourth Squad
Squad Sergeant Val (RR-4-F)
3 Fireteams (14 mechs)

Second Platoon

Platoon CO – Lieutenant Darla (RR-4-F)
Platoon Sergeant – Staff Sergeant Sal (FR-4)

Squad One
Squad Sergeant Sarah (RR-4-F)
4 Fireteams (19 mechs)

Second Squad
Squad Sergeant George (FR-4)
4 Fireteams (20 mechs)

Third Squad
Squad Sergeant Jessa (RR-4-F)
3 Fireteams (14 mechs)

Fourth Squad
Squad Sergeant Jynafer (RR-4-F)
3 Fireteams (13 mechs)

THE BOOKS OF AEON 14

Keep up to date with what is releasing in Aeon 14 with the free Aeon 14 Reading Guide.

Origins of Destiny (The Age of Terra)
- Prequel: Storming the Norse Wind
- Book 1: Shore Leave (in Galactic Genesis until Sept 2018)
- Book 2: Operative (Summer 2018)
- Book 3: Blackest Night (Summer 2018)

The Intrepid Saga (The Age of Terra)
- Book 1: Outsystem
- Book 2: A Path in the Darkness
- Book 3: Building Victoria

- The Intrepid Saga Omnibus – *Also contains Destiny Lost, book 1 of the Orion War series*

- Destiny Rising – *Special Author's Extended Edition comprised of both Outsystem and A Path in the Darkness with over 100 pages of new content.*

The Orion War
- Book 1: Destiny Lost
- Book 2: New Canaan
- Book 3: Orion Rising
- Book 4: The Scipio Alliance
- Book 5: Attack on Thebes
- Book 6: War on a Thousand Fronts
- Book 7: Fallen Empire (2018)
- Book 8: Airtha Ascendancy (2018)
- Book 9: The Orion Front (2018)
- Book 10: Starfire (2019)
- Book 11: Race Across Time (2019)
- Book 12: Return to Sol (2019)

Tales of the Orion War
- Book 1: Set the Galaxy on Fire
- Book 2: Ignite the Stars
- Book 3: Burn the Galaxy to Ash (2018)

Perilous Alliance (Age of the Orion War – w/Chris J. Pike)
- Book 1: Close Proximity
- Book 2: Strike Vector
- Book 3: Collision Course
- Book 4: Impact Imminent
- Book 5: Critical Inertia (Sept 2018)

Rika's Marauders (Age of the Orion War)
- Prequel: Rika Mechanized
- Book 1: Rika Outcast
- Book 2: Rika Redeemed
- Book 3: Rika Triumphant
- Book 4: Rika Commander
- Book 5: Rika Infiltrator
- Book 6: Rika Unleashed (2018)
- Book 7: Rika Conqueror (2019)

Perseus Gate (Age of the Orion War)
Season 1: Orion Space
- Episode 1: The Gate at the Grey Wolf Star
- Episode 2: The World at the Edge of Space
- Episode 3: The Dance on the Moons of Serenity
- Episode 4: The Last Bastion of Star City
- Episode 5: The Toll Road Between the Stars
- Episode 6: The Final Stroll on Perseus's Arm
- Eps 1-3 Omnibus: The Trail Through the Stars
- Eps 4-6 Omnibus: The Path Amongst the Clouds

Season 2: Inner Stars
- Episode 1: A Meeting of Bodies and Minds
- Episode 3: A Deception and a Promise Kept
- Episode 3: A Surreptitious Rescue of Friends and Foes (2018)
- Episode 4: A Trial and the Tribulations (2018)

- Episode 5: A Deal and a True Story Told (2018)
- Episode 6: A New Empire and An Old Ally (2018)

Season 3: AI Empire
- Episode 1: Restitution and Recompense (2019)
- Five more episodes following...

The Warlord (Before the Age of the Orion War)
- Book 1: The Woman Without a World
- Book 2: The Woman Who Seized an Empire
- Book 3: The Woman Who Lost Everything

The Sentience Wars: Origins (Age of the Sentience Wars – w/James S. Aaron)
- Book 1: Lyssa's Dream
- Book 2: Lyssa's Run
- Book 3: Lyssa's Flight
- Book 4: Lyssa's Call
- Book 5: Lyssa's Flame

Legends of the Sentience Wars (Age of the Sentience Wars – w/James S. Aaron)
- Volume 1: The Proteus Bridge (August 2018)

Enfield Genesis (Age of the Sentience Wars – w/Lisa Richman)
- Book 1: Alpha Centauri
- Book 2: Proxima Centauri (2018)

Hand's Assassin (Age of the Orion War – w/T.G. Ayer)
- Book 1: Death Dealer
- Book 2: Death Mark (August 2018)

Machete System Bounty Hunter (Age of the Orion War – w/Zen DiPietro)
- Book 1: Hired Gun
- Book 2: Gunning for Trouble
- Book 3: With Guns Blazing

Vexa Legacy (Age of the FTL Wars – w/Andrew Gates)
- Book 1: Seas of the Red Star

Building New Canaan (Age of the Orion War – w/J.J. Green)
- Book 1: Carthage (July 2018)
- Book 2: Tyre (2018)

Fennington Station Murder Mysteries (Age of the Orion War)
- Book 1: Whole Latte Death (w/Chris J. Pike)
- Book 2: Cocoa Crush (w/Chris J. Pike)

The Empire (Age of the Orion War)
- The Empress and the Ambassador (2018)
- Consort of the Scorpion Empress (2018)
- By the Empress's Command (2018)

The Sol Dissolution (The Age of Terra)
- Book 1: Venusian Uprising (2018)
- Book 2: Scattered Disk (2018)
- Book 3: Jovian Offensive (2019)
- Book 4: Fall of Terra (2019)

ABOUT THE AUTHOR

Michael Cooper likes to think of himself as a jack-of-all-trades (and hopes to become master of a few). When not writing, he can be found writing software, working in his shop at his latest carpentry project, or likely reading a book.

He shares his home with a precocious young girl, his wonderful wife (who also writes), two cats, a never-ending list of things he would like to build, and ideas…

Find out what's coming next at www.aeon14.com

43888368R00192

Made in the USA
San Bernardino, CA
16 July 2019